18.June
5/7/21

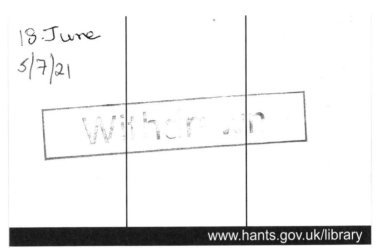

www.hants.gov.uk/library

 Hampshire County Council

 Love YOUR LIBRARY

Tel: 0300 555 1387

CRANBROOK PRESS

CRANBROOK PRESS

Does it matter? – losing your legs?
    For people will always be kind,
    And you need not show that you mind
    When others come in after hunting
    To gobble their muffins and eggs.
    Does it matter? – losing your sight?
    There's such splendid work for the blind;
    And people will always be kind,
    As you sit on the terrace remembering
    And turning your face to the light.
    Do they matter – those dreams in the pit?
    You can drink and forget and be glad,
    And people won't say that you're mad;
    For they know that you've fought for your country,
    And no one will worry a bit.

Siegfried Sassoon
Copyright Siegfried Sassoon by kind permission of the Estate of
George Sassoon

CHAPTER 1

*C*hristopher Shipley woke up to find his mother standing at the foot of his bed, looking at him with ill-concealed criticism.

'Still in bed, Christopher? You know what they say about idleness.' Without waiting for an answer, she pulled the curtains apart, allowing watery sunlight to spill into the gloomy room. 'Remember what the doctor said about not allowing your handicap to hold you back.' She looked away but not before he caught the slight downward turn of her lip when she saw the flat bedding where the contours of his missing leg should have been. He hated pity. More than revulsion.

'I can't let you put off talking to the Walters woman any longer. You won't find a new gamekeeper unless you can offer him the cottage that goes with the job. Offering accommodation is our only hope of attracting a suitable candidate.' She turned to look at him, fixing him with a determined gaze. 'You know that as well as I do, darling.' She studied his face and Christopher felt as though she was searching for something that wasn't there. No matter what he did he would always fall short of her expectations. The one thing she wanted was beyond his capacity to deliver – for him to be his elder brother.

'What's the hurry? The poor woman's lost her husband. Why do we have to harry her out of her home too? Can't we wait and let her get out when she's ready?'

Edwina Shipley tutted loudly. 'For goodness sake, Christopher, sometimes I despair of you. If left to her own devices the woman will never move. That cottage is part of the gamekeeper's recompense.' She moved across to the window and gazed out at the rolling parkland beyond. 'And it's a very superior cottage. Three bedrooms and she's there all on her own. What right does she have to take up so much space with no family? I always said as much to your father even when the husband was alive. Such a waste of space for a childless couple. But George was attached to the Walters man and wouldn't hear of him moving into more modest accommodation. But now – we must find a new head game-keeper. *You* must find one.'

Christopher leaned back against the pillows. 'I don't see why we need a new keeper. I don't even like shooting. I've no wish to hold shooting parties.' He studied her face, wondering why she was oblivious to his repugnance at the idea of holding a gun in his hands again.

She tutted again, her tongue rasping against her teeth, impatience growing. 'How many times, Christopher? It's not just about you. You don't give a damn for anything – the engineering works or the estate. You have a responsibility to the firm, to the Newlands estate, to this family, the servants.'

'I know that, Mother. What's your point? What's that got to do with hiring a gamekeeper?'

'The shooting here is essential to reviving the estate. All part of your job. How else are you going to attract the best kind of people to visit? How else are you to make your mark and expand Shipleys? Your father made his best business deals over a shooting weekend. When your grandfather was alive Prince Albert graced us with his presence and the late King was a frequent visitor. Being able to entertain here has been vital to the growth of Shipley Engineering. You should know this as well as I do.'

Christopher said nothing. There was no point. No matter what he said, his mother would never understand. Never be able to acknowledge that he wasn't interested in royalty staying for a shooting party, that he didn't give a damn about his place in society, and the prospect of discussing business deals left him cold. But if he resisted her she would come back at him stronger, would keep up a constant barrage of reproach until she wore him down, rubbing away his resistance like a blacksmith hammering metal.

Edwina left the room, throwing him one last steely look. 'Just do it, Christopher. It's not a lot to ask.' The door closed behind her.

He rarely wanted to do anything these days, but this task was particularly onerous: he was dreading telling the gamekeeper's widow that she had to vacate her home to make way for a new incumbent. Not only because of the bad news but because he felt guilty he hadn't called on her before now as her late husband had served with him.

He sat on the edge of the bed and looked around the once familiar bedroom. It belonged to another life, another person, another world. He no longer fitted in. Reaching for his prosthetic leg, placed as usual on the top of the trunk at the end of the bed, he strapped it onto the stump, tightening the leather bands so that it gripped his withered skin securely.

The pain wasn't so bad today, more a discomfort, a constant chafing. He wasn't sure which was worse: the days when pain seared and burned through his body, his shattered nerve endings screaming out and blinding him to everything else, or the days like today when pain thrummed away in the background, mingling with the images in his head and wrapping him up in a shroud of misery.

Christopher occasionally considered ending it all. Taking a shotgun and setting off into the woods, sitting down under a tree and blasting his head off his shoulders. But something held him back. His reluctance to hold a gun in his hands again after his experiences in the war rather than his unwillingness to take his own life. And wouldn't suicide be a coward's way out and a mockery of the sacrifices made by the men who had served beside him?

Of course, his mother couldn't understand any of this. After her initial joy that her second son had survived the trenches, Mrs Shipley had grown impatient. Treating Christopher with kindness on his return from the Front, her solicitude had now turned to annoyance. She couldn't understand his reticence, his long periods shut away in his bedroom, his endless gazing into space. Edwina Shipley was a get-on-with-it, no nonsense American, who had no time or sympathy for anyone who failed to share her vision of the world. 'Buck up!' and 'Onwards and upwards!' were her war cries and Christopher couldn't recall a time when he had come across her motionless or lost in thought. She'd no time for thinkers. Edwina was a woman of action, of deeds not words. Christopher sometimes wondered if this was because she was afraid if she stopped to think, to take stock, to weigh up what her life meant, she might conclude that the answer was not very much and her world might crumple and fall apart.

The loss of her husband and firstborn son had caused only a stiffening in her posture, a straightening of the back, a tightening of the lips, before she was busy organising memorial ceremonies and throwing herself into the erection of a pair of marble plaques in their memory on the walls of the village church. Percy, Christopher's brother, had been the heir apparent, adored by both parents. Killed on the first day of the First Battle of the Somme, his death caused his father to suffer a stroke when he heard the devastating news, leading to his own death soon after. But Edwina bore all this with fortitude – to complain or grieve was not in her nature. Christopher knew his own lack of resilience was a constant source of irritation to her.

Now that his mother was gone, he tarried over dressing. The fact that he wouldn't permit his late father's elderly valet to assist him was yet another source of annoyance to his mother. Christopher bridled at the thought of that kind of intimacy, at the idea of another man helping him put on his clothes. He had no wish to expose his missing limb to the scrutiny of a servant; to accept help not only felt inappropriate and old-fashioned, it would be an admission of weakness, an exposure of his disability to the pity of another person. Better to do it himself even if it took him twice as long.

Once dressed, he made his way slowly down the stairs, holding himself erect as he negotiated the shallow sweeping stairway to the hall. He hated the house: its high stuccoed ceilings, draughty corridors, pale sandstone turrets and grandiose wide doorways. It was all so false. His grandfather had built it in the neo-gothic style that was prevalent in his day – a monument to his achievement as an industrialist and an eradication of all traces of his humble roots as a carter turned factory mechanic before he set out on his own, designing, manufacturing and selling machinery to supply the factories of the north of England and latterly across the Empire. The old man had never managed to lose his Yorkshire accent, but Christopher and Percy had benefited from a public school education, rubbing shoulders with the sons of aristocrats. They had never really fitted in, but had been accepted with reluctance by slightly threadbare landed gentry forced to attach themselves to money. He had always suspected that these people left Newlands with a wiping of hands, anxious to rub out all traces of 'new money'.

He made his way to the stable block, glancing up at the huge clock that adorned the decorative brick tower above it. The hands were set at three-seventeen, the moment Percy had met his death according to his commanding officer, now a constant reminder of the family's loss. Those frozen clock hands were a reproach to Christopher, reminding him that he had survived when his braver, more handsome, more outgoing, elder brother had been blown to bits on 1st July 1916. Christopher hadn't even been in uniform then. He'd been in Borneo, studying tropical vegetation, in an all-too-brief fulfilment of his dream of being a botanist and explorer, after completing his degree at Cambridge. The dream had been cut short when he was summoned home by the news of his brother's death and his father's stroke. By the time he reached England his father was dead too, leaving Christopher an inadequate substitute for them both in the eyes of his mother.

The groom had saddled up his horse ready for him to ride out. On horseback Christopher felt a whole man again. It had taken him time to build up the strength and control to apply the necessary pressure to the horse's flank with his prosthetic leg. But now that he had become proficient, riding was a welcome escape and he rarely missed a day.

Newlands was a large estate of rolling landscaped parkland, broad vistas, artificial lakes and acres of carefully curated woodland, where the shooting had once been regarded as outstanding. Since the war and the departure of most of the estate workers to the Front, most never to return, the grounds had been neglected. The formal gardens were overgrown, the parterres now indistinguishable from a rough shrubbery, the lawns unclipped, the ponds empty of water, the greenhouses filled with brown desiccated vegetation, their glass panels encrusted with moss and dirt. This abandoned wilderness was what Christopher was wanted to resurrect, restore, replenish. His mother expected him to recreate the splendours of the pre-war years, but all he wanted to do was get away. Return to his work in Borneo, to his detailed botanical drawings, to the book he was compiling on the flora of South East Asia, to academia, to peace.

He nudged his mount forward, enjoying the cool breeze against his face, the pound of Hooker's hooves on the turf beneath them. He had named his horse after his hero, Sir Joseph Dalton Hooker, the eminent botanist. Christopher had discovered his book, *Rhododendrons of the Sikkim-Himalaya*, one of the many unopened volumes bought by his grandfather to furnish the shelves of the library. As a child he had pored over the pages, admiring the delicate drawings of plants and then taking his sketchbook and pens and meticulously drawing the plants he found in the gardens. When sent away to boarding school, his passion for plants had continued, later cemented by his study of botany at Cambridge. The prospect of abandoning all this to run the estate and the Shipley engineering empire was a life sentence. But who was he to complain when his brother and most of the men of Newlands had lost their lives? His own concerns were trivial compared to their sacrifice.

He steadied Hooker's pace, slowing to a leisurely trot as they entered the woods. The gamekeeper's cottage was in a small clearing a few hundred yards inside the woods, surrounded by beech trees. It was a pretty part-timbered cottage, covered with a scalloped clay-tiled roof in the Arts and Crafts style.

Outside, a neat row of washing hung from a line and a thin trail of smoke drifted from one of the barley-sugar twist chimneys. Behind the house were kennels, and a sitting house for nesting game birds. Swinging himself out of the saddle he felt a juddering through his body as his artificial leg hit the ground first and the impact drove pain through his stump. It was always a harsh reminder, coming back to earth after riding – on horseback he forgot his disability.

Leaving Hooker untethered to crop the grass in the clearing, he approached the house. The sooner he got this job over with, the better. Once done, he might earn a brief reprieve from his mother's constant carping.

Before he reached the door it opened. The woman must have been watching him through the window. A dog slipped out from behind her and sniffed around Christopher before curling up next to a woodpile.

She was older than Christopher. Early or mid-thirties he guessed. Dressed in a drab brown garment, she had scraped her dark brown hair back from her face into an untidy bun.

'The dog's old. Does nothing but sleep these days. I expect he thought it was my husband coming back. He never gives up.'

'I'm sorry about Mr Walters. I've been meaning to come and offer my condolences for some time.' Christopher tugged his hat off his head.

'You're the younger son, aren't you? Master Christopher?'

He nodded.

'I should call you Captain Shipley now, I hear. Come to tell me to get out, have you?'

Christopher felt the blood rush to his face and he started to stammer an answer, but she spoke first. 'I've been expecting you.' She studied him, her face expressionless. Christopher felt his face heating up under her gaze.

The woman gave a shrug. 'Best come inside. Kettle's just boiled.'

He followed her into the house, uncertain why he was doing so, but unsure what else to do.

The door opened straight onto the kitchen, with the scullery beyond it. Mrs Walters prepared the tea in silence as he stood leaning against the door watching her. She was tall, almost as tall as he was, and despite her loose fitting dress he could tell she was of slender build. As she moved about he caught the odd glimpse of her calves above the top of her buttoned boots. She picked up the tray and asked him to hold open the door from the kitchen and he followed her into a small parlour with a scrubbed deal table and a fire burning in the grate. A pottery jug filled with spring flowers sat upon the table. She motioned him to sit.

'You lost your leg in the war I heard. Doesn't stop you riding though. They give you a wooden one?'

Christopher blinked, taken aback by the woman's frankness. He muttered assent. 'Others lost more.' Then feeling the heat burning in his face, he stammered, 'I knew your husband. He served with me.'

'Served for you, you mean.'

'He was my batman.'

'What's that?'

He hesitated. 'I suppose it's a bit like a personal servant. He looked after my uniform, ran errands, did all kinds of tasks for me. He was a good man. The best.' He lowered his head. 'I'm sorry for your loss.'

'Were you there when he died?'

Christopher swallowed then nodded his head.

'Tell me.'

He felt his hand shaking and, afraid he would spill his tea, he put the cup back on the saucer, hearing it rattle against the spoon. 'I don't like to... I can't...'

The woman stared at him, her face still blank, revealing no emotion as she waited for him to collect himself. He imagined what his mother would say if she saw him now, reduced to stammering by a servant.

Breathing in slowly, he said, 'I sent him back to the dugout to get my pocket watch. I'd left it on top of my trunk. Stupid thing to do.' He glanced down at his hand as it shook on the surface of the table, then drew it away resting it under the table on his leg. 'The dugout took a direct hit from a shell. When we went back, there was a crater. Harold... Private Walters was the only man lost that day... if I hadn't asked him to fetch my watch...' He lifted his eyes, then dropped them again under her penetrating gaze.

'So it would have been quick?'

He looked up again. 'Instant. He wouldn't have stood a chance. Wouldn't have known anything.'

The woman frowned then sipped her tea. Putting the cup down, she said, 'What about you? How did you lose the leg?'

'Six months later. Just before the end of the hostilities. In Belgium. Ypres. I stepped on a landmine when we were advancing. A moment of carelessness on my part and it cost me my leg.' He gave a hollow laugh.

Mrs Walters studied him, her eyes green with little hazel flecks. She hadn't smiled once. Pointing at his hand she asked, 'Is that down to the war too? The shaking?'

He nodded. 'Nerves. They said it was shell shock.' He was ashamed as he told her, but felt compelled to answer her questions. 'Stupid, I know.'

'Stupid? Hardly.'

'My mother thinks it is.' He gave a wry smile. 'She keeps telling me to snap out of it.' What was it about this woman that made him open up to her?

Mrs Walters said nothing, but reached for the teapot and refilled their cups.

After a few minutes of silence, she said, 'So when do I have to be out of here?'

He hesitated. His mother had told him to tell her she had to get out by the end of the week. 'Have you anywhere to go? What will you do?'

She shrugged.

'Family?'

'All dead.'

'I see,' he said. 'Perhaps there's a place for you among the house servants. I'll ask Mother. Then you'd have accommodation too.'

She shook her head. 'I've asked already. There's nothing. It's men they need, not more women.'

'I see,' he said again, conscious that he must sound inane.

'I'm too old to find another husband. Not when there are so many young women and not enough men left to go round. I'll have to go to the city and try to find work.' She fingered the sleeve of her blouse, a tiny gesture that revealed that perhaps she was more nervous than she appeared. 'I've lived in this house all my life. It's all I've ever known.'

Christopher was surprised, assuming she must have moved here when she married Walters.

'My father was head keeper before my husband, who was much older than me. He was just turned fifty when he volunteered with your brother and most of the estate workers.'

'I'm sorry. At fifty he could hardly have been expected to serve. Do you think he felt coerced to join up?'

She frowned.

'I mean was he put under pressure to volunteer?'

'No one wants to get a white feather.'

'But at fifty?'

'He wanted to go. He couldn't wait.'

'He was a fine man.'

'You thought so, did you?'

11

'I know so. I suppose the fact that we both came from Newlands was a bond between us… but he was a brave man, a fine soldier.'

The woman's expression was inscrutable. She swirled her teacup, examining the dregs of leaves in the bottom, but said nothing. After a few minutes of silence Christopher stood up. 'Thank you for the tea, Mrs Walters.'

She rose. 'Will you visit me again? I don't have much company. I liked talking to you.'

He felt the blood rushing to his face and neck and he swallowed. 'I'd like that.'

'Come tomorrow. Same time.'

As he clambered onto his horse, Christopher realised that he had failed to give Mrs Walters a date to vacate the property. What would he tell his mother?

MARTHA STOOD AT THE WINDOW, watching as Christopher Shipley mounted his horse. She wondered how he managed it, surprised at his strength in vaulting into the saddle with only one leg and in the absence of a mounting block. As he rode away, a memory of him as a boy came, riding on a little bay pony, galloping around the estate whenever he was home for the school holidays. She'd noticed him, his gritty determination, riding out in all weathers, climbing back onto his rather skittish pony whenever she bucked or reared and dumped him in the bracken.

Here he was now, the master of the estate, clearly uncomfortable in a role that he had never expected to perform, were it not for the war and the death of his brother.

Why had she invited him to come back tomorrow? What had possessed her? It had happened without her consciously planning it. There was something indefinable about him.

Something that drew her to want to know him. Even though she knew she was treading a dangerous path.

Martha sighed. Tomorrow she would give him a cup of tea, settle on a date to move out of the cottage and that would be that. That *had* to be that. In a couple of weeks she would be gone. Where to, she had no idea.

CHAPTER 2

*C*hristopher avoided his mother for the rest of the day, shutting himself away in the library. He was cataloguing his drawings from Borneo, sorting them alongside his notebooks in preparation for when he would begin to compile his taxonomy. He worked until the daylight faded then went to his room to prepare for the ordeal of dinner.

As he shaved, he studied his face in the mirror. He seemed so much older now than he had when he'd reluctantly departed for the Front. If it didn't kill you, warfare added years to a man's face. But worse than the physical changes was the effect on his mind – the nightmares, the shaking hands, the crippling fear and, worst of all, the sense of shame that he had let the side down by living when others much worthier had made the supreme sacrifice. Every day he saw that in his mother's eyes. No Victoria Cross or Distinguished Conduct medals for him – just the regular campaign service medals for showing up. His dead brother had been a real hero, mentioned in dispatches and awarded a posthumous VC.

Christopher rinsed the shaving brush and cleaned his

razor, wiping the blade on the linen cloth laid out by the maid. He had to get away from here. He longed to return to the Far East, to the work he was born to do, to the unfinished business he needed to complete. Away from his mother's plans. Away from the marriage she wanted him to make. Another hand-me-down from his dead brother. He was expected to marry Percy's fiancée, Lady Lavinia Bourne. While it had not yet been discussed, Edwina Shipley treated it as a foregone conclusion. She frequently dropped hints, implying that one day, after a suitable mourning period had elapsed and Christopher had firmer control over the family affairs, an engagement would be expected. Such a marriage would further embed the Shipley family's place in society, uniting Shipley wealth with Bourne blood and helping remove the taint of his grandfather's humble Yorkshire roots and Edwina's American antecedents.

Christopher knew only too well his parents' marriage had not been based on love, but on duty and pragmatism. His mother had turned a blind eye to his father's indiscretions. They had slept in different wings of the large rambling house and once Edwina had delivered her husband the heir and the spare, she was no doubt relieved, and let him pursue his ill-concealed philandering without comment.

Lady Lavinia wasn't unattractive: small, blonde, blue-eyed, with a perfectly formed heart-shaped face and a pale flawless complexion. Doubtless, many men would have happily taken her as their bride. Christopher remembered her as flirtatious, bubbly and, he suspected, empty-headed. He had met her only once, before his departure for Borneo in late 1913, when her engagement to Percy was celebrated with a large ball at Newlands. After they had been introduced, Christopher had been able to slip away, unnoticed by the crowd of visiting dignitaries, to the library where he'd spent most of the evening absorbed in background reading for his forthcoming trip. There would be no such dispensation the next time Lavinia and her family were guests at the house. He would be expected to play the part of the head of the family, the generous host, the prospective husband. He gritted his teeth at the thought and sat down on the edge of the bed.

As he tied his necktie he thought about Mrs Walters. The gamekeeper's widow had been flitting across his mind all afternoon as he was cataloguing his work. There was some intangible quality about her that had intrigued him. An inscrutability, her thoughts concealed by the passive expression on her face, like a mask. Yet he remembered the nervous plucking at her sleeve and the occasional darkening of her eyes, which signalled there was more to her than she cared to reveal. And why had she invited him to return tomorrow? Why had he accepted? He put on his dinner jacket and realised he was looking forward to seeing her again. Even though the prospect was unsettling.

Mrs Shipley was already seated at the table when he entered the dining room. 'You missed cocktails.' Her tone was accusatory.

'Sorry, Mother. It took me a while today getting ready. My joints are a bit stiff.'

'How many times have I told you, Christopher? You must have a valet. It's not seemly to be dressing yourself. Wilson has little else to do and he served your father so well for so many years.'

Christopher took a seat, ignoring his mother's remark. 'Hasn't it been a lovely day? There's a wonderful bank of primroses past the stables on the way to the sunken garden. Have you seen them?'

'Primroses!' She spat the word out in a mixture of amusement and disgust. 'Really, darling. It's time you hired more gardeners to get some herbaceous bedding and shrubs planted again. Sometimes I despair of you, Christopher. You're such a dreamer.' She shook her head as she dipped her spoon into her soup. 'I always said your father should not have permitted you to study all that botanical nonsense at university. You'd have been better off learning from him, getting to grips with the management of the estate, and learning about the running of the factories.' She frowned, as if the likelihood of his being able to run a large industrial empire was remote. She spooned up some more soup. 'And I've never understood why you take so little interest in shooting. And what's the point of riding so well if you never ride to hounds? The whole purpose of hunting is social. Everything is about making connections and using them. Heaven knows, your late father knew exactly how to do that, but all his hard work is going to waste.'

'I've no interest in social climbing.'

'Social climbing?' She leaned back in her chair. 'This family has no need to climb. It's about maintaining our place, furthering our connections. If only you hadn't spent so much time loitering in libraries and hacking your way through jungles, things would be a lot easier for us.'

'Yes, Mother.' They went through this charade almost every evening over dinner. None of it made any difference. He would never be the son she wanted him to be and he wasn't even going to try.

'Did you call on the gamekeeper's wife today? Have you told her she needs to be gone by the end of the week?'

Christopher's hand began to shake. Here it was – the inevitable inquisition. 'There's no need for us to push her out of her house yet. We can find the new man first. As long as she vacates before he starts work.' He swallowed, trying not to stammer. 'Besides, she has nowhere to go.'

'That's her problem, not ours.'

'I've told her she can stay on until we've found a new gamekeeper.'

Mrs Shipley's spoon clattered against the side of her soup plate. 'Really, Christopher, you are the giddy limit. I can't trust you to get anything right. You'll have to toughen up if you want to make a go of being in charge.'

'Maybe I don't want to make a go of it,' he muttered.

'What did you say?'

'Mrs Walters has had enough bad news with losing her husband. We can afford to show her some kindness and patience.'

His mother tutted. 'Why are you so afraid to tell people bad news?'

'I'm not afraid. I've already told more than enough people bad news. I've had to speak to far too many grieving widows, Mrs Walters included. She wanted to know how her husband died.'

Edwina Shipley pulled a face. 'How grisly. Better not to know. You didn't tell her?'

'Of course I told her. She has a right to know. I said it was my fault. I'd left my fob watch in the dugout and sent the poor chap back to fetch it and got him blown to bits as a consequence.'

His mother stopped eating.

'She took it well under the circumstances.'

'I've no interest in how she took it. I can't understand why you should tell her you were to blame for the poor man's death. What good can that possibly do? It won't bring him back and can only serve to make the woman even more unhappy.' She rang the handbell on the table beside her. 'The only person responsible for that man dying is the Kaiser – and the German soldier who fired the shell at him.'

She dabbed her mouth with her napkin as the servant came in to take the plates away and serve the main course.

They ate the spring lamb, cabbage and roast potatoes in silence. Before they finished the course his mother spoke again, brightly – her annoyance gone. 'I almost forgot. I have a surprise for you, darling. Some cheering news. This morning I had a letter from Lady Bourne. Lord Bourne has business in town on Friday so she thought it would be pleasant if she and Lavinia travelled down with him and called in here en route.' She lowered her head and peered at Christopher over the top of her spectacles. 'Of course I have replied to say they must stay for the whole weekend. Lord Bourne will join us from Friday evening.'

Christopher inwardly groaned but said nothing.

'I've invited the Harrington-Fosters and Major and Mrs Collerton to join us all for dinner on Saturday. Anyone else you'd like me to add? I'll need to sort out the numbers so that Cook can make the arrangements. It would have been lovely to have a large party but I think that may be a step too far so soon after the armistice. Perhaps at the end of the summer. Or a winter party? That could be delightful. The run up to Christmas and the end of the year can be so frightfully dreary.'

'I have other plans this weekend.'

'What plans? You never have plans.'

Christopher frowned then mumbled something about being invited to visit an old college friend.

'You have no friends.' In a more conciliatory tone she said, 'I'm sorry, darling, but I'm sure whoever your friend is, he will understand your cancelling. This must take precedence. It's your first opportunity to act as host.' She narrowed her eyes. 'Don't let me down, darling.'

Resigned to his fate, but far from happy about it, Christopher ate the rest of the meal in a blessed silence punctuated only by the clock on the mantelpiece loudly ticking the passing minutes.

CHAPTER 3

*T*he following morning was cloudy and grey, threatening rain. Christopher contemplated abandoning his promised visit to Mrs Walters, but wandered down to the stables anyway, where Hooker was saddled up and waiting patiently in his stall. He stood beside the horse, leaning against him, smoothing his hand down the stallion's neck, feeling the warmth through his silky coat. The horse whinnied at the prospect of getting out in the open and enjoying a gallop.

Relishing the fast ride under the dark clouds, the cold wind cutting into his face, Christopher rode out to the northern edge of the estate, to a small incline where there was a panoramic view of the house and grounds. The huge honey-coloured stone building was like a curse, a drag on his energy, weighing him down with its attendant responsibilities – but from this distant vantage point he had to acknowledge its beauty. It was preposterous though – an enormous multi-roomed mansion with just himself, his mother and a disproportionate number of servants to rattle around inside. What right had he to all this space when Mrs Walters and thousands of other families were homeless, bereaved and impoverished, after the war the nation was supposed to have won?

Newlands was a beautiful white elephant. A monument to the achievements of his grandfather and the empty aspirations of his parents.

The deaths in the war of so many of the landed classes, and the death duties their widows and children faced, meant that many great houses like Newlands were unsustainable. Formerly wealthy families were selling off the silver, consigning the furniture and paintings to auction houses and abandoning their over-large houses in order to pay crippling death duties and avoid the mounting repair bills and property maintenance costs. The Shipleys were different. Their fortune, built on industrial machinery, had grown rapidly during the war and the run-up to it, when George Shipley expanded his business from machinery for the wool and cotton mills into armaments and motor vehicle engine parts. Christopher wished he could walk away from the place, hand the keys to a deserving recipient and sail back to the Far East.

He turned Hooker towards the copse where the gamekeeper's cottage was, squeezing his mismatched legs against the horse's flanks to coax him forward.

There was no washing on the line this morning, but the wisps of smoke from the chimney signalled that the woman was at home. He knocked at the door but there was no response.

'I'm here,' her voice came from behind him.

He turned round to see her wiping her hands on her apron. There was soil on them and under her fingernails.

'The dog died in the night. I've been digging a grave.' She pushed a strand of hair back from her forehead, leaving a dirty streak.

'I'm sorry,' he said. 'Losing a dog is...' He wanted to say it was almost as bad as losing a friend or family member, but in the light of her husband's death that felt inappropriate.

'She was old. And she missed him.' She gave a little hollow half-laugh. 'Pined for her master from the moment he set off to volunteer with the rest of them from the estate. Followed him to the gates, she did. Whined night after night. Watched the door all the time as if she expected him to walk through it.' She shook her head. 'Maybe she's with him now. Do you think dogs go to heaven?'

Christopher was puzzled, uncertain how to reply.

'Well, if they do, she won't meet her master there.' She brushed the hair away from her brow again. 'Can you help me lift her into the hole?'

Before Christopher could ask her what she meant about her husband not being in heaven, the woman had moved away. He followed her round to the rear of the building where the dead dog was lying on an old blanket. The moment to ask her had passed. Perhaps he'd misunderstood her meaning anyway, but he doubted it.

Without speaking, they each took an end of the makeshift shroud and carried it across the grass to the hole she had dug under a tree. They lowered the body into the grave and Mrs Walters watched as Christopher shovelled the soil back into the hole. When he was done, they stood side-by-side, next to the mound of earth.

'That was a deep hole. It must have taken you hours.'

'I was in the Land Army. I volunteered as soon as it started at the beginning of 1917. I got plenty of practice at digging.'

'Hard work, I imagine.'

'Not like the recruitment posters where it was always sunshine, smiles and spring lambs to cuddle.' She gave a sardonic laugh. 'More like slave labour, in all weathers for next to no money. I did like getting to wear breeches though. And I still wear my oilskin coat when the weather's bad.'

'I didn't know the uniform was breeches.' He was surprised. 'That must have raised a few eyebrows.'

'It did. There were many who thought it would be better for us to drag through wet fields with our skirts trailing in the mud. We were doing men's work so we couldn't wear women's clothes.'

'I suppose not.'

'And the boots were awful. They didn't fit properly so we all had blisters. I got through so much Vaseline. In fact none of the clothes fitted properly. A pair of upper-class ladies had their own tailored uniforms from Harrods.' She snorted. 'All right for some.'

'At least they did their bit.'

'Yes. I won't deny that.'

'And if it's any consolation it wasn't any better for the men. The boots never fitted.'

'Did you get your uniform from Harrods, then?'

Christopher reddened. 'My tailor.'

Pushing the door of the house open, she beckoned him to follow her inside. Wordlessly, she prepared tea, as she had done the day before, while Christopher leaned against the scullery wall watching her.

When they were seated at the table, Christopher tried to imagine her sitting here night after night, through the years of her marriage, eating an evening meal with her husband. His heart twisted at the loss and loneliness she must be feeling – and now not even the dog to keep her company. He realised she hadn't mentioned the dog's name.

He took a gulp of tea then asked, 'What did you mean about the dog not meeting her master in heaven?'

She looked up at him, studying his face as though she was weighing him up, deciding what she was prepared to tell him. He had begun to think she wasn't going to answer his question, when she spoke, staring into her cup of tea. 'Harold Walters is burning in hell. At least I hope he is. I've not wasted any prayers on him.' She fixed her gaze on Christopher. 'I've shocked you now, haven't I?'

He didn't know what to say. He was indeed shocked. Not only at what the woman had said but at the tone in which she had said it. Venomous, full of suppressed anger.

'You can't possibly mean that.'

'Why can't I? Don't you think I knew him? Better than anyone? Better than you did.'

'But–'

'I'll bet he was the perfect servant to you. Attentive to your every need. What did you call him? Your batman? He was always good at tugging his forelock to the gentry, but he'd never a good word for his wife.'

Christopher bit his lip, wishing he hadn't come. He was unprepared for this kind of revelation.

'I hated him,' she said. 'Couldn't bear being in the same room as him, let alone the same bed.' She was plucking at her sleeve again. 'Years I had to put up with him. Apart from the blessed release when he went to war. A prison sentence would have been better for me.'

Blood rushed to his face. He didn't know how to respond. His right hand was shaking and he grabbed his wrist to steady it.

'Sorry,' she said. 'You probably don't want to hear this. Not after what you said about him being such a good man, but I'm sick of it. Sick to my guts. Of you speaking well of him. Of the dog pining away in misery for him, while no one knows what I went through with him.'

Instinctively, he put out his hand and touched her arm. Mrs Walters looked down at his hand, saying nothing, until, feeling awkward, he moved it away, letting it lie on the top of the table as if it had landed there by accident. After a few seconds, she placed her hand on top of his. Her touch was light, her skin cool, resting against his only briefly. His stomach contracted and he wanted to feel her hand against his again, but she had moved it into her lap.

'He worked alongside my father,' she said. 'Da took him on when I was thirteen. There were half-a-dozen assistant keepers then and I paid him no more attention than any of them.'

Christopher listened, fearful of what she was going to reveal, but fascinated by the way she was opening up herself and her story to him. She told him how Harold Walters began hanging around the cottage and the sitting house, checking on the nesting boxes when they had already been checked, hovering around the kennels when they had already been cleaned out, or sitting on a fallen tree trunk watching her as she went about her household tasks.

'My mother died giving birth to me, so there was only ever me and my father. He died fifteen years ago and that's when Walters got the head keeper job.'

'I remember your father,' Christopher said at last. 'He showed me how to peel the bark off a piece of wood and make a bow and arrow.'

She smiled. 'That sounds like him. He wasn't a bad man. He only did what he believed was right for me. Pity it wasn't.' She shrugged.

Christopher drank the rest of his tea, uncertain where she was going with this.

Mrs Walters leaned forward and filled his cup again. 'But Da did one thing that was wrong and that I will never forgive him for.' Her eyes fixed on Christopher's. 'He made me marry Walters against my will.'

'Why did he do that?'

'Because Walters had had his way with me. I was only

fourteen and he was thirty-six. He forced himself on me. There was a shooting party and all the keepers, my da included, were out beating the covers. Walters slipped away from the shoot and found me in the sitting house, cleaning the nesting boxes.' Her eyes were hard, defiant. 'Pushed me down and raped me there in the dark on the stone cold floor, among the bird droppings.'

Shocked, Christopher was speechless.

Abruptly Mrs Walters rose from the table. 'Tea's gone cold. I'll make a fresh brew.' She went into the kitchen, moving about, boiling water on the stove, warming the pot, washing and drying the cups.

Christopher studied her as she went about these small tasks. Her spine was straight and her movements fluid. He watched, transfixed, his heart racing, afraid of what else she was about to tell him, afraid of why she was doing so, and even more afraid of how he felt. What would it be like to press his lips against the back of her long bare, elegant neck?

When she had served them both with the fresh, hot tea, she sat down opposite him across the narrow table. 'I had no idea about men and what they did to women. I'd no mother and Da was too embarrassed to bring the subject up. I suppose he thought I'd find out same as most women do, once I was married.'

Christopher frowned, trying to imagine that fourteen-year-old girl, weeping, alone in the dark in the out-building, after being brutalised by a man twenty-two years her senior.

'Da came home and found me weeping and bleeding, still terrified and feeling dirty. Dirty, dirty, dirty. He took a stick and went to find Walters. I wish he'd finished him off, but he settled for giving him a good hiding. Walters couldn't work for a week and was left with a few scars, but no long-term damage. Unlike me. The damage will last all my life.'

'I'm sorry, Mrs Walters.'

'Don't call me that. How can you call me that after what I've told you about him? Call me Martha. That's my name.'

'Martha.' Her name on his tongue sounded strange. The only Martha he had known was in the Bible. His thoughts wandered for a moment as he tried to remember what that Martha did. All he could recall was that her sister was Mary and one of them – he couldn't remember which – had washed the feet of Jesus.

Her gaze was steady, betraying no emotions despite the nature of what she was recounting. 'When my father returned he told me he'd been to the parish church and arranged for the banns to be called for me to be married to Walters.'

Christopher shook his head.

'I cried my heart out all that night and all the next day. I got down on my knees and begged him not to make me marry the man, but he wouldn't listen. Told me that Walters had shamed me and no one else would want me, so I had to marry him.'

Christopher's eyes stung with the threat of tears. He breathed deeply and looked away.

Martha's inflection remained steady, giving no indication of the turmoil her fourteen-year-old self must have gone through. 'So I married him and he moved in here into the bedroom and bed my parents had slept in and my father slept in the room that once was mine. Every night that man forced himself on me. Every night my father must have heard my cries, heard my tears, then heard him hitting me when I tried to resist. But he did nothing. He told me it wouldn't be right to come between a man and his wife. Now that I was married to Walters he was free to do with me what he wished. That's the way things were. Da was an old-fashioned man. He meant well but he believed there was an order to things. Believed that what happened between man and wife was no one else's concern. He tried to make up for it in other ways, bringing me little presents, being kind. It didn't help though. If anything it made me feel worse.'

Christopher gulped in air, as though the oxygen had been sucked from the room. 'I'm so sorry, Martha.' This time when he put his shaking hand on hers he left it there and she turned hers over so they met palm to palm. He laced his fingers between hers.

'I'm sorry to tell you all this but I couldn't bear that you thought so well of Walters. That you believed him to be a good man, a brave man, when he was rotten to the core and a miserable coward who forced himself onto a child. That's all I was then. A child, who didn't even know how babies were made. I hadn't even started my monthlies. I hadn't even realised that what I saw the dogs doing was what men did to women.' She leaned back in her chair and stared up at the ceiling. 'Except with dogs it's over quickly and doesn't seem to cause any pain. Not like what Harold Walters did to me.' She sighed a long slow exhalation of breath. 'You're probably wondering why I decided to tell you all this?'

He met her eyes. 'Yes, but whatever the reason, I feel honoured that you chose to take me into your confidence.'

She smiled at him and he realised it was the first time he had seen her smile. It lit up her face, erased the perpetual frowning and he saw she was beautiful. He swallowed, experiencing a sudden rush of desire. He made himself picture his mother, looking imperious at the dining table, summoning her to help dispel feelings inappropriate to the moment and to what the woman was telling him.

'I told you because you have a kind face. I've carried this inside me for twenty-one years and I needed to tell someone. Somehow I felt I could trust you. I can trust you, Captain Shipley, can't I?'

'Of course.' He squeezed her hand and felt a small pressure back.

'The nightly rapes continued until he gave up when I failed to produce a child. But the beatings got worse. He used to stay out late, drinking in the village tavern, whoring too no doubt, as he never touched me in bed again. Instead he'd come home drunk and beat the daylights out of me. By then my father was dead so he couldn't defend me, even if he'd wanted to. Walters was head keeper and a law unto himself. I had no one.'

'Oh, Martha. I'm so sorry.'

'Night after night he'd come home drunk and call me a barren bitch.'

Christopher winced at her words.

'That's all he thought women were good for. Objects for men's lust and bearers of their children. He wanted a son and when I couldn't give him one he punished me.'

They sat for a few moments in silence. Christopher heard a thrush singing in a tree outside the mullioned window. Her hand was still in his. He began to feel awkward, sitting there like that, hands joined across the scrubbed deal table, tea untouched. His eyes met hers and then they were both on their feet. He moved around the table and took her in his arms. They stood there, locked in an embrace, silent, listening to the sound of each other's breathing, feeling each other's chests rise and fall as they pressed close against each other.

Martha drew away first. 'I'm sorry,' she said. 'I didn't mean that to happen.' She placed her hands on his shoulders using them to keep him a short distance from her body.

'Don't say sorry. I'm not sorry,' he said, his own voice sounding strange to him. 'I'm not sorry at all.'

'You must go,' she said. 'Please forgive me. I stepped across a boundary. Let's forget it happened.'

Christopher pulled her towards him again, then conscious of what she had told him, dropped his hands and took a step back.

Martha's eyes welled with unshed tears. He was about to draw her into his arms again, wanting this time to kiss her, when she turned away. Her back stiffened and she began to clatter the crockery together and moved with it into the scullery. 'I've kept you, Captain Shipley. You'll be late for your dinner. Sorry, it's luncheon you call it at this time of day, don't you?' When she turned to face him it was as if a shutter had come down over her eyes.

He hesitated, waiting for her to suggest he return tomorrow but this time no invitation was forthcoming.

Embarrassed, Christopher was uncertain what to say next. She held the door open for him to leave, but before he could turn around and stammer his goodbye, she had closed it behind him.

MARTHA LEANED her back against the door as soon as she'd closed it. What had got into her? Telling him all that. Telling him her innermost secrets. Things that she'd never told another living soul and should be taking to the grave with her. Why? Why? Why?

There was something about Christopher Shipley that was different from anyone she had ever known. In his presence she felt more herself than she did even when she was on her own. Though she hadn't intended to tell him those things: they had just poured out of her. The caution that had characterised her whole adult life had deserted her. With him this afternoon she had felt calm, peaceful. Her confession of the secret she had carried all these years had felt like a cleansing. Telling him had washed away some of the pain.

But it was impossible to wash it all away. Some things

could never be told. Perhaps she would have been better to tell him nothing. Yes, it would have been better to tell him nothing, than to tell him a partial truth, to open a wound, to let the blood flow, only to staunch it with a dirty cloth, that would not only reinfect her but risk poisoning him too.

Martha moved away from the door and went upstairs. She lay down on the bed, turned her head to the pillow and let the tears flow.

CHAPTER 4

*C*hristopher was troubled by his second encounter with Mrs Walters and unable to stop thinking about her. Her story had moved and disturbed him. He was torn between embarrassment that he had taken her in his arms – hardly an appropriate way to behave with an estate tenant who was his batman's widow, and a wish that he'd gone a step further and kissed her. Touched by the manner in which she had confided the terrible secret of her marriage to him, he longed to offer her comfort, but didn't know how. Nothing could wash away such horrible memories, such damage done to her when so young.

Her face haunted him. The sad eyes, the gaunt features which, when she smiled, were illuminated and transformed into beauty. He felt a sharp longing in his gut, a desire that was almost a physical pain. He remembered how he had felt when he'd held her against him, how he had wanted to kiss her, to keep on holding her, to make things better for her. Yet in evicting her from the only home she had known, he would be making things worse.

Bending down, he unstrapped his artificial leg, rubbing

his hand over the end of his stump, massaging it where it chafed against the prosthesis. How could any woman bear to look at his disfigurement, let alone accept him? He was less than a man now: the war had emasculated him when it had torn part of his leg off but left him to live. Sometimes he wished he'd had a hero's death like his brother and so many of his fellow officers. Better to die than be left crippled. It felt like failure. Yet so many men had lost much more.

He thought of his friend, Douglas Middleton, another captain in the same company. Dougie had taken shrapnel in his face. His handsome looks were brutalised, an empty crater in the middle where his aquiline nose had once been. Blind in one hollowed-out eye, tiny shards of shrapnel embedded in the other to cause constant irritation and itching. Poor Dougie was facing a lifetime of pain and surgery, as well as rejection by the very people who once would have envied him his good looks. He had written to Christopher to tell him his fiancée had called off their engagement as soon as she saw the ugly ruin that had been his face. Men like Dougie who had given their all for their country were now asked to hide their faces in tin masks to avoid upsetting sensitive women and small children.

And then there was Private Biddle, who had arrived at the Front for the first time and, despite the warnings, was unable to resist a peek over the top of the trench at the enemy. Part of his skull was blown off by a sniper. He'd survived but was brain damaged and physically incapacitated and would never work again. An invalid, a living vegetable, for what was left of his life.

Instead of 'a land fit for heroes', England had become a country eager to forget the war, to shovel men like Dougie Middleton and Private Biddle into corners, lest they upset and embarrass others.

And women? They'd featured in the posters that had been

stuck on every tree, wall and building, exhorting men to go to fight the war on behalf of their womenfolk. What had Mrs Walters said? No man wants to be given a white feather. When Christopher had landed in England on his return from Borneo, women were waiting on the dockside, pressing recruitment pamphlets into the hands of disembarking men returning from the colonies. Apart from the expectations of his mother and the responsibility he felt to follow in his dead brother's footsteps, it would have taken a harder man than he to resist those harpies as they encouraged men to take up arms in defence of king and country.

How little he knew of women. He had no sisters. Only his snobbish, self-centred mother, who had always kept him at arm's length as a child. His beloved paternal grandmother had been taken too soon from him. But women as objects of desire? His experience was limited to an unsatisfactory interlude with a Belgian girl, in a hostelry behind the lines. He had turned up with the intention of losing his virginity, but in the end had bottled out, terrified of contracting a venereal disease. A pinched-faced matron in one of the hospital stations had lectured Christopher and a group of fellow officers, encouraging them to instruct their men on the perils of Belgian brothels, lamenting that it was bad enough treating wounds caused by German munitions without having to deal with self-inflicted ones too.

The young Belgian prostitute had spoken little English, appeared barely more than a schoolgirl and Christopher had baulked at the idea of handing over money in exchange for sexual intercourse. He had paid her the cash and headed back to the bar to seek oblivion in wine instead.

But now he was consumed with desire for Mrs Walters. To hold her in his arms, to feel her lips against his, to touch her with his hands where he had never touched a woman before. She was at least ten years older than him. She was uneducated. From another class. So why did he feel this unquenchable desire for her?

He lay back on the bed, drew the covers over himself and tried to shut her out of his thoughts. He closed his eyes and said the prayers he offered up silently every night for those who were dead, lost and damaged. But her face was the last thing he was aware of before he drifted into sleep.

THE FOLLOWING MORNING, mindful of the need to appease his mother, Christopher went to talk to the head gardener, an old man who, during the war years, had single-handedly taken care of the grounds while his workmates were away at the Front. It had been an impossible task. Only four men returned from the war out of a group of sixteen gardeners who had set out together. Nine had been killed, most in the first battle of the Somme. The remaining three were wounded in hospital, unfit to work again.

Christopher found the old gardener, Joe Hobson, in one of the greenhouses, pricking out seedlings. He doffed his cap when Christopher entered.

'Weren't expecting you this morning, Cap'n Shipley.'

'I thought I'd come along and find out how things are going, Joe. Any luck in recruiting more help?'

The old chap shook his head. 'No, sir. There's no workers to be 'ad locally. Looks like there'll just be the five of us for some time. I'd like to talk to you about what you want us to concentrate on. Only there's more work 'ere than we can manage.'

Christopher suggested they take a walk around the grounds. As they strolled, he explained what he wanted doing, conscious of his mother's wish that the area closest to the house should be returned as soon as possible to its former state. Edwina Shipley was keen to have garden parties again, to restore the croquet lawn, to picnic beside the ornamental lake.

The lake had been Samuel Shipley's pride and joy. As well as adding to the beauty of the parkland, its construction had been a feat of engineering. Covering several acres, it occupied a former quarry, created by the diversion of a stream. It was edged with trees on one side, with an open vista up to the house on the other. Christopher's grandfather had stocked the lake with trout and now, sixty years later, it had become a haven for wildlife, including colonies of ducks and Canada geese, the neglect over the wartime years having further encouraged nature to take hold.

They walked on and entered the extensive sunken gardens beyond the stable block. These walled gardens were a nine-acre wonderland of streams and small ponds, ornamental bridges, manicured lawns, summerhouses, pavilions and statuary. The paths were overgrown with weeds and brambles, in some areas impassable. Ivy and bindweed had spread their tentacles everywhere, choking treasured plants and hiding away the various sculptured eagles, Grecian urns and Roman gods that had once presided over the area.

'It's worse than I thought.'

'Aye, it's bad.'

'How long do you think it would take to tidy it up?'

'Months. Nay – years, more like. And without the men to do the work it's not possible. Just keeping the main lawns trimmed is a full-time job, without trying to tackle these in 'ere. There's dandelions everywhere. Ground elder n'all, choking the life out of everything.'

'But couldn't we at least cut back some of the undergrowth?'

The old man snorted. 'Too big a job, sir. Either we do this or the main lawns and shrubberies. Then there's the kitchen garden, n'all. Mrs Shipley is most particular about us tackling that too. Can't do everything. Mrs Shipley and your late father always preferred the rose gardens and the terraces.' He took off his cap and scratched his head.

'Then *I'll* tackle it. Can you spare me one of the lads and we'll see what we can do together?'

'You, sir?'

'Why not? I am a botanist after all. Plants are my expertise.'

'But not a gardener, sir. All due respect but it's not the same thing at all.' Hobson had witnessed Christopher's passion for plants since he was a young boy. 'Digging and hacking back all this mess ain't the same as doing your beautiful drawings.' He assessed Christopher, with a sceptical expression. 'It's 'ard labour.'

'Well, I'm going to try. You may be right, but I don't want to stand by and let this garden go to rack and ruin without doing something. And I did manage to cut my way through dense jungle in Borneo – and in intense heat.'

'So, this is what Mrs Shipley wants?'

Christopher bristled. Why was it so obvious that his mother had the final say in everything? 'It's my decision. I'm running the estate now.'

Joe thought for a moment. 'Maybe young Fred Collins could give you a hand. 'E were too young to serve. Only started 'ere as an apprentice a couple of months ago. 'E's a skinny one, but a good little worker. Stronger than 'e looks. I'd forgotten about 'im. If it's only clearance work Fred should be up to that. 'E's only fourteen, mind.'

'Fred it is then,' said Christopher. 'He can do the full days and I'll join him most afternoons. I have to do other things in the mornings, but we'll see how we go. We can at least make a start while we keep a look out for more hands.'

'Very well, Cap'n Shipley.'

He was about to head back to the house when he had an idea. He called to Hobson. 'What about women?'

'Sir?' Joe frowned, puzzled.

'To work in the garden. Maybe not with the heavy digging, but helping out with weeding and planting.' He was thinking of the large hole Mrs Walters had dug to bury the dog and her experience in the Land Army. She was a strong woman and if there was no situation for her in the house, why not out here? Better than her being thrown workless onto the streets.

'Never 'eard of anything like that, Cap'n Shipley. Don't sound right to me. And what woman would want to do a man's job?'

'Plenty did in the war. We'd have had no munitions if they hadn't gone into the factories. And no food if they hadn't worked the land. And now the men are back from war they're taking back those jobs. There must be women who want to work.' He hesitated then added, 'Widows who need to get by without a husband to provide for them.'

Joe stared at him. Pulling off his grubby cap, he scratched his head again. 'Don't rightly know. Sounds queer to me. But if you think so, sir.'

'There's Mrs Walters, the keeper's widow. I understand she's need of employment.'

'She's a rum one, that lass.' Joe frowned and shook his head. 'Never opens 'er mouth.'

'We're not looking for a talker. Just someone to help out. I'll find out if she's interested. If so, she can assist Fred and me here in the sunken garden.'

The elderly gardener shrugged, his expression sceptical. 'You're the master, sir.'

THAT EVENING at dinner Christopher broke the news to his

mother that he planned to work each afternoon in the sunken garden. He did not mention his intention to employ Mrs Walters.

'Have you lost your mind? You can't labour alongside the gardeners. Sometimes I just don't understand you.'

'I'm a botanist. I've dug up plants in the jungle in boiling heat, working alongside natives. A little work never harmed anyone and it will help build back my strength.'

She snorted in derision. 'And what about running the estate? That's a full-time job.'

'I will deal with estate matters in the mornings.'

'And the business?'

'There is a perfectly competent board to oversee matters and I intend to propose we hire a managing director to run the day-to-day operations.'

'Hire an outsider?'

'I have neither aptitude nor inclination to do it myself.' He took a sip of wine. 'Or we could promote one of the managers?'

She huffed and rolled her eyes.

'You know I'd make a complete hash of it if I tried to get involved myself.'

'You could at least try.'

'I'd have to leave here and live in Yorkshire. Then what about running this place? I can't do everything.'

Mrs Shipley was about to answer but evidently though better of it.

'Anyway, until now I've had no involvement whatsoever in Shipley Industries. That was Father and Percy's domain. But I do know about plants.' He smiled at her.

'Oh, Christopher, what shall I do with you? You are such a trial to your mother.' She gave a loud sigh, then smiled back. 'But you will look after the estate management in the mornings? No shirking and spending your time galloping around on that great beast of yours?'

'I promise. I'll get up early and ride before I start work. And I won't be alone – Joe Hobson has found a lad to help me.'

'I still think it's a waste of energy. That place gives me the creeps. And so old fashioned these days. You and the lad would be much better employed working on the main garden.'

'At least I'll be hidden away if I'm in the sunken garden. I didn't think you'd be keen on me working alongside the rest of the gardeners in full view.'

'There is that,' she admitted. 'And who am I to argue? I'm only a weak and foolish woman.' She said the words in a way to leave her ironic intent in no doubt.

In bed that night Christopher went over what he would say to Mrs Walters. If she accepted his proposal he would be able to spend every afternoon in her company. But would she agree?

CHAPTER 5

*C*hristopher spooned marmalade onto his plate and spread it onto a piece of toast. At the other end of the table his mother was behind her newspaper, absorbed in the Court announcements and society pages. Her two spaniels lay sleeping on the floor in front of the fireplace.

If Edwina Shipley had seen her son holding the gamekeeper's widow in his arms she would have been horrified. Christopher, momentarily amused at the thought of her indignation, then remembered that he had not resolved the problem of removing Martha Walters from her home. And now, with his intent to invite her to work as a gardener, he was risking more approbation from his mother if she found out.

A shaft of spring sunshine fell across the white damask tablecloth, making the silver cutlery sparkle. What was the point of all these things? The finest of everything. A vast estate, an enormous house, the charade of social engagements that were the *raison d'être* of his mother's existence? Most of all, what was the point of his life at all if he couldn't be the person he wanted to be? Defiance bubbled inside him.

After what he had gone through, he had every right to choose how he wanted to live.

His mother placed the folded newspaper beside her on the table and addressed her son. 'We'll have poussin with the Bournes on Friday then when the other guests join us on Saturday, I've told cook to do beef.' She took off her reading glasses, folded them and placed them back in their tortoise-shell case. 'You're not listening to me, Christopher.'

'Sorry, Mother. I was distracted for a moment.'

She tutted. 'Always daydreaming. Thinking about your wretched plants again no doubt. You'd better make sure you're not doing that when the Bournes get here.'

'What?'

'Really, darling, for goodness' sake, listen. I was saying that Lady Bourne and Lady Lavinia will be here for luncheon tomorrow and I expect you to pay Lavinia the attention she deserves. Such a delightful girl.'

She heaved a sigh and Christopher knew she was thinking how much better it would have been were Percy to be sitting here, eagerly anticipating his fiancée's arrival.

'Perhaps you could take her for a walk after luncheon and show her the walled garden and tell her your plans for the estate.'

He felt panic rise and his hand began shaking. 'I can't. I told you. I'll be working in the garden. I start today. I'm afraid I won't be able to join you for lunch either. Today or tomorrow.'

'Don't be ridiculous. You have to be here. These next two days are a golden opportunity for you to prepare the ground with Lavinia. Get to know her. By Sunday morning I'm hoping Lord Bourne will have invited us to visit Harton Hall this summer. I want you to seize every opportunity. You need to win him round. He's a tougher nut to crack than dear Lavinia and Lady Bourne. He was so close to your father and so attached to Percy. If only...' She gave a little cough then smiled at Christopher. 'Wouldn't it be perfect if we could announce the engagement after Ascot? Then a wedding the following May. I do so love a May wedding.'

Christopher dropped his toast onto his plate, appetite gone.

Edwina anticipated his resistance. 'I know we haven't talked about this in detail, darling, but you've always understood that it's the perfect solution. Dear Lavinia is such a treasure. Such a beauty. You'll make a delightful couple...' Her words tailed off and she turned to look towards the sleeping dogs.

'I can't marry Lavinia. She was to be married to Percy. It wouldn't be right.' He tried to keep calm in the face of mounting panic. Why was his mother always wrong-footing him?

'Don't be silly.'

'Please don't talk to me like a child, Mother.'

'Percy is gone but life must continue and we must all make the best of things. We must all do our duty. And your duty is to marry Lady Lavinia Bourne.'

Christopher said nothing. He picked up his teaspoon and twirled the handle round in his fingers. He was starting to get one of the headaches that had plagued him since the Somme.

'Really, darling, anyone would think I was asking you to do something frightful, when most young men would jump through hoops to marry a girl as lovely as Lavinia. You must agree she's beautiful?'

Christopher raised his hands in a gesture of resignation. 'How could I disagree?'

'And she comes from one of the best families.'

'Yes. Her pedigree is impeccable.' He didn't bother to conceal the sarcasm, but his mother was oblivious to it.

'Well then. What more do you want?'

'To marry someone I love? Who might even love me back?'

Edwina Shipley laughed. 'You are incorrigible, Christopher. You're not a servant. No one of our class marries for *love*. If you want love, do what your father did, if you must. Take a mistress. But make sure Lavinia gives you a son first.'

Christopher thumped his fist on the table. 'You're talking about us as if we were a bull and a heifer on the home farm. As if poor Lavinia is good for nothing but breeding.'

His mother rolled her eyes, raising them to the stuccoed ceiling. 'If you put it that way it sounds so vulgar. But you know as well as I do that that's the truth of it. No need to express it so crudely though. You have a duty to our family and to the futures of Newlands and Shipley Engineering. Marrying well is part of that.' She began counting on her fingers. 'Producing an heir is part of that. Making and using powerful contacts is part of that. You're fortunate that you're one of the few who made it though the dreadful war, otherwise—'

'Otherwise a woman like Lady Lavinia Bourne would turn up her nose at the idea of marrying me? A man with a missing leg, and no interest in money or running the estate he was unlucky enough to have inherited. A man who is not his better-looking, braver, altogether more eligible, older brother.'

He pushed back his chair and got up from the table. 'I'm going for my ride before doing the estate accounts and I'll be working in the sunken garden this afternoon. No time for lunch. You'll see me at dinner tonight.' Stepping round the sleeping spaniels, he left his stupefied mother and limped out of the room.

He rode around the grounds aimlessly – through the open fields, over the rolling parkland, skirting the lake, through the woods. His leg was throbbing today, the stump rubbing against his prosthesis, chafing his skin, and there was a phantom itch where his absent left calf should be. He hated that. Hated the way his damaged nerves fooled him into lowering his hand to scratch the leg even though it wasn't there, his fingers making no impact on the wooden substitute.

After a while, he loosened the reins, letting Hooker take him wherever he wished, and found himself riding into the copse of trees that surrounded the gamekeeper's cottage. It was as though his horse sensed it was where he wanted to be.

Martha Walters was sitting on the doorstep shelling peas. Sunlight, filtering through the newly green trees, fell upon her hair, making a dappled latticework. She glanced up at him, her face expressionless. Christopher eased himself out of the saddle and swung himself to the ground, remembering to take most of his weight on his good leg. He looped the reins over Hooker's neck, left him to graze and walked towards Martha. She carried on with her task, offering no greeting until he sat down, sitting on the soft springy turf in front of her, his good leg curled under him, the false one stretching out in front.

'I didn't think you'd come again,' she said at last.

'I almost didn't. You didn't invite me this time.'

'You need no invitation. You own the place after all.' She stated the fact without resentment.

'I wish I didn't.' He leaned back on his arms and looked up at the sky.

'You can tell Mrs Shipley I'll leave whenever she wants me to.'

'No.' He answered quickly, affronted that she realised the truth of his relationship with his mother. 'I've told Mother you'll be staying until I find another head keeper.' He smiled at her. 'And I've no idea when I'm going to get round to doing that.'

'Don't worry,' she said. 'I've started packing. I've not much here that's mine.'

She finished the last of the peas, putting the enamel bowl on one side and gathering up the empty pods into her apron. 'Shouldn't you be having your dinner now?' She corrected herself. 'Your luncheon.'

'We've got guests arriving today and I've told Mother I won't be joining them until this evening. I thought I'd give them time to talk without me.'

'You must be hungry?'

He shrugged. 'Not really. I hadn't even thought about it.'

'Well I am. I'm going to boil these peas up and have them with some leftover stew. You're welcome to join me.'

Christopher accepted the invitation. He picked up the bowl of peas and followed her inside the house.

He watched as she tipped the contents of her apron into a large pan, in which she had already sweated an onion and some wild garlic. 'You're cooking the pods too?'

She added some water. 'They can simmer away. They'll make a good soup. I'll eat that tomorrow and the day after. Have to use what I can. No waste. The thirteen and ninepence I get for a widow's pension doesn't go far.' Her mouth formed a tight smile. She set a saucepan to boil for the peas. 'What will they be eating up at the big house today?'

Christopher shrugged. 'Cold cuts for lunch. Soup, I suppose.' He gave a mirthless laugh. 'Baby chickens tomorrow night, when we have company. Mother seems to think I should be interested in the menus she chooses.'

'And so you should be. You should be thankful for such plenty.'

'You think I'm not? I do know what it's like to be hungry. Sometimes there was nothing but dry biscuits when the supplies to the Front were held up. And the bread was never less than a week old by the time it got up the line to us. Once the war was over I knew I'd never be able to look at tinned beef again. And before that, when I was in Borneo, we ate what we could. Mostly rice and chicken.' He gave a wry smile. 'Sometimes it was wiser not to ask what we were eating.'

When the meal was ready, Martha ladled the stew onto plates and added peas on the side. 'I used the last of the potatoes I'm afraid. Only two left so I put them in the stew. If you're lucky you'll find a piece.'

'I shouldn't be eating your food, Mrs Walters. I'll be leaving you short.'

'I told you. Call me Martha. I won't say it again.' She sounded gruff, annoyed, and Christopher cursed himself inwardly. His intent had been to avoid seeming disrespectful in the use of her Christian name, but he had clearly offended her.

'I'm sorry, Martha.' He picked up his cutlery and began to eat. 'This is delicious. What's in it?'

'Rabbit. I set traps. I told you I make do with what's around.'

He ate, realising how hungry he was after all. 'It's the best meal I've eaten in a long time.'

'Simple food.'

'Simple's good.'

'Tell me about Borneo. Where is it? I've never heard of it.'

'Thousands of miles away. The edge of the Empire. It's part of a huge archipelago of islands, Java, Sumatra, the Dutch East Indies, countless small islands – too many to remember their names, let alone visit them all.'

'Why did you travel there?'

'I went to find and catalogue plants. There's miles of

unexplored jungle and all manner of plant-life that has yet to be discovered and classified.'

She raised her eyebrows. 'You're an explorer?'

'I suppose you could say that. I'd describe myself as a humble botanist. I was working on a book on the flora of the island of Borneo. Then the war came along, my brother was killed and I had to come home. My father died while I was on the voyage back. Then I went into the army.'

'What made you want to study plants? And go all that way?'

'I've loved plants since I was small and used to read about rare species in the books in my grandfather's library.'

'So you got it from him? He liked plants too?'

Christopher laughed. 'I suppose he did. But I doubt he'd ever opened a book in his life. Apart from financial ledgers, I imagine. He bought books by the foot to fill the shelves of the library. All part of his plan to disguise his humble origins. I was the only one who ever read any of them.'

'I used to love to read. I learned at the village school, but when I married Walters I had to leave and there were no books in the house. Da couldn't read and Walters wasn't interested. The school teacher, Miss Edmonds, used to lend them to me. She felt sorry for me having to marry that man. Even tried to persuade my da against forcing me to wed him, but Da wouldn't listen. Said most folk weren't like her and wouldn't look well on a girl who'd already been... Anyway, Walters put a stop to the reading when he came home one afternoon and caught me curled up with a book. *Jane Eyre* it was. He threw it on the fire and gave me a beating for wasting time when I should have been doing housework.'

Christopher swallowed. He wished he had known all this about the man he had believed to be a brave and loyal servant, an exemplary soldier. He felt ashamed that he had been so gulled by his batman. He remembered the eulogy he had given after his death in front of the small band of men beside the ruins of their blasted dugout.

'I'll lend you books,' he said at last. 'Tell me what you want and I'll bring them to you.'

'Thank you. That's kind of you, but I don't want you to get into trouble with Mrs Shipley.'

Christopher pushed his plate away. 'Why does everyone treat me like a child? Even you. I may not want to be the owner of Newlands but that's what I am and if I want to give you the whole damn library I'll do so.'

She was looking at him, her same expressionless face showing no signs of pity, regret or embarrassment.

'I'm sorry,' he said. 'I shouldn't have spoken that way. Shouldn't have sworn in front of you, lost my temper.'

Martha leaned across the table and touched his hand lightly. 'You never need to apologise to me, Captain Shipley.'

'If I'm to call you Martha, you must call me Christopher.'

She met his eyes, her gaze steady. 'Christopher sounds wrong for you. Can I call you something else? Something no one else calls you.'

He was taken aback by her frankness. He thought for a moment. 'Then call me Kit. My grandmother used to call me that when I was a little boy. Mother used to tell her off when she heard her but I loved it. She died before I was twelve and no one's used it since. Percy and Father called me Chris. I hated that.'

'Kit. I like it. Kit.' She smiled at him and he saw again how her face was transformed, lit from within by the uncustomary smile, the warmth in her eyes.

'You were telling me about Borneo. Don't stop.'

So he told her about his journeys through the jungles and equatorial forest of the huge island. Of the caverns filled with stalactites and stalagmites, of mountains rising through the clouds, of rushing streams, houses on stilts high above the surface of the sea, of abundant wildlife, of strange tribal customs, of orang-utans swinging through the trees, of the vibrant coloured plumage of birds so different from the drab monochrome of British birds. She listened to him, spellbound, then watched as he pulled a small sketch book and pencil out of his jacket pocket and drew a picture of the strange dragon creatures he had seen when his boat made a stop en route at the island of Komodo. They sat, facing each other across the table until Christopher checked his watch.

'Oh no. I forgot.'

'Forgot what?'

'The reason for my calling on you today.'

She frowned. 'You don't need a reason, sir.'

'Kit.'

'Kit then. So why did you come?'

'I wanted to ask if you would help me. Work with me? I'll pay you of course. The full rate for the job. The man's rate.'

She seemed puzzled.

'You'd be working alongside me in the afternoons and if you can manage the mornings too you'll be working with a lad called Fred. Fred Collins.'

Her frown deepened. 'I know who he is. But he works as a gardener.'

'That's right. I want to restore my grandfather's sunken garden. It's behind the stable block. Do you know it?'

She shook her head. 'I don't go near the big house.'

Kit explained what he had agreed with Joe Hobson. 'And since you've worked in the Land Army and you're in need of employment, I thought you could help me. Not with the heavy digging. Fred and I will deal with that. But in helping cut back the undergrowth. Weeding. Pruning. Planting. That kind of thing. And only the afternoons if you prefer.'

'Do I get to wear my breeches?'

He laughed, then felt a shiver of desire at the thought of

seeing her clad so improperly. 'I'll order you a new pair from Harrods.'

She laughed too. Then frowned. 'And Mrs Shipley?'

'Doesn't know. And I plan to keep it that way. She never goes near the sunken garden. Says it gives her the creeps. She's not happy about me working there but I told her this morning my mind is made up. There's no point in me riling her further by telling her there's a woman working there.'

'The pay?'

'Twenty-four shillings a week. Eleven and sixpence if you do the afternoons only. But don't mention it – it's more than Fred gets, as he's only an apprentice.'

'Shouldn't I be too?'

'You're not a young lad. And you've more experience.'

'Well, that's very generous. When do I start?'

'I thought I'd take you across there this afternoon. Show you what's involved. And if that doesn't put you off, you can start tomorrow afternoon. Unless you want to do the full days?'

'Afternoons suit me. There's things I have to do here.'

THEY MADE their way through the woods, skirting the far side of the lake so that they would arrive at the sunken garden without being visible from the house. The last thing Kit wanted was to be seen with Martha by his mother.

He showed her the mess that the garden had become, delighted that the monumental nature of the task did not dismay her. The young apprentice, Fred Collins, had already made inroads into clearing the main pathway that ran through the centre of the gardens.

Kit led Martha over to Fred, who pulled off his cap when he saw his employer. 'Afternoon, Cap'n Shipley, sir.' He gestured towards the partially cleared walkway. 'It's taking a long time, sir, but I reckon if I can clear this main path first I can get a wheelbarrow through. That should make things easier.'

'Good show.'

'And then there's the grass.' Fred jerked his head towards what had once been a velvet-smooth lawn between the pathway and a small lake but was now a field of coarse long grasses, dandelions and buttercups, the growth more than waist high. 'It will need scything, Mr Hobson says. And probably new lawns laid.'

Kit decided that even though Fred was still a boy, he was a hard worker and a bright lad.

'One thing at a time, Fred. That's the only way we'll get anywhere with this. And you're right. We need to concentrate on clearing first, then we'll see what plants are left and which ones can be saved.'

Martha had said nothing during this exchange. Kit explained her presence to Fred, who, to Kit's surprise, took the fact that he would be working alongside a woman in his stride. 'My big sister was in the Land Army. You should see 'er muscles.'

Martha gave him a rare smile, then turned to Kit. 'I could start over there.' She pointed to a single-storey building off the main pathway. 'In the gardeners' rooms. Get the place cleaned out, sort through the equipment. See what can be cleaned and used and what will need to go to the blacksmith to be sharpened and resurfaced.' She smiled again at Fred. 'And I'll see if I can find you that wheelbarrow and get the rust off the scythes.'

Satisfied that he had recruited a strong team, Kit apologised to Fred that he had not done his turn that afternoon and assured him that he would be there the following afternoon to lend a hand with clearing the pathways.

Fred appeared nonplussed, evidently still trying to digest

the idea of the master rolling up his sleeves to labour beside him.

Kit clapped a hand on the lad's shoulder. 'Don't worry, Fred. We'll soon transform this place.' But he knew he had taken on a Sisyphean task. There were nine acres to clear, restore, replant, renew, not to mention the buildings and structures. One young lad with the part-time support of a woman and a crippled man. Tomorrow morning he would arrange for a local craftsman to inspect the buildings and determine whether any urgent repairs were needed. He could already see an ornamental wooden bridge, which spanned the small lake to an island, was in need of mending. It was covered in bracken and was collapsing on one side into the water. A hexagonal summer house near the lawn had lost most of its thatched roof and there were pigeons nesting in the rafters.

He glanced at his pocket watch. 'I must go. 'Til tomorrow, Fred, Mrs Walters.' He couldn't avoid using her married name in front of the lad. He nodded at them both, then set off to bring Hooker, who had been grazing outside, back to the stables.

As MARTHA WALKED home from the sunken garden to the lodge in the woods, she asked herself for the umpteenth time what she was doing. Every time she saw Kit Shipley she swore to herself it would be the last time. And then, when he appeared again, all her resolutions floated away, like dande-lion clocks on a breeze.

He was so different in every way from how she had expected him to be. He was the master of the estate, her employer, a wealthy man, rich beyond her imagination, yet a kind, gentle man, an interesting man, sensitive, lonely, damaged. Whenever they were together, all Martha's resolutions evaporated. All she knew was she wanted to be with him.

One thing was clear. He felt the same way about her. Of that she was certain. Martha knew it, just as she knew that day followed night, that bluebells appeared in the woods every spring, and that she had never felt a moment's happiness since the day she was raped in the dark of the sitting house. Yet now she felt blindly, deliriously happy. But her happiness was threaded through with a terrible fear. A fear that, as soon as Kit Shipley found out the truth about her, he would not only withdraw from her, but he would despise her.

Martha could not let that happen. Better to lose him than to have him know the truth. It mustn't happen. He mustn't find out. He must never know. She had to stop it now before it went any further.

CHAPTER 6

*T*he following day, after an early ride around the parkland, Kit rushed through his morning's work before returning to the sunken garden. Knowing that he was about to spend the afternoon in the company of Martha Walters was a spur to his efforts and the previously neglected pile of letters and estate paperwork was significantly diminished by the time he left the house.

Fred was still working on clearing the central pathway through the garden. After offering some words of encouragement, Kit left him to get on with the job and went in search of Martha. He found her in the long brick building used to store gardening equipment and provide shelter to the gardeners.

He stood for a moment in the doorway, watching her as she squatted in front of a pile of plant-pots, discarding the broken ones into a sack beside her. She was wearing her Land Army breeches. He swallowed and took a deep breath, trying to suppress the shock of desire that ran through his body.

Sensing his presence, Martha turned and saw him.

Kit smiled, then looked away, turning his attention to the building, trying to distract himself from her and his overwhelming wish to rush up and take her in his arms.

The structure included a pair of small rooms that before the war had housed the man who had been the undergardener. A bachelor, he had died on the Somme. All that remained of his presence was a photographic studio-portrait of what Kit took to be the man's parents, posing formally to mark their wedding. The image was pinned to the wall, curling at the edges and covered with green mould on one side, where it had been water-damaged by a leak in the roof.

'I got here a little early today to make a start,' Martha said. 'Only I might be late tomorrow. I hope that's in order?'

Kit nodded. 'Of course.'

He gestured at the sparsely furnished room. 'If my mother gets her way and we do have to hire a new gamekeeper, you could move in here. It's not much at the moment, but there's a stove, a table and chairs, and a bed. I could order some furniture, a new mattress. I'm sure you could make it a comfortable home.'

Her expression was dubious.

'Don't you like it?' he said.

'I like it well enough. And I'd love nothing more than to be somewhere that has nothing to do with Bill Walters. No bad memories. But your mother would never agree.'

'It doesn't concern her. I've told you. She never comes here. And what I do with the estate is my concern.'

'I'd heard it said she's got the final say until you're thirty.' She held his eyes, her gaze steady.

'Where did you hear that?'

'Servants talk.' Her expression was challenging. 'Isn't it true, then?'

Kit felt a silent thrill at her boldness in addressing him so directly. Not as a servant. 'Yes, but my mother has no interest in the day-to-day running of the estate. All she cares about is getting it back to what it once was.'

'But the cost of making this place habitable?'

He shrugged. 'I'll make sure it's more than habitable. Money is the one thing I have in abundance. Even if the source of it plagues my conscience.'

'Why?' Again, that steady look, straight into his eyes.

'Armaments. The real winners of the war were companies like Shipley Industries.'

'The war's over. And they've said there'll be no more wars now.'

'I wouldn't lay money on that. As long as men have lived, they've fought wars. The carnage of this one will soon be forgotten. And there are colonies to defend, new ones to acquire. Besides, Shipley's has an automotive branch too. The need for motor cars is going to grow and so will the need for Shipley's engines to power them.'

She stared at him with her habitual inscrutability. Kit turned away, afraid that his own emotions were not so well concealed.

'That pile of tools I've put over there will need to go to the blacksmith's,' she said. 'They need sharpening and re-grinding.'

He turned away, avoiding looking at her legs, their shape visible under the serge breeches.

'I'm meeting a builder in a few minutes,' he said. 'He's coming to do an inventory of repairs. I'll tell him this place needs to be a priority. We'll have it watertight, furnished and ready for you to move into in no time at all.' He went towards the door and turned to look back at her again. 'And I'm going to ask him to include bathing facilities. He can build an extension at the back. A coal store too.'

A few hours later, after he had dealt with the builder – who was now a happy man, eager to return to his office to draw up and price what was an extensive schedule of works – Kit went back to find Martha. The tool store was now cleared, floor swept, useable tools and implements hanging from hooks on the walls. She had even washed the windows.

Fred Collins had gone home for his tea and Martha was putting on her coat when Kit walked in. He stood in the doorway, watching her as she fastened the buttons. One side of her hair was laced with cobwebs. 'Wait,' he said, and moved towards her, lifting his hand to brush them away.

The deep dark pools that were her eyes fixed on him. Fearing she would misinterpret his gesture, he quickly said, 'Cobwebs… in your hair.'

Martha relaxed, but there was a slight flush in her face. His hand shook as his fingers traced the surface of her thick, dark hair, catching up the fine grey lace of the spider's web and casting it aside.

Without a word, she moved past him and he followed her outside. The sun was low in the sky and the clouds were tinged with pink. In silence, they walked together towards the only bench that was not overgrown with moss and grass. They sat down, and Kit was suddenly self-conscious. The badly cut, baggy breeches did nothing to cool his ardour. Her thighs, outlined under the coarse fabric, disturbed him; he wanted to put his hand on her leg. He resisted the urge, crossing his arms instead.

After a few minutes' silence, the tension between them was an electric current. If he stayed there beside her, reaching out to touch her was an inevitability.

He got to his feet. 'I'll be late for dinner. Mother will never forgive me if I don't show up for cocktails with our guests.'

'Cocktails?'

'Fancy drinks. Strange concoctions of all manner of things. Mother thinks it's impressive serving them. But completely wasted on the Bournes. The women prefer champagne and Lord Bourne hates his whisky to be polluted by other ingredients.'

'What an exotic life you lead, Kit. Yours is such a different world from mine,' she murmured.

'A world I don't belong in.'

A ghost of a smile reached her eyes. 'Will you be here again? Tomorrow?'

'I'll try. I intend to be here every afternoon, if possible. But tomorrow it will be hard to escape since there are guests. There'll be more arriving tomorrow evening. Mother is holding a dinner party.'

'And you must pay attention to Lady Lavinia.'

Kit's head jerked in surprise. 'What of her? How do you know of her?'

'Everyone at Newlands knows you're going to marry her. It's common knowledge. She's a beautiful woman.'

'You've seen her?'

'I was there the night she became engaged to marry your brother, before the war. Mrs Harrison had extra servants brought in to help in the kitchen and to fetch and carry. I caught a glimpse of Lady Lavinia when the dining room doors were open. She was the talk of the kitchens. So beautiful. The perfect lady. You must be glad to be marrying her.'

'I'm not marrying her. There is nothing between me and Lavinia Bourne and there never will be.' He picked up his hat from the bench, stood and turned towards the pathway.

She rose, stretched her hand out and touched his arm. 'I'm sorry. I've upset you. I didn't intend to. I wanted you to know that I know. That... that you're going to marry her... because...'

He turned around and, without thinking, pulled her into his arms. This time he bent his head to find her mouth. Then they were kissing with abandon, with hunger, their mouths greedy, their bodies pressed against each other. He felt her breasts against his chest, rising and falling with her breathing.

Martha broke away first. 'Go. You must go, Kit. You'll be late.' She pushed him away.

He stood in front of her, hat in hand, head pounding, then walked with his jerky gait towards the archway and out of the walled garden.

CHAPTER 7

*E*dwina Shipley threw a surly glance in Christopher's direction when he walked into the drawing room, but quickly masked her irritation behind a beaming smile for the benefit of her guests.

'There you are, darling. I was just explaining you had urgent business this afternoon.' She turned to Lord and Lady Bourne. 'Such a bore, but duty calls.' She stretched her hand out to welcome her son into the room. 'Bannister has mixed some Manhattans. You will have one, won't you, Christopher? Do please keep me company – I can't persuade Lady Bourne and Lavinia to succumb. And you know Lord Bourne is as bad as your dear departed father and won't even allow so much as an ice cube in his whisky.' She laughed.

Christopher could tell she was nervous, so he decided the best course was to accept.

From across the room, Lord Bourne bellowed, 'Ice in scotch is an abomination. Something else I fear your fellow Americans are responsible for, Mrs Shipley.'

Edwina's laugh was forced. She hated being reminded of her origins.

Holding Christopher's drink, she pushed it into his left hand. 'Go!' she said, 'Lavinia is waiting.'

Christopher took the glass and moved across the room to greet the guests.

This weekend was the first time Mrs Shipley had formally entertained since the death of her husband, and she was working hard to project the image of the perfect hostess. Christopher felt sorry for her, for her desperation, her determination to play the part of the grande dame flawlessly. It had never ceased to surprise him how much her acceptance by the English upper class mattered to his mother. Under her immaculate and expensive clothes, perfect manners and cultivated cut-glass English accent, there was a large chip on her shoulder and an abiding fear that, as an American, she could never be the genuine article, but always a hopeful postulant, falling slightly short.

Lord Bourne looked as though he wished he were a thousand miles away or, more likely, ensconced within the marble portals of his gentleman's club or in the bar at the House of Lords. He settled himself in a seat in front of the fire and focused his attention on his whisky. Lady Bourne sat down opposite him, beside Edwina Shipley, and the two women were soon absorbed in conversation, leaving Christopher and Lady Lavinia to each other, as was clearly the intent.

Lavinia was undeniably pretty. Tonight she was wearing a gown the same colour as the champagne in her glass. Her figure was slender, and the gown showed it to advantage, with a pearl encrusted bodice above a taffeta skirt, which skimmed her body closely around the waist and hips before falling to a few inches above her ankles. The bodice revealed her shoulders in a way that a few years earlier would have been described as shocking rather than daring. Her blue eyes were framed by improbably long lashes and her lips formed a perfect Cupid's bow. She smiled at Christopher, lowering her gaze flirtatiously. Yet it seemed to be practised rather than natural, and he had no illusions that her manner would have been any different if directed at a man other than him.

They went to stand by the full-height windows that gave onto a paved terrace, beyond which the lawns extended as far as a ha-ha – a completely unnecessary feature in the absence of any cattle in this part of the estate. It was still light, the evenings already lengthening with the promise of spring, and the first signs of sunset were appearing in the rose-tinged sky.

'It's a beautiful evening,' Christopher said after a few minutes' awkward silence.

'I suppose it is.' She gave a little giggle as though he had said something witty.

'Looks as though we're about to get a wonderful sunset.'

'Really? How interesting.' Her tone indicated that she deemed it anything but.

'Mother suggested that I show you around the grounds tomorrow. Would you like that?'

'Actually no.' She rolled her eyes upwards. 'Unless you absolutely insist on it.' She tilted her head on one side and smiled at him in mock apology. 'I suffer from hay fever. It's a frightful bore. I don't care to be outdoors especially near freshly-cut grass or lots of flowers. It makes me sneeze horribly. Winter's all right. But who wants to be out of doors when it's cold?'

'I see.' Christopher tried to imagine what kind of life she must have if she rarely went outside. 'That must be hard for you?'

'Not at all.' She spoke with a drawl, the same lazy, upper class cadence as her father's – as though everything around her, and any possible topic of conversation was too tedious to bear contemplation. 'I spend most mornings in bed.' She peered up at him with her bright blue eyes, then dropped her gaze. He wondered if she practised in front of the mirror. 'Do you think that's awful of me? Mummy says it's very naughty but I think I might as well, while I can. Before I have to be married and get up to do all kind of boring things like telling the servants off.' She giggled again and turned her dazzling smile on him. 'I do go outside to walk my dogs in the afternoon. I have two chihuahuas. I'm heartbroken they're not with me now. I jolly well hate leaving my babies behind.' Her mouth formed a pout and she lowered her voice to a conspiratorial tone. 'Do you like chihuahuas, Captain Shipley?

Christopher swallowed. This was going to be more of an ordeal than he had anticipated. 'I've never actually come across one. Mother has a pair of spaniels.'

'Then I'll have to introduce you to Popsy and Petal. They're completely and utterly adorable. Everyone loves them. Well, apart from Daddy. He's always complaining that they get under his feet. Calls them my little rats. What a beast he is.' She gave a tinkling laugh and told Kit how she liked to hide the dogs in her handbag. He tried to picture this but his imagination failed him.

'I haven't seen you since the night you became engaged to my brother,' he said, keen to change the topic of conversation. Then after a moment's hesitation added, 'It must be hard for you, losing Percy so soon after you were engaged.'

She frowned. 'Yes of course. Jolly rotten luck. Percy was an absolute darling. Such fun. I was so looking forward to marrying him.' She made a little sniffling noise then dabbed at her nose with a handkerchief. 'Then of course everything had to be cancelled. So sad. My brother died soon after. Horrible, horrible war.' She turned to look out of the window. He thought she was going to say something else about Percy but she said, 'My wedding dress was already made. It was so pretty but Mummy said I had to put it in mothballs. It would have worked as well as a ball gown but there weren't any balls once the horrid war started. Now Mummy says I have to wear it when I get married as it was frightfully expensive. Don't you think that's mean of her? That gown is now three years old and fashions are changing all the time. I would so hate to look frowsy and dowdy on my wedding day.'

She smiled at him, again dropping her eyes.

'That would be impossible in your case, Lady Lavinia,' he said. She smiled in acceptance of the inevitable compliment.

Barely a word to spare for his poor dead brother. Christopher slugged down his Manhattan. He was going to need several drinks to get through this evening. Especially as all he could think of was the memory of kissing Martha and how desperate he was to rush out of the room, saddle up his horse and go to her.

He was about to replenish his drink, when Bannister came into the room and announced dinner.

Over the course of the meal, Christopher made further attempts at conversation with Lavinia but failed to find a sustainable topic. The only subjects that seemed to enthuse his prospective fiancée were her dogs, her collection of porcelain dolls – she told him she now had thirty-six, which were displayed in a glass cabinet in her bedroom – and her recent trip to Paris with her mother. 'Daddy told me to make the most of it,' she whispered. 'Funds are a teeny bit tight at the moment. Such a bore.' She clapped a hand over her mouth then whispered to him, 'Gosh. I wasn't supposed to say that. Mummy will be jolly cross. Do you think she heard me?'

Christopher told her it was unlikely, and assured her that the secret was safe with him.

He asked what she thought of the granting of the suffrage to women the previous year.

'I'm not thirty,' she replied, sounding outraged.

'I didn't intend to imply that you were. I merely wondered whether you were pleased that the struggle is over.'

'I find politics boring. And as for the suffragettes, I think they behaved disgracefully and should still all be in prison. Politics is one of those things like war and driving motor cars that should be left to men, don't you agree, Captain Shipley?'

Christopher swallowed, scarcely believing what he was hearing.

They passed the rest of the meal with little more to say to each other, while their mothers kept up a valiant attempt at small talk, drawing them in where possible.

When the ladies retired, leaving the two men to port and cigars, Lord Bourne got straight to the point.

'So, you're intending to marry my daughter?'

Christopher swallowed, shocked at the bluntness and the speed at which his lordship had got to the crux of the matter.

His hands shaking, he put down his port and stammered, 'I barely know her. Tonight's only the second time we've met.' He quickly added, 'Lady Lavinia is a charming woman.' He realised he had had too much to drink in his attempt to make the evening tolerable, and Lord Bourne's face was slightly out of focus.

The older man puffed on his cigar. 'Damned good cigars. George always did keep a good Havana. You not smoking?'

The thought of a cigar made Christopher feel nauseous.

Lord Bourne returned to his chosen topic. 'Lavinia's an empty-headed creature. Her mother's always spoiled her. Pretty little thing though. That's all that matters in a woman, I suppose. She certainly knows how to twist me round her little finger.' He inspected the end of his cigar. 'So, young man. What about it?'

Christopher opened his mouth like a fish, at a loss for what to say.

'I don't believe in beating about the bush. I'd have preferred her to marry your brother. Good man, Percy. Chip off the old block. Just like George. Clubbable. Damn shame he copped it. My son too. Terrible business.' He shook his head and refilled his glass from the decanter. Christopher saw it was already half empty.

'I hear you're a botanist. What kind of nonsense is that?' Without waiting for an answer, Lord Bourne added, 'But your mother says that from now on you'll be devoting yourself to the management of the estate and the family business.' He spoke the last word as if it was slightly grubby. 'Never really understood commerce myself. But you can always pay someone else to manage the company for you while you concentrate on getting Newlands back to its best.'

'I haven't decided yet what I will do. I've been concentrating on recovering my health.'

'Ah, yes. Lost a leg. Shame about that. Don't suppose Lavinia is too thrilled about having a one-legged husband.' He drew on his cigar, then rolled it around between thumb and first finger. 'Still, she'll have to get on with it. Same as you're doing. Sacrifice for king and country. Can't ask more than that, eh?' He swirled the port around in his glass. 'Damn fine port too.' He took another sip, then added, 'Leg won't stop you, you know, doing what you need to do, if you follow my meaning? Didn't lose any other parts I hope?'

Christopher felt the blood rushing to his face, wondering how to reply, but Lord Bourne evidently didn't expect a response.

'I'd like to get this settled soon. Have to follow proprieties, but you and I can agree, man to man, and let the ladies sort out the finer details later. I thought we'd announce the engagement in a couple of months. I've invited you and your mother to come to Harton Hall. End of June. After Ascot. In the meantime you can take the gal to the theatre or dinner a couple of times. Go through the motions – she can't abide the theatre – who can blame her? – but she'll play the game. Like her father in that regard. Can't stand opera either. Once you're married you can do what you like.'

Christopher listened, barely able to take in what he was hearing.

'Told you about her blessed dogs, has she? Horrible little things. I swear to God, one day I'll accidentally step on one and squash it to death. Can't say she hasn't been warned.' He chuckled to himself. 'Good luck to you with them. Horrible, yappy little creatures.'

He tapped the top of the table with his knuckles. 'Your late father and I had already sorted out all the financial aspects when she and Percy became engaged, so we'll stick to those. No need to waste any more time. Percy, or you – makes no difference in the end. Not when I have a roof that needs mending. The place will be yours and Lavinia's when I go anyway. No son to leave it to any more. Need you and Lavinia to provide an heir to my title.' He was in full flow now. 'No entail on the estate or the title so Lavinia's children will inherit. As to the house. Draughty old place. Damp too. So it makes sense to get the repairs done sooner rather than later. These days we spend most of the time in the town house. My wife and Lavinia hate the country. But Harton Hall has been in the family for centuries so we can't let it go to rack and ruin.'

Christopher didn't know how to respond to being so overtly described as a fair exchange for a new roof on a country house.

Lord Bourne leaned back in his chair and puffed on his cigar. 'Well?' he said at last.

'As I said, I've not had an opportunity to consider all this. I've only been home from the rehabilitation hospital for a month.'

'What? Nothing to consider.'

'I happen to think there is.' Christopher got to his feet, trying to ignore the way the room was spinning. 'Now, Lord Bourne, I believe the ladies will be expecting us in the drawing room.'

After they drank a hurried and awkward tea with the two older women, Lavinia having already excused herself and gone to bed, Christopher was approaching his bedroom when his mother intercepted him on the landing. 'Well?'

'Well what?' He realised his speech was slurred.

'Don't be tiresome, darling. How did it go with Lavinia? And what did you discuss with Lord Bourne?'

'Lavinia surpassed all my expectations.'

'Oh, that's wonderful, darling.'

'She's not only dim, she's completely unable to think about anything other than herself and her beloved dogs.'

'Really, Christopher, you're such a tease. Be serious.' She peered at him. 'Are you intoxicated?'

'Yes, I am indeed intoxicated. Only way I could get through the bloody evening. And I'm deadly serious. That was the dullest evening I've ever had the misfortune to spend.'

'You don't have to find the girl interesting. You just have to marry her. How hard can that be?'

'Hard? It's impossible.'

'We'll talk about this tomorrow,' she hissed. 'When you're sober. In the meantime, please, please, be civil to the woman.'

'I've never been anything but civil, Mother. The model of manners and courtesy.'

'Well, thank heavens for that at least. Goodnight.' She proffered her cheek to be kissed and went back along the corridor to her room.

Safely inside his own bedroom, Kit leaned against the back of the door for a few moments. He staggered towards the bed, slumped on top and fell into an immediate sleep. He hadn't even removed his leg.

CHAPTER 8

The following morning, nursing a sore head, Christopher went down to breakfast in the morning room. To his relief, only Edwina was there and she told him that Lavinia and her mother had not yet risen and were unlikely to appear before luncheon and Lord Bourne had left for a round of golf with Geoffrey Harrington-Foster, one of the dinner guests expected that evening.

'I hope you're in a better frame of mind this morning, Christopher?'

'My mind is perfectly framed.'

'Do you have to joke all the time? You know exactly what I'm talking about. I must say you do look dreadful. You and Lord Bourne gave the port a hammering last night. Bannister says you demolished a whole decanter.'

Christopher chose not to respond.

'So? Did Lord Bourne raise the question of you marrying his daughter?'

'He did indeed. Rather bluntly, I thought. Told me the arrangements would be exactly as agreed between him and Father for Percy; that it made no substantial difference to him

71

which of us married her, although he made it clear that Percy would have been the preferred choice; told me being a botanist was no profession at all; that you had assured him I would be more appropriately occupied in the management of the estate in future, and that he would like to conclude matters as quickly as possible in order to have the funds for a new roof.'

Edwina clasped her hands together. 'How splendid! I hope you told him that would be ideal for us too.'

'For *us*? I think you mean for *you*. Marriage to Lavinia on any terms is not ideal for me. In fact, it's not going to happen.'

His mother's hands flew to her face. 'I hope you didn't tell him that!'

'No. I told him I needed time to think about his offer, that I had only just finished my convalescence. He managed to squeeze in the fact that apparently Lavinia is rather put out by my lack of a leg. I wanted to say not nearly so much as I am.'

'He said that?' Her eyes widened.

'Along with some mutterings about sacrifices for king and country and his belief that the girl will eventually come to accept the missing leg. As long as she doesn't ever have to look at it. He meant the stump, presumably.'

Edwina walked over to the sideboard and helped herself to another portion of kedgeree. She sat down again and shook her head. 'Don't take it to heart, darling. She'll come round.'

'I hope she doesn't. It might be my best chance at her turning me down. That is if she has any say in the matter, which I imagine she hasn't.'

'Your marrying Lavinia is the perfect solution for everyone. We've been through this so many times.'

'It's the perfect solution for everyone except me – and

probably Lavinia. Please, Mother, for once, can we have a proper conversation instead of flinging platitudes across the table?'

His mother frowned, puzzled and reining back her annoyance.

'Let's talk about why you want this marriage so much. About why you want to push me into doing something that runs completely counter to everything I want and everything I believe. Does my happiness not even enter into your calculations? Not even *slightly*?'

'Your happiness? What about your duty? What about the family honour? What about your responsibility?'

'Don't you think serving my country and losing my leg in the process was sufficient discharge of duty and honour? Spending two years in the trenches, sending other men to their deaths and narrowly avoiding my own? As to responsibility, my only one is to see that you are provided for, Mother. I don't give a fig about uniting the Shipley name with the Bourne family tree. I happen to be proud of my heritage. Proud of the fact that my granny worked in a woollen mill and my grandfather started off pushing a cart round the streets of Huddersfield.'

'Don't be vulgar.'

'Vulgar? Sometimes you are a complete mystery to me.' He poured himself a cup of tea and reached for the sugar. '*Your* father worked in a factory and then made his money from using his powers of invention. What is there to be ashamed of? And your grandfather was an immigrant to America from Poland.'

'Stop it at once. You're distressing me now, Christopher. Are you deliberately trying to make me unhappy?'

'Unhappy? I'd like to understand why it's perfectly acceptable for *you* to consign *me* to a future of unhappiness.

Tell me why this matters so much to you. Explain to me why it will make you happy to see me in misery.'

'Don't be ridiculous.' She pushed her plate away, having barely touched the kedgeree. 'Once you get used to the idea, marriage to Lavinia will be perfectly fine. Misery indeed! No one expects to marry for love, except the lower orders. Marriage is a business arrangement, and marrying a woman as beautiful as Lavinia should make that less burdensome. Your poor dear brother understood that perfectly and so should you.'

'Poor old Percy. I discovered last night that the only thing Lavinia is sorry about is that his dying meant she didn't get to wear her wedding gown. And what good is her beautiful face if I can't bear to be in the same room as her?'

Edwina's face twisted with pain at the mention of Percy. She was silent for a moment then said, 'Your brother was awfully fond of the girl. Why are you saying such terrible things? Lavinia was fond of him too. Everyone said so. They were a beautiful couple.' She sniffed and dabbed at her nose with a lace trimmed handkerchief. 'As you get to know her better, you will grow fond of her yourself. Give her a chance, Christopher.'

'If a "good marriage" is so important to you, why don't you make one yourself? Now Father's dead there's nothing to stop you. But please forget about trying to arrange mine. You can live here in peace for the rest of your life off the dividends from the business. I'll hire a manager to run the estate if you want to keep it on, but I'll have no part of it. I may even go abroad again.'

Edwina rose from her seat and flung her napkin on the table. 'I have a headache. I'm going to lie down. I suggest you reflect on the terrible things you've said. I'll expect your apology before dinner.'

THIS TIME he didn't hesitate. He pointed Hooker in the direction of the woodland as soon as they walked out of the stable yard and he rode across the park by the most direct route, uncaring if anyone noticed where he was heading.

When he reached the little house in the copse, there was no smoke from the chimneys and no sign of life. He pressed his face against the windowpane and saw that the fire in the tiny parlour was laid but unlit. Where was she? He moved around the back of the dwelling, opening the doors to the empty sitting house, store rooms and wash-house, then went down the slope to the long brick building that housed the kennels. When Walters had been alive and the shooting a regular occurrence, there had been birds in the nesting boxes and more than a dozen dogs in the kennels. Now there was only dust and cobwebs.

Behind the house, there was a small plot with rows of vegetables. The soil appeared to have been freshly weeded. The clothes-line hung, limp and empty, across the patch of thin grass between the cottage and the vegetable garden.

Kit hadn't prepared himself for the possibility that she might not be at home. Had she gone for good? Changed her mind about working in the garden? Was it the kiss?

Filled with anxiety, he took off his hat and sat on the step, looking up hopefully every time he heard a twig snap from the movement of a bird or rabbit in the undergrowth.

It was more than an hour before Martha appeared. Kit's stomach lurched as she approached down the dirt track that led from the village. She was wearing a coat over her usual drab brown dress and her hair in its loose bun was partly hidden beneath a shabby felt hat.

Lost in thought, she didn't notice Kit at first, as he watched her approach. When she saw him, she halted for a moment, then came slowly up to where he was waiting on her doorstep.

'You shouldn't have come,' she said. 'We have to stop these meetings.'

Ignoring the remark he asked, 'Where were you?' His anxiety that she'd gone away lifting from him.

She told him she had been taking flowers to lay on her father's grave in the village churchyard, as she did every Saturday morning.

Unbuttoning her coat, she settled beside him on the step and he reached for her hand. His own was shaking but this time it was because of her proximity rather than his shattered nerves.

She paused, then reached up her other hand and stroked his hair away from his forehead where it was flopping over one eye. 'What's wrong? There's something the matter, Kit.'

He gave a long low sigh. 'I'm being put under pressure to agree to marry Lady Lavinia.'

'Is that such a bad thing?'

'It's the worst.'

'No, Kit. It's not the worst. Believe me.' She stared into the distance.

'I'm sorry. I didn't intend to compare my situation with what you went through.'

She got up from the step and opened the door. 'I'll make some tea.'

How had they come to this? In a few short days, Kit had already formed a habit of visiting Martha, of their tea-drinking ritual. The thought that a day might come when he arrived at her house to find it shuttered up and empty was too much to bear.

She stood behind him when he sat at the table, placing her hands on his shoulders, and bent over to drop a kiss on the top of his head. He pulled her into his lap and she leaned her head against his chest. They sat there silently, until the whistle of the kettle on the range drew her into the kitchen.

She sat down again, this time opposite him.

'I can't marry her. I won't marry her.' He faced Martha across the table, realising that he loved this woman whom he had only known a few days. 'I want to marry you.'

He had been afraid she would laugh at him, or accuse him of patronising her, but she had sadness in her eyes.

'You know that can't happen. Wealthy men don't marry their servants' widows. Please don't say that again. I beg you.'

'Even though I only met you a few days ago, I feel I know you, really know you, and that you know me too. That you understand me. That we understand each other.' He breathed slowly then said, 'I think I love you, Martha, and I want to be with you all the time. I can't stand to think of life without you. When I got here today and you weren't here, I didn't know what to do. I couldn't bear it. The thought of you being gone. It's unimaginable.'

He saw her lip trembling and he thought for a moment she was going to cry. Reaching across the table, she clasped his hand. 'There is a strong feeling between us. I can't deny that.'

'You feel the same?' he said, eagerly.

'I like to be with you.' She hesitated then barely above a whisper added, 'This week has been the happiest I have ever known.'

Kit made a small choking sound, relief flooding through him. 'I want to make you happy all the time.'

She shook her head. 'Stop it, Kit. Don't torture yourself. Don't torture me. We both know there's no possibility for us. Being together is a beautiful dream. There's nothing wrong with dreaming. Sometimes it's the only way we get through life. But that's all it is, Kit, a dream.'

He moved around the table and knelt at her feet, heedless of the pain in his stump. He clutched her hands. 'No. It's not dreaming. I'm serious. We could go away. I'd be glad to see the back of Newlands. It means nothing to me. Money means nothing to me. Reputation, connections, commerce, hunting, shooting and fishing, drinking drinks with stupid names, dining with boring people, making trivial conversation while eating too much food. I despise it all.' He gulped. 'And as for being married to that simpering, baby-faced halfwit who wants only to talk about her dolls and her dogs and refuses to ride, or even walk in the garden for fear it will upset her sinuses. Oh, Martha, it's unthinkable.'

'Then don't marry her. No one can force you. There'll be someone else for you, one day. Someone more congenial. Someone of your class. But forget about me.'

'Why? Why must I forget about you? How can I? I love you.'

'We're from different worlds. I'm ten years older than you. Your mother would have a heart attack.'

'My mother would get over it. She's hardly out of the top drawer herself. She's an American – the landed gentry love nothing more than enjoying American money while feeling superior. Her father was a factory worker who happened to invent a piece of kit that made my grandfather's weaving machinery work more efficiently and cost less to produce than the competition. He made a fortune until Grandfather bought his business and my father got Mother as part of the deal.'

The pain in his leg now biting hard, he got up, pulled her out of the chair and sat down, drawing her onto his lap. She leaned her head against his chest and pulled his hands in front of her waist, girdling her, her own hands on top of his.

'Don't stop,' she said.

Kit hesitated a moment, distracted by the warmth of her body against his, then went on. 'My mother and her family mistook wealth for status and she got a rude awakening when she discovered Father wasn't a bona fide member of the upper classes – people like the Bournes look down on the Shipleys as social-climbing tradesmen. It's been Mother's life's work to put that right, and my marrying Lavinia was to be the clincher. But Mother will survive – she's weathered worse than this. Not least losing Percy.'

'Your mother married your father as an arrangement, so it's understandable she should expect you to do the same. Is that really so bad, Kit?'

'How can you even ask that? How can you expect me to look at Lavinia Bourne across the table every day?'

'She's a beautiful woman. Looking at her should be no hardship.'

He groaned in frustration. '*You* are beautiful. Yours is the only beauty I can see. She's a painted doll.' He lifted one hand and ran it down her face, his open palm caressing her skin. 'So beautiful. I want to look at you all the time. I see your face when I close my eyes to sleep.'

'I'm not beautiful, Kit. No one would say that about me.'

'I say it and I'm the only one that matters.'

She shook her head in frustration. 'I'm only telling you what I'm certain is best for you. It's because I care about you. Marrying Lavinia Bourne is what you must do.'

'Why does everyone think they know better than I do what's best for me?'

She stroked his hair. 'Because it's how things are done. It's the way of the world.'

'The war has changed everything. We fought for freedom. Better men than me lost their lives. For what? So that the same old ways carry on? All this stupid, empty posturing and jockeying for position. What does it mean? What's the point? No, Martha, after what I've seen and done I'll never settle for a dynastic marriage. I'll never compromise on my dreams.'

'And what are your dreams?'

'To be with you,' he said quickly. 'To travel with you. To

pursue my career as a botanist. Imagine, my love, sailing to the East, seeing strange and wonderful things together. I want to live that life again and I want to share it with you. Only you.'

'I'd not be much of a wife to you. Ten years older. Little education. Unable to bear you children.'

'I don't care about any of that. Not a damn thing. If we can't have children then so be it. You're more than enough for me.' He stopped, thinking for a moment, then said, 'But you don't even know that you can't have children – it could be that it was Walters who was infertile. Why do women always have to take the blame?'

Martha said nothing. Her face was pale. Kit felt her shiver. They went to stand together by the window at the rear of the cottage, looking out at the sunlight streaming through the trees and patterning the grass like embroidery.

'I won't go back there tonight. I want to stay here with you.'

'No, Kit. Just because you don't want to do your mother's bidding, it doesn't justify being rude to her and her guests. You told me she has a dinner party tonight. You can't abandon her.' She turned to him, running her finger down his cheek and over his mouth.

He made a low moan then bent his head to kiss her. 'Will you grant me this one thing? Will you take me to your bed?' he said.

Martha pulled away. 'That's not a good idea. It will make matters worse.'

'You don't want me?'

She looked into his eyes and whispered, 'Of course I do. You've no idea how much. But I can't.'

'Are you afraid? Because of what Walters did to you? I'd never hurt you. I couldn't hurt you.'

Martha pulled back, the mention of her late husband making her recoil. 'I know you wouldn't.'

'It's my leg, isn't it? You don't want me because I'm not whole.'

She moved against him, pressing her body up against his. 'No, no, my darling. Why would you think that?'

'Lord Bourne told me that Lavinia had misgivings about marrying a man with a missing leg. And who would want to look at it? I can hardly bear to look at it myself.'

Martha gasped. 'Show me. Show me now.' She reached for his hand and led him from the room, opening the door that concealed the stairway to the upper floor.

Her bedroom overlooked the forest. Outside, birds were singing, but Kit was conscious only of the soft sound of her breathing.

She told him to sit on the bed and she knelt before him on the floor, removing his riding boots.

'Are you sure?' he asked. 'I don't want to put you through this. Seeing my disfigurement. It would be better if you didn't look. It's not pretty.'

She ignored him, unbuttoning his jodhpurs and sliding them down over his lower body. She saw his hand was shaking so she kissed his palm, opened her blouse and pressed his hand against her breast. He groaned as his palm settled over the contours. Then she unbuckled the leather strap that attached his wooden leg to his stump and eased the prosthesis off. He turned away, not wanting to witness her inevitable disgust. But she ran the palms of her hands over the scars and the puckered skin, then lowered her head and kissed him there, her tongue and her lips setting his nerve endings on fire.

'It's part of you,' she said, 'so I can only love it.'

Kit gasped and lifted her chin so he could kiss her.

AFTERWARDS THEY LAY in each other's arms, exchanging kisses and caresses.

'That was the first time I have made love,' he admitted.

'It was for me too,' she answered.

He raised himself on one elbow to look at her.

'I can't call what Walters did to me making love. It bore no resemblance to what we just did. You've washed away the stain of the man who raped me. You've given me a beautiful gift and I will remember this afternoon and what we did together until my dying day.' She rolled over and examined at his face with intensity, her own face serious.

'What are you looking at? What's wrong?' he said.

'I'm learning you. Learning your face. Drinking it in so that every inch of it is imprinted on my mind, and I can carry the memory of how you look now, like a treasure in my heart.'

He laughed. 'You don't need to do that. You're going to come away with me.'

Her eyes were sad. 'How can I do that? Don't say that, Kit, it makes it worse.'

He fixed his eyes on her. 'I mean it. We'll go away together. We'll marry and travel to the Far East. I'll work on my cataloguing. I can teach you about it and you can help me.'

'I'd like that,' she said, stroking his hair back from his eyes.

'We'd have to live simply. Prospecting for plants is not as lucrative as panning for gold. There's no money in it. My father didn't trust me. He knew I'd want to head off and follow my dreams, so he did everything possible to prevent that. He's doing it now from beyond the grave. As you know, the estate is held in trust until I'm thirty and Mother holds the purse strings. Until then I have only a small monthly allowance and that's contingent on my being fully involved in the management of Newlands and the family business.'

'Won't you need money to fund the trip?'

He nodded. 'Maybe I can get a bursary from my college. I was planning to go to Cambridge next week to see my old tutor. I could talk to him and the dean of studies about it. And then there's the Royal Horticultural Society. I've lots of avenues to investigate.'

Martha rolled onto her back. 'I've never had money. What you haven't had you don't miss. All I want is you. Now that we are together like this I don't want to think of being without you.'

'Then don't.'

'But it will happen. Even if your college pays for your trip they won't pay for mine.'

'Then I'll wait until I have enough put by. I won't go without you. We can finish the work on the sunken garden. You'll move into the cottage there and I will visit you every night.'

'That's daft,' she said. 'And if you let me get in the way of your dreams you'll come to resent me. Maybe hate me in the end.'

'That can never happen. You are my dream now. My life without you is meaningless. My life until now has been meaningless. You've changed everything.'

She turned to him with her solemn face and her sad eyes.

He stroked her hair. 'The two years I was in the war were the worst kind of living hell. Men climbing over the top of the trenches, walking forward, blindly, following orders, knowing with every miserable muddy step that they were moving towards certain death.'

She was listening intently.

'Every day I would wake up convinced it would be my last. I used to pray that I would take a "Blighty" and get sent home to recuperate. We all did. None of us wanted to be there. So much for being brave. We were all terrified.' He laughed but it was hollow. 'If it was bad for us officers it was so much worse for the enlisted men. Many of them were boys.'

Kit closed his eyes, trying to blot out the memory. 'Some days the smells were the worst thing: the foul stench of decaying flesh, the sulphur like rotten eggs, the stink of too many unwashed bodies crammed close together in filthy conditions. But was that really worse than how it *felt*? Water-logged feet, lice in your clothing, blisters, boils, trench foot, the rub of your uniform against broken skin, the shiver of rats as they climbed over you while you slept. And my conditions were luxurious compared to what my men had to put up with.'

He went on to tell her about the sounds. The thud and pounding of guns, sometimes distant, sometimes close. The scream of shells. The ear-splitting sound of an exploding mortar. The weeping of young men as they tried to sleep the night before an attack, knowing they were unlikely to see home again, unlikely even to see another night.'

He turned his head and stared up at the ceiling. 'I'm sorry. You don't want to hear this.'

'I do,' she whispered.

But he shook his head. 'I don't want to think about it any more. I don't want you to know. Better to try and forget. You help me forget.' He rolled over and kissed her slowly, then moved his hands over her skin.

CHAPTER 9

*B*y the time Christopher returned to Newlands Hall and changed into evening wear, his mother and her guests had begun dinner. When he entered the room, he was greeted by a stony silence. Lord Bourne narrowed his eyes at him and didn't return his greeting. Lavinia and her mother talked to each other, ignoring him, Lavinia's little retroussé nose lifted as though there were a bad smell in the room. Only Mr Harrington-Foster and Major Collerton pushed their chairs back and got up to shake his hand.

He sat down, drawing his napkin onto his lap as Bannister placed a plate of soup in front of him. Seeing that the rest of the company had by now been served with the fish course, he waved the soup away and asked to proceed straight to the fish.

'I apologise. My horse stumbled taking a ditch, landed awkwardly and I think he's slightly lame. I didn't want to take any chances so I dismounted and walked him home.'

His mother appeared relieved that he had deftly covered up his tardiness for their guests, but was clearly not convinced herself by his lie. She knew that the chance of

Hooker stumbling in clearing a ditch was as unlikely as her son allowing it to happen.

The tension at dinner was eased by the presence of the other guests. Harrington-Foster was a blustering bore, but his wife, a plump smiling matron, regaled them with stories of the goings-on in the village, where she had evidently established herself as benefactress-in-chief over the poor and needy. Christopher plied her with questions, gratified by the fact that this line of conversation was of no interest whatsoever to Lavinia, her mother or his own mother. In between, he talked across the table to Major Collerton, who had been too old for active service during the war, but professed a hobby interest in horticulture and wanted to hear about Christopher's experiences in Borneo.

Annoyed at being neglected by all the gentlemen present, Lavinia, having failed to spark any interest among them to hear about her dogs and her doll collection, eventually enquired as to where Borneo might be. She was going through the motions, evidently intending, once she had secured an entry point, to manoeuvre the conversation in her own direction. When Christopher explained that it was a large island in South East Asia, beneath the South China Sea, her eyes glazed over.

'I can't imagine why anyone would want to go there. It sounds absolutely horrid. Full of natives and wild animals and creepy crawly insects and things.'

'Isn't that rather the point?' said Collerton. 'That's why Captain Shipley has been so keen to visit the place. Not much of interest for a botanist to study around here.'

Lavinia smiled, as if she were thinking that Christopher would not be doing any more exploring once they were married. She said, 'Well the only animals I'd ever want to study are Popsy and Petal.' She threw a dazzling smile at Christopher. 'Once you meet them, Captain Shipley, you'll find them absolutely fascinating. Perhaps they might even tempt you to study them too! Then you wouldn't need to go all the way to that horrible place.' She clapped her hands and waited for the appreciative laughter which the assembled company provided on cue.

Christopher stretched his lips into a smile, then, duty discharged, resumed his conversation with Major Collerton until it was time for the ladies to withdraw.

As she left the room, Edwina pulled him aside and hissed at him, 'Where were you? You were more than an hour late. And you haven't even combed your hair. You look as if you've just got out of bed.' Without waiting for a reply she swept out of the room.

HE WAS RELIEVED that the Bournes departed early the following morning for the trip back to the leaking roofs of Harton Hall.

His mother was far from pleased. She sat in grim silence all through her breakfast, then, as they drove to the service in the village church, she castigated his behaviour, speaking quietly to prevent the chauffeur hearing.

'I was absolutely mortified. You missed cocktails altogether and were over an hour late to table. And don't expect me to believe that ludicrous tale you spun about Hooker getting lamed. I've no doubt you'll be saddling him up as soon as we get back from church.' She slapped her gloved hand against his sleeve. 'You talked to Major Collerton and Mrs Harrington-Foster throughout the entire meal and had barely a word for poor Lavinia. I could tell she felt humiliated, poor child.'

'She's not a child. She just acts like one. She's older than me – she's twenty-seven.'

'Whatever. You might have made an effort. After dinner,

she seemed positively glum. She went to bed early, for pity's sake.'

'She was missing her lap dogs. Nothing to do with me.'

'A woman like her needs to be paid compliments. You really must make more of an effort, Christopher. Sometimes I despair of you.'

They pulled up outside the parish church and walked under the lychgate and along the stone-paved pathway into the building.

As soon as they were inside he saw her. It hadn't even entered Christopher's head that of course she would be there at church, along with the rest of the village and the Newlands estate. Strange how, in all those years of going to the Sunday morning service, he had never noticed her. He must have walked past her, Sunday after Sunday, as he did past all the other members of the congregation, seeing them as a collective entity and failing to register any as individuals. Even her. That seemed impossible now.

She was wearing the same brown felt hat and coat. As he and his mother passed her pew, on the way to his family's designated seats at the front of the church, he looked at her, hoping for an acknowledgement, but she kept her head lowered as if she hadn't seen him. Of course she would have been expecting to see him there, accustomed to seeing the arrival of the Shipley family every Sunday morning.

Throughout the service he wrestled with himself, but couldn't help turning his head whenever he thought he might be unobserved by his mother, hoping that once he might look in Martha's direction and find her looking back at him. But every time he turned towards her, she had her head bowed in prayer or was gazing straight ahead at the altar and the vicar as he officiated.

Afterwards, he steered his mother out of the church quickly, hurrying outside where he hoped to find Martha –

maybe even manage a few words while his mother was having her customary conversation with the vicar. But once he reached the churchyard there was no sign of the gamekeeper's widow. Christopher looked from one group to another then went and stood in the lane looking up and down in vain. She had vanished.

When his mother appeared at his elbow, he said, 'Go ahead without me, Mother. It's a fine morning so I've a mind to walk. I'll stop off at the stables and take a look at Hooker's leg.'

Edwina Shipley tutted. 'Please don't insult me, darling. I've told you I know there's nothing wrong with your horse's leg.' Then she smiled at him and slipped her hand through his arm. 'But you're right. It is a beautiful day, so I'll walk with you. Rawson can take the motor back without us.'

He cursed inwardly, but could think of nothing to say to dissuade her.

As soon as they had left the village and entered the Newlands park, she took her hand from his arm and slipped it into the pocket of her coat, a habit from her youth she had never managed to lose. 'Are you going to tell me what's going on?'

He was surprised but nervous about what might be coming.

'I saw you. Turning your head to look at that woman. All through the service. The whole church must have seen you. Your head was like a swivel.'

'I don't know what you're talking about.'

She sighed in irritation. 'The Walters woman. The gamekeeper's wife. The one you're supposed to have evicted by now. Is that where you've been spending your time? Is that why you were so late last night? And gone most of the days on these mysterious rides.'

Christopher said nothing.

She sighed again. 'I suppose you've been having sexual relations with her?'

He didn't know what to say. There was little point in denying it.

Edwina shook her head. 'Maybe it's not such a bad idea. Get it out of your system. Being a widow means she has experience. No bad thing, for Lavinia's sake.' She spoke briskly. 'I was always grateful that your father wasn't a virgin. Doesn't make the act any pleasanter but at least if the man is experienced he knows how to get on with it. None of that fumbling about, working out what to do next.' She gave a brittle laugh. 'And with your handicap... it means you can work all that part out. Must be awkward – managing the mechanics of it.' Again she laughed. 'Listen to me. I can't believe we're having this conversation! But since your father isn't here to discuss such matters with you, I–'

Christopher stopped. She walked a few steps further then stopped too, waiting for him.

'What's wrong now?' She was irritated.

'I love Martha, Mother. You may as well know it. You'll have to find out sooner or later as I mean to marry her.'

This time her laugh was a hearty one.

'Stop laughing. I'm serious. In fact I've never been so serious about anything. I'm going to Cambridge tomorrow to find out if I can get funding from the college to go back to Borneo. Then I'll sort out everything here. I'll find an estate manager. I'll talk to the board at Shipley's about appointing a managing director. I'll make sure I don't leave you in the lurch, Mother.'

She was staring at him, open-mouthed. 'Stop it, Christopher. Stop it at once. It was amusing at first but I don't find it the least bit funny now.'

'I'm not joking. And I'd be grateful if you would authorise the trust to continue my allowance until I reach thirty and have control.' He touched her arm. 'And don't worry – even then all I want is my allowance. That will be enough for Martha and me to get by. I'll make the necessary arrangements to transfer everything else over to you. You can do what you like with the money. Sell this place if you wish.' He saw the anger in her eyes and risked stoking it further. 'You can even pay for Lord Bourne's new roof. That should help smooth the waters there. I imagine Lavinia will be relieved to be off the hook.'

Edwina turned on her heel and walked rapidly up the driveway towards the house. He let her go and set off in the direction of the little cottage in the woods.

CHAPTER 10

*K*it pushed the door open. Martha was waiting inside, her hat and coat thrown carelessly over the back of a chair as though she had not long arrived.

He pulled her into his arms and they kissed each other hungrily. He started to move her towards the stairs, but she leaned her back against the door so he couldn't open it. 'Wait. We have to talk.'

'What's the matter?' he asked. 'I've thought of nothing all morning but being here. Of carrying you upstairs and making love all day long. I couldn't stand it in church. Seeing you. Wanting you. Then when you disappeared I thought I'd go mad. I thought you didn't want to see me.'

'You made it so obvious, Kit. The whole parish must know. That's why I slipped away before the service finished. I didn't want people to see us talking. Your mother could see what was going on. What on earth were you thinking?'

'Of you. Only of you.' His gaze was locked on her face.

Martha sighed. 'You're being rash. You're risking everything. Your mother... she won't like it. You'll make her angry.

What's the point of upsetting her? Oh, Kit, why are you being so headstrong about this?'

'Because I love you and I don't care who knows it.'

She shook her head and went to sit at the table. 'Shall I make us some tea?' she asked, looking up at him, her eyes, solemn.

'I don't want any tea. I want to kiss you.' He moved towards her and pulled her back onto her feet, holding her against him. 'Anyway it's too late for caution. Mother knows. We talked just now. I've told her I intend to marry you.'

Martha seemed alarmed, but he bent his head and kissed her tenderly.

'There's nothing she can do. I've said that she can have everything. All the money. The dividends from the business. Everything. I don't need it – *we* don't need it.'

'She'll never agree. She'll find a way to stop you.'

'My love, you worry too much. I'm twenty-six and in four years I'll have full control of my affairs.'

'Four years is a long time. Plenty of time for your mother to foil your plans. Oh, Kit, why didn't you wait?'

He sat down, pulling her onto his lap. 'Because since I met you I have become like a mad man, crazy for love of you, so that I can I barely think straight.'

Martha laughed, and he cupped her face in his hands. 'I love you so much. Your sad and solemn face that bursts into life when you laugh or smile. It makes me feel like it's something for me only. Do you smile for anyone else? Please say no, my darling. Please tell me it's a secret gift to me alone.'

She laughed again and stroked his face. 'You are indeed crazy, my beautiful man. And you have made me crazy too. Crazy with happiness. And until you came along I had little to smile about.' Then her face clouded over.

'What's wrong?'

'I feel too happy. That makes me nervous, I'm scared that

such happiness is more than I deserve. More than I've ever had before. It can't possibly last.' She sighed. 'And I'm frightened your mother will make sure it doesn't.'

He noticed the reflexive plucking at her sleeve that she did whenever she was nervous. His heart swelled with love for her.

'Tomorrow I'm going to Cambridge. I'll be gone for two days then when I come back, no matter whether I manage to convince them to give me a bursary or not, we will be married. We'll go away and marry elsewhere – somewhere my mother won't find us. Then once you're my wife there's nothing she can do about it.'

'I wish I shared your confidence, Kit.' She frowned.

As he studied her face he marvelled that less than a week ago he would have seen that frown creasing her brow and thought her plain. Now he wanted to kiss it away and thought her beautiful.

'You don't need to. I have enough for both of us. And do you know why?'

'No. But I think you're going to tell me.' Her face lit up again with a smile.

'Because the way you have made me feel has already changed my whole life beyond recognition. It was only a week ago that I saw you for the first time. That I talked with you. Then I started to fall completely and utterly in love with you. When I rode here on Monday morning my heart was heavy. I didn't want to meet you, to tell you about what had happened to your husband, to ask you to leave this house. But more than that, I was weary of life, of the burden of responsibility on my shoulders. I was weighed down with misery and self-pity about what had happened to me in the war. There didn't seem any point to anything.' He lifted her hand, turned up her palm, then bent his head and kissed it.

'You changed all that. You gave me my life back. You gave me purpose, meaning, love.'

He looked into her eyes and saw that they were brimming with tears. As they ran down her cheeks, he took out his handkerchief and wiped them away. This time, when he lifted her into his arms and moved towards the stairs, she didn't resist.

'I LOVE LISTENING TO YOU TALK,' Martha said. They were lying entwined, in a tangle of bed sheets. 'I thought you'd be quiet, have little to say, but once you start, you talk so beautifully. Words flow out of you. I could listen to you like this all day long.'

He laughed. 'I never run out of things to say to *you*.'

'Do you really think we have a possibility of being together, of always being this happy? Or is this the best it can possibly be and from now on, every day a tiny little less happy, until eventually we aren't happy at all?' She smiled at Kit but her eyes were sad.

'As long as we are together, I will always be happy. The idea of being with you and not being happy isn't possible.'

She ran her fingers over his chest.

'Besides,' he said. 'My grandmother foresaw this for me.'

Martha rolled over and lay propped up on her side, looking at him. 'What do you mean?'

'It was when I was about ten years old, not long before she died, she said to me one day "Your brother must marry for the family but you will marry for love".'

She smiled. 'Tell me about her.'

'She was small, rather plump. Big smiley eyes. I loved being with her because she always held me on her knee and cuddled me. My mother never went in for any physical

95

contact beyond holding out a cheek to be kissed but Grandma was warm and loved to show affection to me and Percy – especially me. I think she saw that he was the favoured son so she always tried to make it up to me, to redress the balance.'

'She sounds a good woman.'

'I loved her because she never tried to be anything different from how she'd always been. My grandfather played the part of the landed gentleman, always trying to fit in. Grandma never bothered. She wore finer quality clothes than she had done before they were rich, but nothing fancy, and that was about it. If it had been left up to her she'd have stayed living in Yorkshire in a little terraced house on a street with all her friends and family around her. She never liked Newlands. Apart from the sunken gardens. She loved to sit in the shade under the big sycamore tree on the south lawn there, near the stream, and do her tatting – making little bits of silk lace.' He smiled at the memory. 'I always thought Mother and Father were slightly ashamed of her. Didn't much like the house guests having anything to do with her. They thought Grandma's presence and her York-shire accent were embarrassing evidence of Father's working class roots. But she wasn't keen on mixing with their friends either. She much preferred to be with the hoi polloi, but since my grandfather decided it wasn't done for her to be over-familiar with the servants and the villagers, she kept to herself most of the time or visited Percy and me in the nursery.'

Kit glanced at his watch, sighed and said he had to leave. Martha told him she would walk with him part of the way. They set off through the woods, hand-in-hand.

He bent down and cleared some dead leaves away from the base of a beech tree. 'Look,' he said, revealing a cluster of pale cream coloured toadstools, with pinkish gills on their undersides. 'Make sure you don't put those in a stew.'

'Deadly fibre caps. I know they're poisonous. You're talking to a country girl, Mr Botanist. I never take risks with mushrooms. My father taught me well.' She smiled at him. 'But thank you for the warning.'

They walked on through the beech copse, and took a path up a hill, past a ruined folly, its bricks tumbled down and covered with grass, and with ivy growing over what had once been an ornamental tower.

'I used to play here when I was a child,' she said. 'I loved scrambling over the walls.'

'So did I!'

'I know. I saw you. This was my secret place. When I was older I used to come up here to read books, sitting on the grass, there behind the wall, where Walters wouldn't find me, and then one summer – I must have been about eighteen – I came here as usual one day, only to find a little boy playing in my refuge.'

'Me?'

'You. Home from boarding school for the summer. I was annoyed that you'd taken possession of my secret hideout.'

'I'm sorry. You should have come in. I wouldn't have minded.'

'Don't be daft,' she said. 'Of course you would! What small boy would be willing to share his secret hiding place with a grown-up? And especially with a servant.'

He felt his skin prickle, uncomfortable with the way she was highlighting the difference in their age and status.

She went on. 'I used to watch you riding your pony. A little bay mare. I always thought you had a kind face. And you smiled at me when you saw me. Unlike your brother, who was aloof. Haughty. People like me were invisible to him.'

Kit said nothing.

'I never dreamt back then that this would happen. That

you would come to mean so much to me. So quickly. So absolutely.'

'Martha, I have something to tell you.'

'Yes?' she said, her expression curious, perhaps even anxious.

His face was solemn, frowning, his eyes serious. 'I have no recollection of you whatsoever back then.' He burst out laughing and she slapped at his arm. 'Seriously. I find it impossible to imagine now, but I hadn't even realised that Walters was married to the last keeper's daughter. You simply hadn't registered in my consciousness. When I rode over to talk to you on Monday I hadn't the faintest idea what you looked like. How is that even possible, my love?'

She smiled. 'I hope I've made more of an impression since?'

'Oh yes.' And he pulled her into his arms and kissed her again. 'So much so that I don't know how I will survive for the next two days while I'm in Cambridge without you.'

They walked on, past the ruined walls and up a grassy slope.

'Tell me more about Borneo,' she said.

He raised his eyebrows. 'Are you really interested?'

'Would I have asked if I wasn't?'

She was right. There was nothing about her that was pretence. No room for feigned interest, idle small talk. She said what she thought and did not dissimulate. That was one of the things he loved most about her.

So he told her about the first time he came upon the giant rafflesia flower and how he had spotted it when climbing through the rainforest, close to a waterfall. He told her how the five-petalled parasitic flower could reach more than three feet wide but lived only for a week or less, capturing insects inside its fleshy red heart. 'Its petals are covered in raised spots like warts. And it stinks to high heaven!'

'A flower?'

'The pong attracts flies. That's how it pollinates. Smells like fish that have been rotting for days.'

'How horrible. It sounds revolting. I won't be in a hurry to see that then!'

'See it you must – but I won't mind if you choose not to smell it.' He laughed, already imagining scrambling through the undergrowth with Martha by his side. 'You can hold your nose!'

She asked him again what the plant was called. 'It's common name is Corpse Flower but its proper name is rafflesia.' She repeated the name experimentally.

'After Sir Stamford Raffles. It was on his expedition that it was first found in Sumatra. His wife was with him. Just as one day you will be there with me.' He squeezed her hand. 'I long to show you the beauty of the island. To have you by my side.'

Martha leaned her head against his shoulder. He placed his arm protectively around her and his heart soared in his chest.

They reached the top of the slope and there through the trees, in the distance, they could make out the west wing of the big house as the sun caught the pale stones.

Remembering his mother and their recent quarrel, Kit said, 'I must go. I have to try and appease Mother. Pour oil on the raging waters. I'll be back on Tuesday night. Wednesday at the latest. And then, my darling girl, we will make our plans.'

He kissed her quickly, then broke away and walked off, down the slope towards the distant mansion house. He didn't turn back to look at her, fearing that were he to do so he would lack the resolve to leave her at all.

MARTHA WATCHED him until he was no longer in sight.

As soon as she wasn't in Kit's presence the hollow fear and dread returned. She was playing with fire. Risking everything. She should never have let it get this far. But how could she have prevented it? There was no doubting their feelings for each other. Her resolve disappeared the moment she was in his company, making her lose her reason, drawing her into his arms as if it were her natural home.

Now that his mother knew about them she was sure to cause trouble. Perhaps Mrs Shipley knew Martha's secret. But that wasn't possible. Was it?

CHAPTER 11

When Christopher walked into the house, Bannister appeared in the hall and asked him to join his mother in his father's study, where she was waiting for him. Puzzled, as his mother had never used the room – even when George Shipley was alive – he made his way there. The room was sombre and masculine, panelled in oak with carvings in the shape of Tudor roses between the panels and mirrored in plasterwork on the ceiling. It was dominated by the huge mahogany desk.

Edwina was sitting behind it, a pile of papers in front of her.

'What are you doing, Mother?'

'Looking for something. I know it must be here somewhere. Have you been moving things?'

'Of course not. I haven't set foot in here in years.'

As he said the words, he remembered how much he used to dread receiving a summons from his father to attend him here – sometimes as the result of a poor school report, but more often to be punished for a trivial misdemeanour such as lack of punctuality. How many times had he been here, arms by his side, standing rigid, terrified at incurring the wrath of his parent. His father had never punished him physically, but being on the end of what Percy used to refer to as a 'parental tongue lashing' was as bad. Christopher had never grown out of his fear of his father.

Edwina Shipley signalled him to take a seat in one of the two winged chairs in front of the mullioned windows, then followed him over there. She perched on the cushioned window seat.

'You've been with that woman all day.' It was a statement not a question.

He stared her straight in the eye, summoning defiance, but feeling nervous. His mother knew exactly how to get under his skin.

'Has she told you anything of her history?'

'Yes,' he said, already feeling defensive.

'She told you how she came to be married?'

He nodded.

'What exactly did she tell you?' Her arms were folded.

Christopher bridled. She had no right to ask him. 'What she told me was in confidence.'

Edwina narrowed her eyes and tutted in irritation. 'She has evidently spun you a yarn. If you were aware of the truth you wouldn't be persisting in the relationship.'

'Stop. I don't want to hear any more.' He lifted his hands, palms outward. 'I've told you I intend to marry Martha and nothing you say can possibly dissuade me from that. I love her.'

She studied his face, then said, 'I hate to shatter your tender dreams, darling. You're such an innocent. Always seeing the best in everyone.' She gave her head a little shake then said, 'So, Mrs Walters hasn't told you that your late father paid her father and Harold Walters a substantial sum each, in order for Walters to marry her?'

Christopher tried to swallow but his mouth was dry. Where was this going?

His mother shook her head again. 'I'm sorry to be the bearer of bad tidings particularly as in this instance I have to tell you something that will make you see your father in a different light.'

Suddenly cold, he shivered.

His mother got up and walked over to a side table, where she poured whisky into a glass from a decanter and handed it to him. 'Here, you're going to need this.'

He took the drink from her and placed it on the small table in front of him, without drinking. It was water he craved, not whisky. 'I've told you, I don't want to hear – and whatever you say, nothing will alter my feelings for Martha.'

'Your father – how shall I put it – always had an eye for a pretty face. Sadly, the younger the better. I learned early on in our marriage that I was never going to be enough for him. After you were born, it was effectively the end of that side of our marriage. Something I never missed. When I tell you what I am about to tell you, you'll understand why.'

She turned her head away from him to stare through the window at the advancing dusk. 'I am finding this difficult so I will be as blunt and as brief as possible. Your father had sexual relations with Martha Tubbs, as she was known then. She was little more than a child. Only about fifteen.'

'Fourteen.'

'So she told you?'

'She told me the truth, which was that she was raped by the man her father forced her to marry. Harold Walters.'

'Harold Walters married her because he was paid to do so by your father to prevent a scandal. And her father was paid too. Not to go to the police.'

Christopher got out of the chair. 'I won't hear any more of this. You've gone too far. I'm not listening any more.'

'I warned you you wouldn't like what I had to say.'

'You're sick, Mother. To come up with a packet of lies like that. To impugn the reputation of my father, your husband of thirty years, to try to stop me marrying Martha because she's not of our class. I'm disgusted with you. You're beneath contempt.'

She reached out a hand and gripped his arm. Pushing him back into his chair she said, 'There's proof. That's what I was looking for when you came in.'

He threw her a look of unconcealed loathing, picked up the tumbler of whisky and drank the contents straight down.

'The girl was in the sitting house, cleaning out the nesting boxes. George knew she was in there and did what he did to her there.'

'You're lying.'

She shook her head and fixed her eyes on him. He shivered.

'I'm not enjoying this, Christopher. Not one little bit. Telling my son that his father was a rapist. That he violated a young girl and then paid off her family.'

'I don't believe you. Why would you even know this? Father would hardly come back here and tell you what he'd done if it was true.'

'He didn't. Of course he didn't. I only found out because the girl's father burst into the house brandishing a shotgun and screaming the place down.'

She got up and walked over to the desk again. 'After they had finished talking, I came in here and confronted your father. He tried to fob me off but I'd heard enough not to let him get away with that. Eventually he told me that the matter was resolved and he had paid off the father and the Walters man.' She pointed at the papers on the desk. 'Somewhere here will be the evidence. He was always most meticulous in accounting for everything and kept the counterfoils for every cheque he ever paid. One hundred and fifty pounds to each of them – and that was worth more than twice what it's worth now. They were only too happy to go along with helping him cover up what he'd done.'

Christopher sat in silence, too stunned to speak. He felt nausea rising in him and his mouth was sour with the taste of the whisky he had gulped down.

Eventually, he said, 'I don't care. It makes no difference to my feelings for Martha. What my father did to her was not her fault.'

'You may choose to believe that. I tend to think she brought it on herself. She's not exactly pretty. The only way your father would have done what he did was if she led him on.'

This was more than he could take. He got to his feet and picking up the whisky glass from the table, flung it against the wall where it shattered into shards. He moved towards the door.

Edwina got there first and leaned her back against the door panels. 'Wait. I've not finished.'

He stood in front of her, hating her, wanting to make her disappear. Wishing he had never come home tonight. Wishing he had never let his mother speak to him. Wishing he had never heard the poison that had come from her mouth.

'Tubbs and Walters came back with demands for more money. Three months later. The girl was expecting a baby and they both swore it was your father's. Apparently Walters had never been near her since the wedding. He had more scruples than your father had about violating a child, even if the child was his now his wife.' She paused then added, 'Although your father always suspected women were not the Walters man's first choice.'

'None of this is true.' Christopher stood in front of her, his eyes closed. 'It's not what she told me.'

'I can't help what she's told you. Maybe she's created an alternative story for herself. Or more likely she's lied to you because she knows you wouldn't want anything to do with her if you knew she'd been your father's fancy woman.' Her eyes were angry. 'He used to go down to that little house in the woods and have his way with her, all the darned time.' She screamed at him. 'Don't you think I didn't know! I was his wife.'

He had never seen his mother like this before. Pent up anger released like a shaken-up champagne bottle, uncorked.

'Percy was eight. You were four years old. I wanted nothing more to do with George Shipley. Told him he was no longer welcome in my bed.'

Christopher felt his knees buckling. He moved towards the chair and slumped down, a sharp pain bursting up through his missing leg. He saw the tremors in his hands.

'I found out that she was expecting a child, because by then I was so suspicious about everything your father did that I regularly went through his desk. I found the cheque stubs paying the monthly fees to the institution.'

The room was spinning around him. He bent forward, head in his hands. Without looking at her he asked, 'What institution?'

'Martha Tubbs was little more than a child. Both mother and baby nearly died. She was too small to give birth. Too narrow. The baby got stuck in the birth canal.'

She reached across the desk, opened a mother-of-pearl box and removed a cigarette which she lit. Christopher had never seen her smoke before.

'The labour went on too long – nearly four days and the girl was so weak the midwife was afraid she was dying, so Tubbs ran over here and asked your father to pay for a doctor to attend her. The baby's skull was damaged by the forceps when the doctor delivered it.'

'Martha had a child?' Kit was finding it hard to assimilate all the information.

His mother said nothing. She stared back at him.

'The baby survived?' Kit's voice was barely a whisper.

'It was brain damaged but yes, it lived. A girl.'

Christopher struggled to comprehend the import of her words. Martha had a daughter. By his father. A bilious feeling swept through him and he gagged. He had a half-sister. He took a deep breath. 'You said she was in an institution?'

His mother nodded. 'She's still there now. Must be twenty.'

'And Martha knows this?'

Edwina shrugged. 'Probably not. But it's possible she found out. I've no idea. At the time, they felt it best to tell her the child had died.'

Christopher was numb. 'How can you possibly know all this? All these details?'

'Because ever since I discovered your father's true nature, I made it my business to know everything that happened on this estate. As I still do now.'

Christopher shivered at the implication of her words. She probably knew about Martha working in the sunken garden. A dull throb was hammering in his temple. 'Martha told me she couldn't have children. She said her husband beat her because of it. Called her barren.'

'Maybe that's true and she can't. After what she went through having that child it would have been a miracle if she could have had any more. But your father never went near her again after she was pregnant. Learnt his lesson. And as I said, the rumours were that Walters wasn't interested in women.'

Feeling wretched, Christopher got to his feet and went to

the door. 'I don't believe you. You're telling me all this to wreck what I have with Martha. There must be something wrong with you to want to say such terrible things. You want to rule my life. No – worse – you want to destroy it.'

'I only want what's best for you. And the best thing for you is for Martha Walters to leave here, for you to forget she ever existed and marry Lady Lavinia Bourne. Don't you see, darling, it's the only way to put all this behind us.'

'I will never marry Lavinia. And I don't believe what you've told me. It's all lies. Nasty, twisted lies.' He ran his hands through his hair, which was damp with sweat.

Edwina Shipley handed him a piece of paper. 'If you don't believe me, go and see the halfwit who is her daughter.'

He stared at the sheet of paper.

'That's the address of the place where they keep her. The fees are paid from the Shipley estate account. Her name is Jane Walters.'

He stuffed the paper inside his jacket pocket and left the room.

Back in the sanctuary of his bedroom, Christopher flung himself into a chair. The last of the daylight had gone and the dusk was illuminated by the magnificence of a blood red sunset. Looking out over the rolling land that one day would be his, all he wanted was to be thousands of miles away. To be free of Newlands, his mother and everything they stood for. More than that, he wanted to travel further than earthly miles – he wanted to go back in time, to wind the clocks back to the time before the poison had passed from his mother's lips and polluted his mind, souring his image of Martha.

He should have never returned home but stayed in the cottage with Martha and gone straight from there to Cambridge, taking her with him. He tried to blot out the things his mother had told him, but they could never be unsaid. Worst of all, he feared them to be true.

Why had Martha lied to him? Why had he believed the tangled web of untruths she had spun for him? Was his mother right and she had deliberately sought to entrap him, to win him over to her cause with her tale of a brutish husband and a barren womb? With her story of Walters raping her. And how could it be possible that she didn't know she had had a child? A living child. Not only had she lied to him about the baby's survival, she had lied about its very existence at all.

Her betrayal was devastating. He struggled to breathe. He had never felt so alone – not since lying in a mud-filled crater at Messines with a blasted leg, as the Third Battle of Ypres went on without him. Lying in agony in that muddy hole, shaking with terror as shells burst around him, he had fully expected to die. Now, he was trapped in a limbo with no way to move forward and his retreat cut off by the shocking words his mother had spoken.

He didn't know whom he hated most – his mother for her cruelty in telling him all this, in shattering his illusions about both his lover and his father – or Martha for the way she had lied about everything. An hour earlier he had felt sheer joy, happiness and love for her. He had had his future ahead of him and had been brimming with hope for it. Now he was squirming in a bottomless pit with no obvious way to escape.

And the future? He had none now. He was only too well aware that his mother had told him all this, intending that despair would make him weak and thus susceptible to her pressure for him to marry Lavinia. It was working. All the fight had gone from him.

He got up and paced the room, in front of the windows, his thoughts contradicting each other.

He wouldn't give into his mother. Never. Not after what she had done to him. He would go back to Borneo alone. Lose himself in the sultry heat of the rainforest, far away from the shame George Shipley had brought upon him and the family. Maybe eventually he'd find comfort in his work. It wouldn't remove the pain, the hurt – how could that ever heal? But distance and displacement might one day ease it.

As he tried to force these thoughts, these rational responses, to the surface, an overwhelming sense of loneliness, desolation and despair swamped him, so that he struggled again to breathe and his whole body shuddered.

He remembered the poisonous mushrooms he and Martha had come upon under the tree. How long ago was that? Less than two hours, but it felt like a lifetime. How easy would it be to return there, pluck those toadstools and eat them? He relished the idea, taking satisfaction from the prospect of his mother finding his body and knowing that she had driven him to take his own life.

But he was enough of a scientist to know that such a death would be an agonising and protracted one. If he was going to kill himself there were less messy and painful ways to do so. He slumped back into the chair, his head in his hands.

He forced himself to remember a time before the war when he had felt differently. Back in the forests of Borneo he had always been full of purpose, every day had felt fresh – new things to discover, new sights to see. The people around him were uncomplicated – or the fact that he had been limited in his means of communicating with them kept interactions down to a simple level. He could go back there – recreate that feeling of freshness and discovery. Such a feeling might seem impossible and unattainable now, but surely he could recapture it if he went back.

A wave of anger swept over him. Anger at Martha, at his

mother, at the whole damned world which was rotten to the core. He remembered a German word he had learned at school – *weltschmerz* – pain at the world and weariness with it all. He let the anger seep into him, drawing strength from it. His mother wasn't going to get her way. He wasn't going to give in like that. Capitulate. Bend to her will.

Through the window, he saw a deer running across the grasslands beyond the ha-ha and into the woods. It made him think of Martha again. Had she really lied to him? Was their brief love affair a confection to allow her to manipulate him? Everything his mother had said led to that conclusion. But he couldn't believe that Martha was so devious, so calculating. Instead she had seemed vulnerable, trusting him despite her innate cautiousness. He thought of her that afternoon, lying in his arms, looking into his eyes. He remembered the little cries she had made when he had moved inside her, the tenderness in her eyes. How could that have been simulated? The more he thought about it the more convinced he was that it wasn't.

His mother must be lying. That was the only possibility.

He must visit the mental institution and find out if Martha's daughter did exist. After all, his mother hadn't actually managed to find the proof she had been seeking in the drawers of George Shipley's desk.

A half-sister? The addle-brained child of a violent and abusive relationship. How was that possible? Going to the place where this Jane was supposedly kept was the only way he could be absolutely sure of the truth of his mother's words. He looked again at the sheet of paper she had given him. The place was called St Crispin's and was in a small market town about sixty miles away. He would go there tomorrow. Cambridge could wait. He would go alone – there was no possibility he could risk Rawson driving him and word getting out among the servants about the visit. But if his mother was telling the truth, then perhaps all of Newlands already knew about his father's behaviour?

Tossing and turning through the night, he gave up the battle for sleep, rising before six. He left the house before his mother had stirred, without taking breakfast. His stomach was rumbling with hunger and he remembered he had not eaten the previous evening. He would stop at an inn on the way.

CHAPTER 12

*T*he growth of mental asylums had burgeoned during the nineteenth century, with over one hundred thousand patients living inside these institutions in England by the time of Queen Victoria's death in 1901. The inmates were labelled, not always correctly, as lunatics. Women were disproportionately represented – many with nothing wrong with them but an illegitimate pregnancy or an ill-fated love affair.

After the war, the return of thousands of injured combatants from the Front meant many asylums were repurposed as military hospitals to treat both physical and mental injuries. It was deemed appropriate, since mental illness was viewed as shameful, for the civilian mental patients to be rehoused, to remove any indication that these were now anything other than military hospitals. The original inmates were cast out onto the mercy of their families or communities or shunted into other asylums which consequently became overstretched and overcrowded.

The sun was shining on the huge brick structure of St Crispin's as Christopher drove between the tall gateposts and down a long tree-lined driveway, through parkland that was not unlike Newlands. His nerves were jangling and he asked himself again why he was doing this.

The drive ended in a large turning circle in front of the imposing facade of the institution, its frontage dominated by a central clock tower. It appeared a forbidding and unwelcoming place. Yet in contrast to the severity of the buildings, offset to one side was a cricket pitch and pavilion with tennis courts on the other.

Christopher parked the Bentley and made his way across the gravel to the front door. He passed under the engraved stone portal which proclaimed the virtues of the original benefactor who had founded the place in 1821.

Inside, he was immediately assailed by the smell of carbolic soap and disinfectant, transporting him back in an instant to the months he had spent in the military rehabilitation hospital in Sussex.

A nurse in a starched apron and cap walked past and he called out to her. 'I'm here to visit a patient. Where do I find out where to go?'

Wordlessly, she pointed him towards a door. He knocked and entered, unsure what to expect of this visit. Part of him wanted to turn around, get back in his motor car and drive away before it was too late. Another part of him was full of curiosity. So he told the woman behind the desk that he was here to visit Miss Jane Walters.

The woman looked up in surprise, appraising him. 'I don't believe poor Jane has ever had anyone visit her before. May I enquire who you are and the purpose of your visit?'

Christopher hadn't even thought about the inevitability of this enquiry. He stared at her, momentarily uncertain, then quickly mumbled that he was from a firm of solicitors acting for Miss Walters' family.

'And your name, sir?' She thrust a visitors' book in front of him.

'Bell,' he said, choosing the first name that came into his head, that of his housemaster at school. 'Her family would like me to provide them with a report as to Miss Walters' welfare.'

'I see. When we admitted her we were told the family didn't want to receive any reports on her progress – or lack of it in her case.'

'Since so much time has passed, my client has indicated that a visit would be in order.' Christopher narrowed his eyes and glared at her. 'After all, my client funds her care here.'

His words and expression had the desired effect. 'Of course,' she said. 'Perfectly understandable.' Then looking uncomfortable, she added, 'Jane, er, Miss Walters, used to be kept in a private room but we have found that she responds better to being on one of the women's wards. Having the company. It's a ward for paying patients,' she added quickly. 'Not one of the public wards.'

Christopher felt out of his depth. He suspected that the long term incarceration of Jane Walters and the absence of relatives had led to St Crispin's saving on the cost of her care. 'Could you tell me exactly what her condition is?'

'She's been here since childhood. She was transferred from an orphanage when they proved unable to cope with her.' The woman rose from her desk and opened a filing cabinet behind her. She flipped through the folders and pulled one out. It was thin. 'Here we are. Chronic brain damage, occasioned at the time of her birth, rendering her an idiot.'

She put the folder back in the drawer. 'When she came to us, aged seven, she was unable to talk. Now she responds to her name and can say a few simple words. Would you like to see her?'

He said he would, the words out before he could think what he was doing, curiosity overcoming his fear.

The woman rang a bell and another uniformed nurse appeared.

'Take this gentleman, er …Mr Bell… to Sycamore Ward. He is here to see Jane Walters.'

She turned to Christopher again. 'Perhaps you would like to have a word with the doctor in charge of her case?'

'I don't want to trouble him.'

'It's no trouble. And as you are the first person who has ever been to visit the poor girl it's the least we can do.'

The nurse led Christopher along a series of long austere corridors, their walls lined with brown glazed tiles. Sycamore was the last in a series of wards running off the main female wing to the left side of the central administrative building. Its heavy oak door was locked. The nurse took out a key and opened the door. Seeing Christopher's discomfort she said, 'A precaution. Some of them tend to wander, but none of those in Sycamore are dangerous.'

He followed her inside. They entered the large ward, past a nurses' station on his left and a store room on his right. The ward was lined with beds, around a dozen on each side, some of them occupied, most not. Christopher studied the occupants, one or two sleeping or comatose, others lying groaning in pain, perceived or real, one curled up in the foetal position on the floor beside her bed. As he passed, an elderly woman got up from her bed and moved towards him, clutching at the hem of his jacket. Her hair was matted, her eyes sunken inside their sockets with dark shadows around them, her teeth blackened stumps. She said something incomprehensible and reached to grab at his hands.

'Get away, Gracie!' the nurse told her. 'Go back to your bed or we'll have to tie you down.' Then to Christopher she said, 'She thinks you're her husband, poor soul. But he's been dead thirty years. She's been here ever since. Never got over it. She's a chronic case. Harmless though – apart from to herself.'

Christopher shuddered at the thought of spending one's whole life shut away in a place such as this.

The end of the long dormitory area gave onto a large day room, flooded with light from tall windows on three sides. Outside were lawns, dotted about with patients, walking around or sitting on benches in the morning sunshine.

Round the circumference of the day room, several of the ward's inmates were seated, some slumped forward, appearing to be semi-conscious, others alert and upright. There was the buzz of incoherent voices, some singing, some crying, some mumbling to themselves, while others stared blankly into space.

The nurse stopped in front of a chair occupied by a woman who had her face turned away. 'This is Jane Walters.' Then to the patient, 'Come on Janey. Say hello. You have a visitor.'

Turning again to Christopher, she said, 'Jane can sometimes manage to say her name but not much more. Depends what mood she's in.'

The young woman in the chair turned her head and her eyes moved in his direction. She was wearing the same striped, serge dress that most of the women on the ward wore – her hair was parted in the centre and tucked behind her ears and appeared not to have been washed in weeks. Her eyes were vacant and her head was lolling.

Christopher experienced a surge of guilt. He searched her face in vain for similarities in looks to either his father or to Martha, but could find nothing to confirm the familial relationship.

'May I sit with her a while?'

The nurse told him he was free to sit with her as long as

he wished and told him to call at the doctor's office on the way out, informing him it was back along the corridor towards the central administrative block.

He pulled up a chair and sat down opposite Jane. Her eyes were lowered and he tried in vain to make contact with them, but she appeared to see nothing and to lack the ability to focus. Her hands fidgeted in her lap – the only parts of her body that showed any animation. Christopher struggled to imagine what her life had been thus far, and what it might have been had she not spent it incarcerated. If this woman was his sister, he felt no affection or kindred spirit towards her. Looking at her sitting here, slumped in her chair in front of him, she reminded him of a rag doll, limbs floppy, facial features fixed and unchanging. He'd had a rag doll himself when he was an infant, a hand-me-down from Percy, its cloth body already grubby and losing some of its woollen hair. Then he remembered how he had loved that doll, made by his grandmother. He tried to remember its name but it eluded him.

Feeling awkward, uncertain what to do, whether to try to talk to the young woman or to leave, he acknowledged to himself that this had been a wasted journey. He was no more certain that Jane Walters was the daughter of his father and Martha than he had been before he came. And yet how could she not be? George Shipley was too careful a businessman to commit funds for this girl's care if he had not felt an unavoidable obligation. Christopher sat beside Jane, in silence, the two of them bathed in a stream of sunlight coming through the metal-framed windows.

A passing nurse smiled at him and turning back said, 'Jane hasn't had her walk yet. That usually raises her spirits. We're short-staffed today. Two nurses down with the influenza.'

'Perhaps I could walk her around the garden?' he said, not knowing what had compelled him to offer.

'If you can spare the time, sir.'

Christopher offered a hand to the woman in the chair and to his surprise she took it. Her own hand was thin, bony, with long tapering fingers and it felt so delicate in his that he feared crushing it. He helped her to her feet and they shuffled together through the French window into the garden. A large paved terrace gave onto an extensive lawn surrounded by trees. He could hear birds singing. With her thin-boned hand resting in his, he led her around the expanse of garden. As they walked, she became steadier on her feet, as if she were drawing strength from the air, from the sunlight, from the growing plants around them.

When they were a distance away from the other inmates, they came to a natural halt by a bench under a spreading oak tree. The ground about them was covered in a carpet of acorn cups that crunched underfoot. They sat down, her hand still holding his. Suddenly and unaccountably, he began to feel calm, experiencing no tension between them from the lack of speech.

St Crispin's was a peaceful place, removed from the buzz of daily life. A backwater, forgotten by the rest of the world along with the people in it. Not what he had expected, fearing some latter day reincarnation of Bedlam. He decided he liked the place.

It was only when she let go of his hand to reach down and pick a buttercup from the edge of the lawn that he remembered she had been holding it. She turned and offered the flower to him, a ghost of a smile playing on her lips. He was reminded of Martha and how her stern face was transformed when she smiled. For the first time he saw a resemblance.

Raising her hand, Jane tapped her fingers to her breast and made an attempt to say her own name, but it emerged as only 'Juh'. She tapped her fingers against the front of his jacket and turned her head towards him. The dead eyes now seemed to show a slight glimmer from their dark, unfathomable depths.

He felt a wave of sadness sweep over him, as he told her his name was Kit. The sadness was not only for this poor lost girl, trapped inside the prison of her damaged mind, it was for the mother who must have denied her existence. It was also for the whole rotten world that they were living in, for the terrible pointless war he had fought in, for the lives of all the young men who had died in the mud and the cold and the rain. He was sad for his mother, for the way her husband's infidelities had eradicated any capacity for compassion, for love, for empathy in her. He grieved for the loss of the father he had believed he had known, but now realised had never existed. The stern, ambitious dynamic man by whom he had always been intimidated, had proved to be a hollow man, a weak and cruel man who used and abused and then wrote cheques to hide away the consequences of such abuse. He found himself stroking his half-sister's hand and for the first time since he had set eyes on her, he felt an affinity with her.

Jane made a little snuffling sound, then, her head nodding in rhythm, she formed the plosive consonant of his name, repeating the 'k' sound over and over again.

He smiled at her and said his name again, gratified when he saw a hint of a smile play about her lips. Surely these tiny signs indicated a possibility of Jane being helped to speak. He was convinced that there was something more than a mute idiot inside her.

As they sat there in silence in the sun-dappled garden, Christopher was transported back to the day the previous year when he was wounded. It had been a very different day from this one: torrential rain that blinded the men as they marched along the muddy track, churned up and ploughed under the weight of hundreds of vehicles and thousands of boots and hooves. The muddy roads and devastated farmland had taken on a new and changing form, as shells and mortars lifted the ground, throwing it skywards, altering the landscape. Distant explosions lit up the sky in a fiery furnace. Fire and rain. He had lifted his head to witness the terrible beauty of the burning sky, and didn't notice the tell-tale signs of unexploded ordnance. A careless moment of inattention. Whether it was seconds, minutes or hours later, he did not know, but when he was conscious again he was lying on his back at the bottom of a crater, flung there by the power of the explosion underneath him.

He had felt no pain at first, unaware that his foot was no longer attached to his leg. Above his head, he had seen only smoke, a thick pall of it, blotting out the sky. Underneath him the ground was shaking. All around he could hear the thump of guns, the scream of shells and the roar of retreating vehicles. He heard no voices, saw no faces, friend nor foe, looking over the rim of the crater to search for him. By now the pain had won out over the shock and he lay on his back in agony, his leg feeling as if it was being slowly and simultaneously burned in a furnace and crushed in a vice. He tried to call out, thought he was screaming but could hear nothing but the sounds of the battle. The pain intensified. Burning. Searing. Cutting. Killing him in a slow relentless torture. Had his own men forgotten him? Were they dead or wounded too? All around him and above him the war went on without him. He had felt utterly, completely alone. Abandoned. Forgotten.

But he had not been forgotten or left to die. He had no idea when or how, but they came for him. Hands reaching out, lifting him, digging him out of his hole, his mud-mired tomb, and laying him gently on a stretcher. They had carried him behind the lines and into the haven of a hospital where an angel in white had bent over him, wiped his brow and eased his pain with morphine to send him into the blessed peace of sleep.

Now here today in this tranquil garden, holding Jane Walters' hand, he remembered how it had felt to be rescued. To be released, not so much from the fear of death, but from the fear of being alone, forgotten, ignored, abandoned. How must it be for Jane? Until today, no living soul had visited her, walked with her and held her hand. She had grown up, unknown, unloved, untouched by anyone save those paid to care for her. Christopher's heart swelled and he knew at once that he must get her out of here.

A bell rang and Jane got to her feet in a reflexive response to the sound. Seeing the other inmates move across the lawn towards the house, Christopher helped steer her back to the ward.

A nurse came forward and shepherded Jane along with the others out of the ward and down the corridor. 'Dinner time,' the nurse said, pointing to the clock on the wall which showed it was half an hour past noon.

Jane didn't give him so much as a backward glance. It was as if the shutters had come down inside her brain and she had reverted to the passive, inscrutable being, with dead eyes and an absence of any facial expression. He watched her move away, her feet shuffling, her head lowered, in clothing indistinguishable from her fellows.

When they had all gone, apart from those who were comatose or sleeping on their beds, Christopher went back along the corridor, knocked on the door of the doctor's room and was invited to enter. The man behind the desk was older than he was – probably in his forties. He wore a black patch over one eye and had a neat moustache. Evidence of a military man. In confirmation, Christopher noticed a regimental tie.

'Dr Reggie Henderson,' the man said, offering his hand to Christopher.

'Without thinking, he replied, 'Captain Christopher Shipley.' Then realised his mistake at once.

'They told me your name was Bell. A solicitor?'

'I'm sorry. I intended to keep my identity concealed... I wanted my visit to be discreet.'

The doctor waved his hand. 'No need to explain. Quite understandable.' He indicated a chair and Kit sat down.

'Problem with the leg?'

'Left it in a muddy hole near Messines.'

The doctor nodded. 'Lost my eye back in '14. Mons. That was the end of the war for me.' He extended a wooden box of cigarettes towards Christopher, who declined. The doctor lit one himself and exhaled the smoke slowly. 'After they patched me up I was posted here in 1916, when it was a military hospital and I stayed on after the Armistice. So, you'd like to know about Miss Walters?'

Christopher decided the truth was the best course. 'I believe her to be my half-sister but I only learnt of her existence yesterday.'

The doctor passed no comment, merely nodding and puffing on his cigarette.

'What exactly is wrong with her? All I've been told is that her brain was damaged at birth.'

Henderson shrugged. 'I know nothing of her history before she was admitted here. She was one of the few who remained during the war years when most of the civilian patients were removed. There are houses in the grounds where a small number of private patients, unable to return to their families, were kept, and she was cared for there throughout the war. After the Armistice, she moved back here when the place was decommissioned as a military hospital. This is a private ward, much less crowded than the public ones, and with more staff. We now tend to use the houses for staff – I live in one myself – with a few reserved for those patients who are ready to return to their families. Most of them have jobs and we can still keep an eye out for their welfare. Obviously Miss Walters does not fit into that category.' He tapped his fingers on the top of the desk. 'Sad case. Neglected since childhood. I don't see why she couldn't have learned to speak. Complete lack of stimulus. Anybody would turn into a vegetable if they were treated that way.'

'You mean she's been neglected here?' Kit gripped the edge of the desk.

'No more than many of them. And she only moved here when she was seven – the damage was already done by then. The methods used in places like these was rather crude in the past. It used to be little more than a prison. There's a new regime here now. We look at things in a more enlightened way these days. Instead of locking them up and forgetting about them, we're trying to get them to the point where they can return to as normal a life as possible.'

'You think Jane might have a normal life?'

'Sadly, no. Not her. She's too far gone for that.' He consulted a folder. 'Chronic idiocy. Since birth. We might eventually get her to manage a few simple words and phrases. May even moderate the diagnosis from idiocy to imbecility. Perhaps she can reach a level you might expect from a small child. Not able to read and write or sustain a conversation, but better than she is now.'

'I see.' Christopher was uncertain how he felt.

'More significantly, I'm sure we can build up her trust and help her to be less afraid. More able to respond to stimulus. That should make her poor miserable life a little more bearable.'

Christopher got up and stretched a hand out to the

doctor. 'Thank you, Doctor. I will return. That is, if you think it might be beneficial for her to see me?'

'I think it would be extremely beneficial. But on one condition.'

Christopher sat down again.

'That if you do return you must do so on a regular basis. It would be detrimental to the poor creature if you were to visit for a while and then stop. It would be harmful for her to become familiar with you...' He thought for a moment then added, 'Or maybe, in her own way, became fond of you, and then you were to vanish from her life.'

'I understand. I wouldn't do that.' He rose again and moved to the door. As he opened it he turned back. 'One more question, Dr Henderson. Could you envisage it ever being possible for Jane to live in the care of her family? Given the right level of support?'

The doctor raised his hands, palms upwards. 'Again I would urge caution. Change is a great disruption to a patient like Miss Walters. She is institutionalised and would find it extremely difficult to adapt. And if having done so, for whatever reason, it was decided that the family could not cope, it would be a serious trauma for her to return.' He reached for another cigarette, tapping it on the surface of the desk. 'Don't underestimate the toll on a family, caused by having a person such as her in their midst. She requires full-time care. She's unable to dress or wash herself. Needs help feeding. She's like a small infant in terms of her capacities. Without the means to provide a nurse to care for her I fear the situation would be detrimental for all concerned.'

'We have the means,' Christopher said. 'Goodbye and thank you.'

CHAPTER 13

*W*hile Christopher was meeting his half-sister and discussing her care, Martha, unaware, made her way to the sunken garden, where she set about pruning some climbing roses which had grown rampant along the north wall of the gardens.

She didn't see Mrs Shipley approaching and nearly fell off the step ladder in fright at being addressed.

'So it's true, he's put you to work in here.' Kit's mother looked Martha up and down, her lip curling in disgust at the sight of her former gamekeeper's wife, clad in breeches. 'I wish to speak with you. But not now. Not here. Come to the house as soon as you have put on some respectable clothes and cleaned yourself up.'

Without waiting for Martha to reply, Mrs Shipley was gone.

An hour later, Martha Walters was shown into the library by the butler. She walked around the enormous room with its full-length windows along one wall, the others lined with oak shelving, crammed with leather-bound volumes, most of which appeared to be in pristine condition. Martha remembered Kit's offer to lend her any books she wanted to read and wandered over to the shelves to browse. Her hand was raised to take a volume from the shelf, when she became aware of someone watching her from the open doorway. She dropped her hand, guiltily, and moved away from the bookcases.

Edwina Shipley sailed into the room and took up a seat behind a large oak table, waving her hand imperiously to signal that Martha should approach and stand in front of the table. She did as she was bid and Mrs Shipley pointed to an envelope on the table.

'Take it. It's to tell you to be out of the keeper's cottage by the end of the week.'

Martha glanced down at the envelope but made no move to pick it up.

'My son wrote it before he left this morning. He's more generous than I am. I would prefer you to leave immediately and will make it worth your while to do so.' She reached for the cheque book that was already beside her on the table. 'It's made out to cash. You will need to take it to a bank. There's enough for you to pay for food and lodgings for a few months or more. It will tide you over until you can make arrangements for yourself.' She fixed cold eyes on Martha. 'And before you ask, my son was unable to convey his letter to you himself, as he is away.'

'I know where he is. He's in Cambridge.' Martha stared straight at her, defiant.

'You're mistaken, Mrs Walters. He might well have been planning to go to Cambridge today – until he was made aware of the truth about you. That has changed everything. Right now he is in Northington visiting the lunatic asylum there. St Crispin's.' A half-smile ghosted across her face. 'Do you know why he should be there? Why he should be visiting St Crispin's?'

Martha had no idea, so she said nothing, but had a mounting sense of fear.

'He is establishing for himself whether what I told him about you and my late husband is true.' She watched Martha curiously. 'Were you trying to protect my son from the knowledge that you were the mistress of his father – or were you, as I suspect, only too aware that if you'd told him the truth he would have gone nowhere near you?'

Martha felt her knees weaken. 'I don't know what you're talking about.' Her hands gripped the edge of the table. She was frightened now.

'Don't lie. My son may fall for it but it cuts no ice with me. I may have turned a blind eye to what went on between my husband and you but I will not stand by and watch you ruin my son's life.'

Martha said nothing, her head lowered. Dizzy. Terrified.

'Captain Shipley has gone to visit your daughter today. He refused to believe me at first. Wanted to see for himself.'

'I don't know what you're talking about.' Martha's words were faint, barely audible, even to herself.

'The child you gave birth to twenty years ago. Jane Walters. I understand the girl's brain was damaged at birth and she is classed as an idiot. My son wanted to establish the scale of your deception: that you gave birth to a daughter fathered by my husband and that the child has spent the last twenty years shut away in a lunatic asylum.'

Martha swayed and struggled to remain standing. But she wasn't ready to let this woman intimidate her with her lies, so she forced herself to remain on her feet, her head held high.

Edwina smiled. 'You knew it was alive, didn't you?'

Martha gulped.

'Didn't you?' Mrs Shipley tapped her fingers on the surface of the table.

'No.' Barely a whisper.

'Is that what they told you?'

The room spun around Martha. Waves of nausea rushed up from the pit of her stomach. A dark place. Shut away – locked inside her. Sudden memory of death coming to her, waiting to take her, as she begged it to come, to release her from the pain. Unbearable pain. Ripping her apart. *Let me die. Oh, God, please make it stop. Let it be over. Let me die.*

But she had lived. Only to be told the child that the doctor had dragged out of her small broken body had been born dead.

Martha had buried the horror of what had happened to her twenty years ago. But now it surfaced, bringing back all the pain and torment she had gone through: the searing grief at the loss of the baby she had never wanted while she was carrying it. Standing here now, unsteady on her feet, the agony overwhelmed her. Her legs crumpled underneath her and she fell to the floor.

Revived by the application of smelling salts, Martha found herself sitting in an armchair near the tall windows, with Mrs Shipley standing over her. She was disoriented at first, then remembered the terrible things the woman had told her. She opened and closed her eyes then said, 'Where is he? Where is K… Captain Shipley?'

'I told you, he's gone to confirm the whereabouts of your daughter. And as soon as he has done that, he will be travelling on to make amends with Lady Lavinia Bourne and her family for his absence over much of the weekend. I have no doubt that once he has smoothed matters over, arrangements for his marriage will proceed as originally planned.'

Mrs Shipley walked back to the table and picked up the envelope and the cheque and thrust them at Martha. 'It won't take him long to get over his foolish infatuation for you. Once he comprehends what an accomplished liar you are he'll be only too glad to see the back of you and marry Lady Lavinia. If she'll still have him.'

Martha stared at the envelope and gave a little sob. 'I don't want your money.'

'No, I'm sure you don't. But I insist you take it. I can't have you wandering the streets or hanging around the village. One of the grooms is going to drive you into Ledford and put you on the next train to London. Whether you stay there or move on somewhere else is up to you. But don't come back here.' She glanced at her watch. 'You'd better hurry.'

Martha got to her feet.

Mrs Shipley had moved towards the window and had her back to her. Over her shoulder, she said, 'And don't try to contact my son. He doesn't want to hear from you. He certainly doesn't want to see you again. I only wish I had disillusioned him sooner, before he had the misfortune to follow his father into your bed.'

CHAPTER 14

*C*hristopher drove down the driveway from St Crispin's, his head full of conflicting thoughts. He had travelled here today in the expectation that he would either disprove what his mother had told him, or that he would see the woman who was his half-sister and be filled with disgust and loathing for her.

Now he knew. Jane was definitely who his mother had told him she was. When they had sat under the oak tree he'd seen Martha in her eyes and there was something about the line of her jaw that was unmistakably a Shipley inheritance.

But to suggest to the doctor that Jane should come to live with them? What had possessed him? What had he meant? How could he possibly bring her home to Newlands and force her presence on his mother? And what about his plans to go abroad?

He tried to see the situation from Edwina's point of view. He abhorred the manner in which she had told him about Jane's existence, the way she had been heedless of hurting him. But he couldn't help but feel some pity for his mother in being forced to live for twenty years in the knowledge that her husband had betrayed her and fathered a child with one of the servants on the estate, a child herself at the time. How had she accepted it? How had she lived with that knowledge for so long? But he knew the answer to that. Edwina Shipley would never have contemplated the scandal of a divorce or the shame and disgrace of the circumstances that had occasioned it. Nor would she willingly have forgone the status and wealth that marriage to George Shipley and the bounty of his vast industrial empire bestowed upon her. No wonder she wanted rid of Martha now. He speculated as to why she hadn't done it before and could find no satisfactory answer. Perhaps she'd felt it was inappropriate for her to be dealing with such matters. Had she wanted to pretend she didn't know anything about what had taken place? And to avoid a scene with Martha? Discretion had always been a by-word for his mother.

But Jane? She was a different matter. At first Christopher had felt fear and, yes, even a little disgust at the creature with the blank dead eyes and the slumped posture, but their walk in the grounds had changed all that. He remembered the way her small hands had felt in his, the way the light had eventually come into her eyes, how she'd responded to being outdoors, to being awoken by the presence of the natural world.

When she'd offered the buttercup to him, he'd felt a surge of affection for her. It was as if, under the layers of what the doctor had described as her idiocy, she had a dormant sensibility. He felt in his pocket for the buttercup. It was still there.

What he had not yet managed to confront, was how all this made him feel about Martha. What had changed since yesterday to alter how he felt about her? Until yesterday, he had wanted her physically with a passion he had never experienced before – but he was unsure if he could feel that way about her now, knowing she had lied to him and borne a child with his father and possibly colluded in Jane's incarceration. Yet everything in Christopher's head and his heart screamed out that Martha would never knowingly have denied her daughter's existence nor conceded to her being locked away. And never willingly succumbed to his father's advances, no matter what his mother might think or say. Something inside told him that he must trust his heart, not listen to his head.

Driving through villages and towns, past farmland and forest, factories and railway stations, Christopher asked himself over and over again what he should do now. Confront his mother? Talk to Martha?

He knew what he *wanted* to happen. He couldn't go to Borneo any more, and instead he knew with a certainty that was unsupported by any practical plans to make it a reality, that he wanted to live in the little house in the copse, with Martha and, God willing, eventually with Jane. He wanted to be the one who would unite mother and daughter, be the means by which his sister might one day be able to function away from the institution in which otherwise she would be condemned to see out her days.

And yet, his head told him such a plan was fraught with impracticalities. How could he live on the estate under the nose of his mother, inflicting what she would see as a terrible humiliation upon her? And Jane? How would Martha herself react? How much did she know? Over and over he mulled these points in his head until his temples throbbed and his palms were clammy on the steering wheel.

The war may have changed many things, but he knew it wouldn't have lessened the tendency of people to gossip, to criticise, to condemn. Any attempt to bring Jane Walters to live on the Newlands estate would result in the shaming and dishonouring of Martha and he couldn't put her through that. The only way he could make his wish a reality would be for the three of them to leave Newlands and move somewhere where no one would know them.

As he mulled the idea over in his head, the more it appealed to him. He could earn his living pursuing his research at the university or for the Royal Horticultural Society – or failing that, become a teacher – and forgo any claims on the estate. He could marry Martha. No one need know that Jane was her daughter – she could easily pass as her sister. His mother would be furious, but he wasn't going to let her reactions rule him. It was his life not hers.

Christopher reached the gates of Newlands by early evening. The sky was aflame in a brilliant sunset with ripples of red and orange cutting through the tracery of clouds. He drove the motor car off the main driveway and onto the gravel track that led to the cottage in the woods.

There was no light coming from the windows. He walked across the grassy clearing and knocked on the door, impatient to find out the truth from Martha. She had lied to him about his father but what of Jane? He could believe she had lied about George Shipley, probably out of shame and fear, but he refused to believe that she had allowed her child to be locked away in an asylum.

Silence.

He walked round to the rear of the cottage. The curtains were undrawn and the rooms were all in darkness. He heard a fox barking and jumped. His nerves were raw.

He tried the handle of the door and it opened. He walked inside and checked the downstairs rooms but there was no sign of Martha. The kettle on the stove was cold, and the grate was full of cold ashes and did not appear to have been cleared and laid since the previous night. Opening the door to the stairway, he bounded up the stairs as quickly as his wooden leg would permit him. Memories of their walk the previous day past the toadstools chilled his blood. Panic that his mother had talked to Martha sliced through him. No. Please, God. No.

He didn't know whether to be relieved or disappointed when he didn't find Martha in the bedroom.

'WHERE IS SHE?' Christopher burst into the library where his mother was enjoying one of her favourite cocktails. She was standing in front of the fireplace, twirling a swizzle stick inside the concoction.

'Calm down, darling. We don't want the servants to hear. You know what this place is like. As soon as you say anything it's all over the kitchens and within five minutes the whole village knows our affairs.' She tutted. 'Let me get you a drink. I'm having a Gin Fizz. You?'

Christopher ignored her and went to the sideboard and poured himself a large scotch. He was beginning to develop a taste for it.

'You're as bad as your father, Christopher. I'll never understand why Englishmen are so dreary about cocktails. At least dear Percy would indulge me once in a while. But you... Really, I despair. And according to the papers today there's growing pressure to prohibit alcohol altogether in the United States. What kind of a world are we living in?' She flung herself into an armchair. 'What did we fight a war for if we can't even enjoy the peace?'

'Why do you have to trivialise everything, Mother?' Christopher moved to stand in front of the fire opposite her. 'I asked you a question, so answer me. Where is Martha?'

Mrs Shipley took a sip from her drink and narrowed her eyes. 'I have absolutely no idea where the gamekeeper's wife is – if it is she to whom you are referring.' She crossed her legs. She was wearing a dress in green chartreuse silk, and the movement showed off her trim silk-clad ankles. She flexed her foot to admire it. 'All I can tell you is she left on the train from Ledford to London this morning. But don't worry, I made sure she was amply compensated. She was only too willing to accept a nice fat cheque.'

Christopher felt sick. His hand shook and he struggled to form words. Nothing his mother was saying rang true about Martha. Being bought off? He couldn't believe it. He wouldn't believe it.

The arrival of Bannister to announce dinner cut short any reply Kit might have made. Walking into the dining room he felt hollowed out and empty. Life at Newlands had seemed empty and pointless after his experiences on the Western Front, but now, in the face of his mother's refusal to confront the truth of what George Shipley had done and the legacy he had left in the form of Jane Walters, he could tolerate it no longer. He despised his mother, with her devotion to fine clothes and cocktails, her nostalgia for the pre-war days, her obsession over her position in society, and her vicarious pleasure at her son's matrimonial prospects. But how could he hate her? She was his mother. Despite her faults, her vanity, her insatiable hunger for acceptance, wasn't he duty-bound to feel love for her? But he couldn't. Maybe he never had. He'd always respected her but he no longer knew what respect for her was either.

As soon as the servants had left the room, he said, 'I will find her. Wherever she has gone, I will seek her out and find her. I intend to marry Martha Walters and you won't stand in my way. I don't expect you to understand my reasons. I realise that love is an alien concept to you, but it's what I feel for her and why I want to spend the rest of my life with her.'

'Nonsense. Love?' She spoke with a cross between a sneer and a snarl. 'I've told you before. Love is not for people of our class.'

Putting down his knife and fork he said, 'And what's more, I intend my sister to live with us. With her mother and me. As soon as I can arrange for the necessary care. When I've found Martha, we will be married and the three of us will move away from here. You're welcome to the whole damn place. Do with it what you will. All I ask for is my allowance.'

'You ask too much.'

'What do you mean?'

'I can't do anything about the choices you make when you are thirty, but until then the provisions of your father's will established that I have full control over your inheritance. And I have determined that you will not have a penny of your allowance unless you are living under this roof.'

'You can't do that.'

'I think you'll find I can and I will.'

'Why? Why would you do this, Mother?'

'I ask in turn why you want to do everything to flout my wishes? I expect you to *do your duty*.' She emphasised the words. 'I expect you to marry Lavinia Bourne. I'm prepared for you to sow your wild oats and, once you're engaged, even delay the marriage for a year or so. But I will not permit you to see that woman again.'

'Permit me?' Christopher felt his voice rising and the veins on his temples began to throb. 'I am twenty-six, not twelve, Mother. You can't tell me what to do. I've fought for my country, risked my life, lost my leg and still you persist in treating me as a small child.'

'Because you behave like one. As for the idea of bringing the lunatic bastard child of that woman to live with you – you must have lost your mind too, Christopher. Now I don't wish to discuss this any more.' She jangled the bell for the second course.

The rest of the meal took place in silence as Christopher

tried to figure out what to do next. His priority was to find Martha. He had to bring her back. She had to meet her daughter. He dreaded to think what his mother had said to her. If she had believed her child had died, as he was certain she had, she must now be in a state of shock. She must think he'd abandoned her. He would find her wherever she was and make everything all right with her.

Lying in bed that night he longed to be with Martha. In turmoil as he lurched between blind faith in her and anger that she had lied to him, he was sure if she were with him she'd be able to explain everything. But how? She had lied to him with a cock and bull story about her husband. Lied about having a child. And yet, he refused to accept that she had done so deliberately or maliciously. There had been no mistaking the love he had seen in her eyes.

Turning on his side he punched his fist into the pillow. He couldn't help himself. He loved her anyway and longed to be lying here with her in his arms, the fresh scent of her hair as it spread on his pillow, the feel of her skin under his hands, the touch of her lips on his and the memory of how it felt to be inside her.

CHAPTER 15

*C*hristopher spent the next three weeks searching for Martha Walters. He established from Michael, the groom who had taken her in the cart to the station at Ledford, that he had been instructed by Mrs Shipley to purchase a one-way train ticket to London and wait to see Mrs Walters onto the train. Heading straight for London, Christopher stood on the platform at St Pancras, wondering where to start his search.

Crowds of people thronged the station, all rushing towards their trains, or disembarking from them, only to be absorbed into the vast ocean that was the capital.

He began by questioning staff on the station, but no one had seen her. Most of the porters he spoke to laughed at him.

'You got any idea 'ow many people come through 'ere each day?'

'She wouldn't know where to go. She might have enquired about places to lodge.'

The porter shrugged. 'I'm a porter, not a bleeding travel agent.'

Christopher visited lodging houses in the vicinity of the

station, but no one had any recollection of a woman of her description.

Footsore and dispirited, he broadened the search and tramped his way every day around employment agencies, hostels and guest houses throughout central London, everywhere being greeted by raised eyebrows or shrugs of indifference.

'You reckon this lady would want to be found?' asked a landlady, putting down the cloth she was using to polish a brass bell on the counter, in order to study him. 'You say she took off without warning?' She smiled and said, 'Sounds to me like she wanted to disappear. Nowhere in the world easier to do that than in London.' She shrugged, turned away from him and went back to polishing the brass.

He went to several police stations. If the railway porters, hoteliers and employment agency staff were dismissive, it was nothing compared to the reception he got from the police.

Defeated, Christopher finally admitted to himself that he was getting nowhere and called on the services of a private investigator.

The man, a Mr Pontefract, was not encouraging. 'A name and a description is not much to go on,' he lamented. 'You've no idea how many people come to London and disappear. She may even be using a different name if she doesn't want to be found.' He fixed his gaze on Christopher. 'You sure there's no relatives? Friends? And you say she has no occupation?'

Christopher replied in the negative, beginning to lose heart.

'What's she going to live on then?'

Cursing his own stupidity, Christopher remembered that his mother had said she had paid off Martha with a cheque. 'There's the bank,' he said. 'She will have drawn a cheque on my mother's account. Perhaps that will give us a clue as to her whereabouts.'

'That's more like it. Get me the account details and I'll see what I can find out.'

'But will the bank give out such information?'

'You leave that to me. Best you don't know. My methods are trade secrets.' The man winked and Christopher felt as though he were conspiring in something nefarious. But there was no possibility of moral quibbles – finding Martha was all that mattered.

TWO DAYS later Mr Pontefract called to say he had unearthed the information.

'The lady drew the sum out from a bank branch in Northington on the same day that you said she travelled to London. It appears she got off the train from Ledford before she reached London.'

'Northington? Are you sure?'

'Are you questioning my integrity, Mr Shipley?'

'Of course not. It makes sense. I should have known. You have done an excellent job.'

'That all? Don't you want me to go to Northington and try to pick up the trail there?'

'That won't be necessary. I'm confident that I know where to find her.'

He handed over some notes to Pontefract, who counted them out, grinned and stuffed them into his wallet. 'That's most generous, sir. I'm happy to have been of assistance. I trust all will go well between you and the lady concerned.' He tilted his head and gave an almost imperceptible wink and Christopher felt himself reddening.

He drove straight to St Crispin's. As soon as he set foot inside the building, the disinfectant smell assaulted his nose.

He made his way along the interminable, brown-tiled corridors to Jane's ward. Looking through the glass panel in the locked door, he saw that Jane was sleeping, head slumped forward, chin on chest and mouth slightly open. Her hair was clean – glossy and tied back neatly with a ribbon, rather than hanging in the greasy rats' tails of his previous visit.

A nurse was sitting at a desk at the top of the ward. It was a different one from his last visit. She opened the door. 'Can I help you, sir?'

'I've come to visit Jane Walters, but I can see she's asleep. I haven't picked a good time.'

'She always has forty winks after she's eaten her dinner. Might I ask who you are?'

'My name is… Shipley, Captain Shipley.' There was no point in continuing with the story he had used last time. 'I'm a relative. I called on her about three or four weeks ago. I'd intended to return sooner but I had urgent business to attend to.'

'Isn't Jane a lucky girl? Another visitor. There's a lady who's been coming. Every day for the past few weeks. Isn't that strange – no visitors in a whole lifetime and then two of you appear out of nowhere.'

He hesitated for a moment, then decided to plunge onwards. 'I presume you mean Mrs Martha Walters?'

'You know her then? Well, of course you do. You said you were a relative.'

'Has she visited today?'

The nurse smiled at him. 'All morning. Stayed with her until after dinner. Feeds her she does. Said she be back later once Jane's had her nap.'

'Any idea when that will be?'

The nurse lifted her fob watch and checked the time. 'In about half an hour or so. She likes to be here ready, as soon as Jane wakes up. Devoted she is. Apparently she only recently found out the poor creature was in here. I suppose it's the same for you?' She was evidently eager for him to tell her more about this sudden convergence of relatives on a previously neglected inmate.

'Thank you for your help, Nurse. I'll return another time.'

Christopher hurried back along the corridor. He would sit in the motor car and watch and wait for Martha's return.

He saw her approaching long before she saw him. He watched her tall slim figure as she moved up the drive in her familiar brown coat and shapeless felt hat. Kit felt a surge of desire as she moved towards him, oblivious of his presence in the parked car. When she was a few yards away she saw him through the windscreen and stopped in her tracks.

Kit got out of the car and took her arm, steering her towards the vehicle. 'Get in,' he said. 'We can talk inside.'

Martha hesitated for a moment, glancing nervously towards the front door of St Crispin's, and then slipped into the passenger seat. 'I've never been inside a motor car.'

He turned to face her and then, unable to stop himself, pulled her into his arms and kissed her. He held her face in his hands and gazed into the dark pools of her eyes, looking for the truth in them. 'I've searched high and low for you. I was desperate. Terrified I might never see you again. That I'd lost you forever.' He stroked a finger down her cheek and ran it over the contour of her lips. 'Oh, my darling Martha, I don't know what I'd have done if I'd lost you. But why? Why did you tell me all those lies?'

Martha turned her head away, leaning it against the windowpane. 'I didn't lie. I'd no idea about Jane. Do you think I'd have abandoned her if I'd known? I thought she was dead. That's what they all told me. Then I think I wiped everything that happened out of my mind. When Mrs Shipley told me I'd had a child I thought at first she was lying. But I knew about Mr Shipley. That he was the father. That he was the one who did those things to me.' She put her hands over her face. 'But how could I tell you that?'

Kit stared ahead out of the windscreen. He knew she was telling him the truth, but it still hurt.

'Walters never touched me. Not that way. Not as a husband. But he was responsible for the beatings. That was all true. They only stopped when Da died and he moved into the other bedroom. I think sharing a bed with me was a source of shame to him.' She paused, running her finger down the glass window. 'But Jane. How can I forgive myself for what happened to her? Why didn't I insist on seeing her body when they told me she was dead?'

'You were in shock. You'd suffered so much. Everything my father did to you. The beatings from Walters. And, according to Mother, you almost died giving birth. She said your labour lasted for days. And you were a child. It's no wonder you wanted to blot it all out.' He reached for her hand and held it, stroking it. 'The mind can do strange things. I know that from what I saw in the war. Men who one day were laughing and brawling, next day reduced to blubbering babies. Men who forgot their own names. How to talk. Some even became blind or deaf with no physical damage to the eyes and ears.' He bent his head over her hand and kissed it.

'If people go through an experience that is truly shocking to them, or terrifying, their mind can completely block out the memory, as if it never happened. I think that's what happened to you.'

Her eyes filled with tears and he pulled her towards him, holding her with her head resting against his chest. He felt the warmth of her breath through his shirt.

'Martha, my love, you must come away with me. I want us to go back to Newlands and I will confront my mother. Later we will bring Jane back too. I want to marry you and then together we can care for Jane.'

He felt her body stiffen.

'I won't leave her. Not ever. Even for a day.' She pulled away from him. 'I need to go now. She will be waking and I want to be there.'

'I'll come with you. I promised I would return to see her again.'

She nodded. 'I've asked them to find me work here. As a cleaner. So I can be with her. I start next week.'

Kit grabbed her arm. 'No. I won't have you doing that. I'll pay for your lodgings until we can make the necessary arrangements to bring Jane out.'

Her eyes were brimming with tears. 'She can never come out of here. The doctor told me she's completely institution-alised. She would be distressed at the change in her surroundings. I can't allow that to happen. Staying here is the best thing for her.' Martha took the handle of the door and stepped outside the motor. Impatient, Kit followed her.

As they walked through the building he spoke again of his dream that they marry and live with Jane.

Martha stared straight ahead as she answered him. 'Your mother would never permit it. She made her position abso-lutely clear to me. And you can't possibly expect her to accept Jane, knowing her origins, quite apart from the shame of her idiocy.'

She was right. And his mother could veto his allowance until he was thirty. He couldn't even afford to set up house with Martha somewhere else. It was imperative he reach some form of accommodation with Edwina. He couldn't bear to think of Martha scrubbing floors to be close to her daughter.

As soon as they entered the ward they heard Jane crying. Martha threw him a glance, full of recrimination, and rushed towards the young woman where she was sitting in the chair, thrashing her arms about. He watched, mesmerised as Martha knelt before Jane, wrapped her daughter in her arms and cooed words of comfort to her until the sobbing subsided.

Martha turned to look at him. 'You should go, Kit. It will take me some time to calm her. She must have thought I wasn't coming back. She's so fragile and so trusting. It's taken time for her to accept me and I can't risk hurting her. Please go, my love. Please.'

'What time will you leave here? Where are you staying?'

'I'm in lodgings opposite the gates. I'm staying with an elderly lady.'

'I'm going to wait for you. I'll book us a room in a hotel.'

'I can't walk into a hotel with you. What would people think?'

'If anyone asks, we'll tell them we're married. But I'm sure no one will. I'm going to book the room now and I'll be back later to fetch you.' He spoke quietly, looking around to make sure there were no nurses within earshot.

She nodded.

Taking a last look at his still sobbing sister, he ran his hands over Jane's hair, bent and kissed the top of her head then left the ward.

KIT WAS RIGHT about the hotel. The place was so busy no one gave him a second glance when he booked in. Northington was a bustling market town and he had been lucky to secure the last available room, tomorrow being market day. He walked around the town to kill time and then arranged for a plate of sandwiches and a flask of tea to be left in his room for later and returned to St Crispin's to collect Martha.

She told him she had eventually calmed Jane and left her

sleeping. They drove the short journey into the centre of the town in silence. As soon as the door to their room was closed behind them they were in each other's arms.

'I was so afraid,' she said at last. 'Afraid that you would hate me because of your father. I was scared your mother would convince you that I went with him willingly.'

He frowned. 'She tried. I didn't believe her. But it still cuts me to the quick, Martha, that you lied to me.' He dropped his embrace.

'What else could I do? I was ashamed of what he'd done to me. And when I got to know you, I was terrified you wouldn't want to have anything to do with me if you knew your father had…' She began to cry. 'I never meant to fall in love with you, I tried to stop seeing you but I couldn't.'

He felt as though his heart was breaking. 'I'm so sorry, Martha. My father was a monster. And as for my mother – what did she say to you?'

'She told me you didn't want to have anything more to do with me once you knew I'd lied about your father and the baby. But I didn't lie about Jane. They never even let me see her. When they told me she'd died I tried to put the whole terrible experience out of my head. And as I had no baby to show for it, I must have convinced myself it had never happened. How was I supposed to tell you?'

'Why did you take her money?' Kit began pacing up and down in front of the window.

'I had no choice. I needed some money to travel here to find Jane and to support myself until I found work. And Mrs Shipley gave me a letter she said you'd written, telling me to get out. That you wanted nothing more to do with me.'

'Martha, I swear to you I never wrote you such a letter. Yes, I was shocked that you'd hidden the truth from me, but I knew there was no possibility you would have willingly let your own child be incarcerated here.'

'Never. No matter how she was conceived, Jane is my daughter.' She hesitated, looking into his eyes, seeking reassurance. 'You don't mind about her? That I had her? That she's the way she is?'

He held her against him. 'At first, I didn't know what to think. I didn't want to believe Jane was your child. But then she held my hand and I saw you in her. I saw her loneliness and her gentleness and I think I loved her then. I love her now, poor creature.'

Martha gave a big gasping sigh. 'No matter what, Kit, I will be happy for the rest of my days that we found each other. That we had a few brief hours of happiness. That we have loved each other.'

'Don't talk like that. You make it sound as if it's all past.'

'Then we won't talk at all. Take me to bed.'

With a cry he drew her towards him, lifted her into his arms and carried her to the bed.

KIT WAS WOKEN EARLY by the sunlight creeping under the curtains, which were too short for the window frames. Kit woke first, disorientated for a moment by the unfamiliar surroundings and the warmth of Martha's naked body next to him in the bed. He had never felt so happy. When he was with Martha, everything made sense. The war was a distant memory and he lived in the moment, relishing every second in her company.

He moved his body against hers and she stirred and woke. He smiled at her, ready to reprise the pleasures of the previous night, but Martha sat upright, reaching over to the chair by the bed to gather her discarded clothing together.

He told her she didn't need to get up yet, tried all the blandishments he could think of to lure her back into the warmth of his embrace. But she would have none of it, pushing him away.

She got out of bed. 'I need to get to St Crispin's and I want to talk to you first, but not in bed where you'll try to divert me from what I intend to say. It's too important.'

Reluctantly, Kit dragged himself upright and leaned against the pillows, looking at her warily, dreading what she might have to say.

She spoke as she was getting dressed. Kit watched her as she pulled on her clothes, longing to reach out and draw her back to bed.

'I'm going to stay here in Northington with Jane,' she said. 'I want you to go back to Newlands. Make your peace with your mother and follow your dreams – go back to doing the work you love. Go to Borneo. If life were perfect I would be going with you, but I always knew that was a dream too far. Better that you go than you don't.'

'I won't leave England without you, Martha. My mind's made up. I'll continue my studies here in Britain. I'll find a job – maybe with the Horticultural Society, or my old college, Kew Gardens… We could manage. We can live together.'

'You know that's not possible. Your mother is adamant you won't get any money. We couldn't afford to live. Certainly not to pay Jane's fees. She has to stay at St Crispin's – she could never manage outside. She'd be distressed. I can't let her suffer.'

'She won't if she's living with us. Not if we're there to love her and care for her.'

Martha shook her head. 'You're a dreamer, Kit. That's one of the reasons I love you so much. But right now I have to be practical. I have to think of my daughter's welfare above everything else. Jane lives in the moment. Her affection towards me is fleeting. The things that matter most to her are her surroundings. They anchor her. Much as it pains me to admit it, I have had to accept that I am only as important to her as any of the nurses over there. She can make no distinction.'

His heart contracted as he saw her eyes well with tears. 'Then marry me anyway. I'll live here too. We'll visit Jane every day.'

Martha turned her head away. 'You make it sound reasonable but it's not. I've told you, my daughter is now my priority. I've lost twenty years. Who knows how Jane might have been now, had I been with her since birth?'

'That's not your fault.'

'I know it isn't – but the result's the same. She was abandoned at birth, neglected, unloved, uncared for in the most important years of her life.' She wiped her eyes on her sleeve. 'Even if I'm with her every minute for the rest of our lives it can't ever make up for what we've both lost. I can't give her back her childhood, wipe away the pain and loneliness.' She made a little sobbing noise. 'But I'll try my best to do what I can. That means me living at St Crispin's. It means being with her as much as possible.'

Kit stared at her in disbelief. 'But you can't sacrifice your own life like that.'

'It's no sacrifice. It's what I want and what I must do. There's nothing you can do or say that will change that. It doesn't mean I've stopped loving you. I will never do that. But it does mean I have to put Jane first.' She turned to look out of the window. 'Dr Henderson said people with Jane's condition usually live very short lives. I've no idea how long I will have with her. But the chances of her living a long and contented life are greater if I'm here to show her the love and affection she's lacked until now.'

Kit opened his mouth to speak, but she lifted a hand to silence him.

'That's why, my dearest darling, this morning we must say goodbye for ever. I hope and pray you will understand.'

'Understand? Never! I won't accept it.'

'If you love me you will.' She stretched out a hand and laid it on his arm. 'I will only have the strength to go on, to do what I have to do, if I don't see you again. I need to forget you. To lock you away inside my heart. Otherwise it will be a constant torture of seeing you, wanting you and being forced to say goodbye to you, over and over again. I can't do that. I'm not strong enough. I can't do it, Kit, I just can't.'

'But that's unreasonable. Surely it's better that we agree to wait until we are free to marry. I'll wait for you. As long as I have to.'

'That would be like saying we would be waiting for Jane to die. How can you expect me to agree to that? No.'

Kit started to speak again, but she interrupted. 'There's a woman in the village whose son joined up with the rest of them at the beginning of the war. He was reported missing. For months she wrote to the War Office, desperate for information, but all they would say was that he was missing. Then after almost a year they told her he was presumed dead. But she had earlier received a letter from a friend of his saying he had witnessed her son being stretchered away to the hospital tents. So she wouldn't believe the army. She kept on writing. Must have written forty or fifty letters. She wrote to nurses in the field hospitals, to the Red Cross, to his regiment, to anyone who might be able to help her. All the time she kept on believing that he would come home to her.' Martha turned to look at him. 'Hope is a terrible burden. When someone is faced with death they can at least grieve, adapt to life without the loved one. But to live on in hope that one day...' She shook her head. 'No I couldn't bear that.'

'But I'm not dead. I'll be here, waiting for you.'

'I won't let you make that sacrifice. I won't let you throw away your life waiting in the hope that one day–'

'It wouldn't be a sacrifice. The only sacrifice would be to be without you.' He reached out to her, but she stepped away, out of his reach.

'Then do it for me,' she said. 'I can't do what I must do until you accept that this is the end. Please, my dearest love, please, do this for me. Let me walk out of this door and don't try to follow me. Don't come to St Crispin's again.'

She turned to face him and he saw that she was weeping. He shuffled down the bed until he could reach her then he pulled her down to sit beside him on the edge of the bed.

Martha looked at him and Kit could see the love in her eyes. His heart was thumping and he tried desperately to find words that would change her mind, but none would come.

She kissed him tenderly, then got up, took her coat from the hook on the back of the door and without looking back, left the room.

CHAPTER 16

*C*hristopher drove back to Newlands in a state of grief and despair. Deep inside, he knew Martha would not budge in her determination to end their relationship, but try as he might, he couldn't understand why. There had to be a way for them to be together. But after tossing ideas around in his head on the long drive home, he had to acknowledge that he could find no alternative to move her away from the course she had set.

He glanced at the clock in the hall as he entered the house. He had forty minutes to get ready before his mother would be taking her customary pre-dinner drink in the drawing room. He'd hardly seen her these past weeks, while he'd been pursuing his search for Martha. He could put off the moment no longer.

When he entered the drawing room, she was standing in front of the glowing fire, where one of her spaniels was sleeping, while the other was chewing at the edge of the rug. Edwina was wearing a black gown with an over-blouse, studded in tiny glass beads that shimmered in the firelight. His mother was still a beautiful woman.

In an effort to be conciliatory, Christopher accepted the drink she pressed into his hands and was met with a beaming smile.

'It's so lovely to see you home again, darling. I've barely seen you in weeks – you've been away more than you've been home.'

'You know why, Mother.'

'No, I don't but I imagine it has something to do with that woman?'

'The woman I am in love with and would dearly love to marry. The woman you threw out of house and home and so casually told about the most traumatic experience of her life. Do you have any idea how much damage you could have caused?'

'I've no idea what you're talking about.'

'I'm talking about you bluntly telling her she has a daughter, fathered by my father.'

'Don't be silly. That can't have been news to her. She was there, after all. Committing adultery with one's employer and giving birth to his child is not something one forgets about.'

Christopher turned away and went to sit down in one of the big leather chairs that stood either side of the fireplace. 'You have no idea, do you? Martha was so traumatised by what happened to her that she buried the memory. She had no idea her child was alive. They told her her daughter was born dead. And she'd been through so much pain. My father brutally raped her. She was forced to marry a man she despised, a man who beat her. Then she almost died in a long and painful labour. And she was a *child*! No wonder she wiped it from her memory.'

His mother burst out laughing. 'Christopher, oh, Christopher. You are so gullible. Speaking as someone who went through childbirth twice, I can assure you that's not something you can ever forget!'

He felt an animosity towards her, akin to hatred.

Before he could respond, she spoke again, 'I mean, really, darling. It's preposterous. No one could possibly forget giving birth.'

'Then you've never seen a badly shell-shocked patient. Not only can they forget what they saw on the battlefield, some even forget how to speak, turning mute and deaf, paralysed even when there was nothing physically wrong with them. That's what happened to Martha. She couldn't cope with what happened to her as a fourteen-year-old, so her brain wiped it away and she never knew it had happened. Then you came along and told her all that.'

'Well, if that's the case, somebody had to. Where is she now? I suppose you are going to tell me?'

'She's with Jane, my half-sister.'

'Please, Christopher, don't call her that. That simpleton has nothing to do with us now. Your father discharged any obligations by paying her upkeep all this time. I think it's time we drew a veil over it all.' She moved away from the fire and sat down in the chair opposite him. 'In fact, I am going to give instructions to the bank to stop the standing order. The wretched creature is now Mrs Walters' responsibility. After twenty years, I feel this family's duty is discharged.'

Before Christopher could reply, the door opened and Bannister entered to tell them dinner was served. Edwina rose and said, 'Let tonight be the last time either of them is mentioned in this house.'

'You can't stop the payments. Jane depends on them.'

Mrs Shipley turned and hissed at him to shush, while they were within earshot of the servants. Only after they were seated in the dining room and served with the cold poached salmon, did she answer him. 'I have made it clear to you, that while you are living under this roof, under the age of thirty and unmarried, you will do exactly as I say. And I say that I've had enough with us supporting that person, that... lunatic. Once you attain thirty – or sooner if you marry Lavinia Bourne and provide me with a grandson, things will be different.'

'I'm not thirty for four years. How will Jane's fees be paid until then?'

'I've no idea. It's up to Mrs Walters to worry about that. It's no concern of mine.'

Christopher flung down his knife and fork and pushed his plate away. 'You can't do that. How can you be so cruel?'

Mrs Shipley shook her head and looked at him pityingly. 'Once you marry Lavinia and she is safely delivered of a child – a male child – you can do whatever darned thing you like. Like father, like son, I suppose. I will have to live with that, just as I did with your father. But until then, the only way I will continue to pay those maintenance fees is if you announce your nuptials with Lavinia. If at any time there is the slightest indication the wedding will not happen, believe me, your allowance and the payments for the girl's upkeep will cease immediately. It's your choice. I'm sorry, Christopher, but I've lost patience with you. You have left me no alternative.' She rang the bell to summon the servants to clear away their plates and serve the main course.

When they were alone again, Christopher said, 'Why do you hate me so much?'

She jerked her head up. 'Hate you? How can I possibly hate you? I adore you, Christopher. I know your father always seemed to favour Percy, but you were always my darling little boy.'

He snorted in disbelief.

'It's true. And I'm only doing what I know is the right thing for you. You're young. You're headstrong. You've been through so much, heaven knows. And thank God you came through the war. Now you need to think of the future. One day you will thank me. You may not think so now, but believe me, you will.'

'How can I possibly thank you for forcing me to marry a woman I can't bear?'

'Don't be dramatic. Lavinia may not be the brightest star in the constellations but she's a beautiful girl. Anyone in his right mind would find her attractive. Look at her! She's gorgeous. I could understand if I was asking you to marry an old trout.' She stopped and he knew that she was thinking that was exactly what Martha was. 'I mean a plain girl, or a fat girl or... well, you know what I mean. And if you don't snap her up quickly, someone else will. A stunning woman like her won't be left on the shelf.'

'Not even when her father has squandered his inheritance and is marrying her off for a new roof?'

'What?' She glared at him. 'That's preposterous.'

'He told me as much himself.'

'Well, whatever his reasons, we should be thankful. Lavinia's the kind of woman who will do her duty and be the soul of discretion. She's a well brought-up gal. She knows the drill. As long as she's kept in frocks and fripperies she'll leave you to do what you want. Once she's given you a son, if you still have a hankering for the Walters woman, then there's no reason why you shouldn't put her up in a house somewhere and visit her occasionally.'

'Martha would never consent to be treated like that.'

'Like what?'

'A kept woman.'

Mrs Shipley raised her eyebrows. 'I'm not even going to

bother to contradict that. But I of all people should know what she would consent to do.'

'But that's it. She never consented. And you are suggesting that I should use her the way my father used her.' He scraped back his chair. 'I'm turning in.' He flung his napkin on the table and left the room.

CHAPTER 17

artha was sitting with her daughter on Jane's favourite bench under the oak tree in the asylum grounds, when Dr Henderson approached and asked if he might join them.

Martha nodded, and he settled himself at the other end of the bench and lit a cigarette.

'You're very fond of Jane, Mrs Walters.'

Martha frowned at him, then said, 'She is my daughter. You know that already.'

'But why did you never visit her before?'

Uncomfortable at the line of questioning, she said, 'They told me she was dead. I had a hard labour and was sick for some time afterwards. They said she was born dead. They said that's why the labour was so long.'

'They?'

'The doctor. The midwife. My husband.'

'You must have been very young. I'd have thought you and Jane sisters, not mother and daughter.'

'I had just turned fifteen when she was born.'

'I see.' He puffed at his cigarette, frowning. 'Too young.' After a few minutes he added, 'The age of consent is sixteen.'

'But not the age of marriage. My father forced me to marry my husband. Consent doesn't apply if it's your husband.'

'And Captain Shipley? What is his connection?'

She felt herself reddening. 'My late husband was the gamekeeper on the Shipley family's estate.'

'And was it Captain Shipley who discovered that your daughter was alive?'

Martha blushed again. 'It was Mrs Shipley.'

'Ah, he's married then? I didn't realise that.'

'No.' Her denial came out faster than she intended. 'Mrs Shipley is his mother.' She paused, reaching for Jane's hand. 'But if you don't mind, Doctor, I'd really rather not talk about what happened. I'm grateful to have been reunited with my daughter.'

The man nodded. 'As is she. Of that I've no doubt.'

'You think so?'

'I know so. Jane has improved to a remarkable degree since you began to spend time with her.' He seemed about to say something else, but must have thought better of it.

Sensing his concern, Martha said, 'I'll not be parted from her again. You can count on that. Not ever.'

'I understand from Matron you are working here as a cleaner? Working during the night?'

Martha nodded.

'You must be exhausted. Spending the days with Jane and then working all night.'

'There's time to sleep when she has her nap in the afternoons. And it's not all night. I only work from midnight 'til six – so I try to sleep as soon as Jane goes off at night. I mostly get in a couple of hours and then one or two more in the morning.'

Dr Henderson shook his head and stared towards the building. Martha felt uncomfortable, wondering what he wanted and why he had chosen to sit with them.

After several minutes of silence, he spoke again. 'What do you think of St Crispin's, Mrs Walters?'

Taken aback, she replied, 'It's not such a bad place.'

'Better than most of its kind. Mainly because such a high proportion of the patients are privately funded. At this end of the wing anyway. It's overcrowded on the public wards.'

'I know. I'd hate for Jane to be in them.'

He drew on his cigarette. 'The superintendent here is more enlightened than most. He's the only reason I agreed to stay on after the war ended. He is a progressive. Open to new ideas. New ways of doing things. Thanks to him we now have clinical examination rooms for all the wards. Before, the doctors had to examine patients out on the wards in view of everyone – including new admissions. Not very discreet or respectful. Most men in his position would have taken the view that privacy was not something worth affording to the mentally ill.'

'That's good, sir.' She wondered why he was telling her all this.

'Have you ever thought of becoming a nurse, Mrs Walters?'

'A nurse? Me, sir?'

'St Crispin's would benefit greatly from having someone like you as an auxiliary.'

'Auxiliary? I don't know what that is.'

'Someone who has not been formally trained. Someone who assists the other nurses. I don't imagine you would wish to leave Jane in order to attend a nursing school?'

'No, sir.'

'But you could become an auxiliary without having to go to nursing school. It's an exciting time to be involved in the care of the mentally ill.' He leaned forward, hands on his knees. 'The war has given us the chance to learn about many aspects of madness. It convinced me that severe trauma can be a trigger for mental illness. Even grief.'

Martha listened, uncertain how to respond.

'The United States is much ahead of us in many aspects of treating lunacy. New drugs. New treatments. ' He lit another cigarette.

Martha turned to Jane, anxious that her daughter might be feeling excluded, but Jane was smiling and as her mother acknowledged the smile, the young woman rested her head against Martha's shoulder.

'I'm thinking of giving talks in the afternoons to some of the nurses. You could participate.'

'Me? But I know nothing of medical matters.'

'That's the point. It's a chance to learn. Even trained nurses know little about mental illness. It's why I'm instituting the classes.'

He turned sideways on the bench so he was looking straight at her.

'I believe our attitudes towards the mentally ill need to change. The men who gave the money to build places like this one did so in the belief that it would be a means to helping these unfortunates get better. Instead, we have used them as places to hide people away, out of sight and out of mind. Our mental asylums are often more like prisons than hospitals.' He was excited now, moved by his passion for his work.

He paused, smiled at her. 'Will you think about it, Mrs Walters?'

'About what? I'm not sure I really understand.'

'About becoming an auxiliary nurse. You would wear a uniform. You'll need to come to the training lectures. And you would take instructions from the ward sister and the official nursing staff. But if you learn quickly – who knows? You may eventually become a trained nurse.'

'But, Jane? I want to be near her.'

'We'll assign you to this ward. You will be within sight of her all the time. In fact you'll be able to do more for her. Be more directly involved in her care. And in the care of others on the ward. Have a think about it. That's all I ask.' He got up from the bench, gave her a nod and moved away across the lawns, back to Sycamore Ward.

OVER THE FOLLOWING WEEKS, Dr Henderson was relentless in his encouragement of Martha to become a nursing auxiliary.

'I see in you the qualities I'm looking for in the mental nurses of the future. Kindness and compassion. Patience. Diligence. Attention to detail. Some of the nurses are too set in their ways to change. People like you and me will eventually swing the ship around and set a new course. One day it will be accepted that doctors study the causes and cures for insanity, as now they do for medical conditions. We need to get past the stigma of lunacy. Please, Mrs Walters. Will you help me? Will you at least give it a try?'

'You promise I can still spend time with Jane?' Her tone was hesitant.

'Of course. Eventually I am hoping we will build a nurses' home for all our nursing staff to have accommodation on the premises. Meanwhile I see no reason to stop the arrangements you already made with Matron for the care of your daughter. I understand your own lodgings are close to the gates?'

She nodded.

It was agreed that she would become an auxiliary. Martha was grateful – cleaning the day rooms, refectory and kitchens every night had been hard work, no easier for being done during the night hours. Being able to work near to Jane was all she asked for, but she soon found that the care of these patients was rewarding in a broader sense.

Each patient was different. Sycamore Ward housed a wide range of patients of different ages, conditions and behaviours. None were considered dangerous, but the causes for their incarceration ranged from depression and disturbances brought on by grief at the loss of a husband or a child, to women sent here long ago, and since forgotten, as a result of what was described as 'immoral behaviour'. There was a small cadre of elderly ladies with senile dementia, who slept most of the time.

Most of the cases on Sycamore had become institutionalised over the years and were in a state of passivity, worn down, broken, bereft of the capacity to look after themselves. Martha saw how easily she herself might have ended up in a place like St Crispin's. Perhaps it was better that her father had settled on marrying her off to Walters after she'd been raped by George Shipley, if the alternative would have been permanent incarceration. Anything to protect Shipley from prosecution for violating a minor.

Martha found the twice-weekly afternoon lectures from Dr Henderson enlightening. They included explanations for the various classifications of mental illness, illustrated by examples as well as detailed explanations of the anatomy of the brain and the nervous system. As the weeks passed, Martha became increasingly fascinated by what she was learning. She was grateful for the doctor's kindness in offering her this opportunity. Nothing could assuage her pain over separation from Kit, but at least this work filled her days and offered her some consolation, as did the camaraderie and support of the other nurses and the presence of her daughter in her life.

MARTHA HAD BEEN SO ABSORBED in her care of Jane, her growing interest in her nursing duties and her grief over the absence of Kit, that she failed to register the cessation of her monthly periods. But her thickening waistline and constant fatigue eventually caused her to register what was happening within her body.

With mounting panic, she had to acknowledge that she was with child. This was a calamity. She would be dismissed from her work as an auxiliary nurse, even prevented from working as a cleaner.

One evening, at the end of her shift, after holding Jane's hand as her daughter went to sleep, she remained at her bedside, trying to run through the alternatives open to her. What alternatives? She had to admit there were none. The most likely outcome, once her condition became known, was dismissal, forcing her to seek shelter in the workhouse. Where else would open their doors to a widowed woman, who had presumably committed adultery with the father of her unborn child?

For a moment she thought of seeking Kit's help. But how could she? Mrs Shipley had threatened to stop Jane's maintenance if she made any contact with her son. Jane would be moved to the public wards, amid the noise, dirt and over-crowding. She'd never survive the shock and upheaval. Martha couldn't let that happen.

Could she appeal to Mrs Shipley for help? But as soon as the thought formed in her head, she knew it was impossible.

Watching the innocent and calm expression on Jane's face was too much for Martha. Once the tears formed they wouldn't stop. She sat there beside her sleeping daughter's bed, eyes swimming, vision blurred, oblivious to Dr Henderson, who had appeared at the other side of the bed.

'Nurse Walters? Will you come to my office please?'

Heart thumping in fear, she followed him across the

ward. He must have noticed her condition. He was going to dismiss her. It was happening already. What was she to do? She put her hands over her swelling belly.

Martha followed Dr Henderson into the room and was about to stand in front of his desk, but to her surprise he waved her towards a seat. He came around the front of his desk and perched on the edge, watching her intently.

She squirmed, waiting for him to deliver the blow, to tell her that she must pack her bags and go immediately, that she had let him down after the trust he had placed in her.

But he looked at her with kindness and compassion. Reaching into his jacket pocket he brought out a box of matches, took a cigarette from the wooden box on the desk, lit it and smiled.

'You're expecting a baby, aren't you?'

She jumped in fright. He did know. Terrified at what lay in prospect, her mouth was unable to form words, so she nodded, mutely.

'Is it Captain Shipley's?'

Martha gasped. 'What do you mean?'

'I mean what I say. I'm asking if Captain Shipley is responsible for your condition. I know your husband was killed in the war. I was puzzled by Captain Shipley's interest in your daughter. And then on the last occasion he visited here, I chanced to see you driving with him in his car towards the town. Then, when I suspected you were with child, I put two and two together. Was I wrong to do so?'

Martha sobbed. 'Oh please, Dr Henderson. Please let me stay a little longer. I don't know what I shall do. I need a little time.'

'I suppose marrying Captain Shipley is out of the question?'

She nodded.

The doctor frowned and Martha guessed he was

assuming Kit had slept with her then abandoned her.

'It's not his choice. He wants to marry me. He wants nothing more. It's his mother. She's threatened to cut him off without a penny and cut off Jane's maintenance here. I couldn't let that happen, sir.'

'I see.' He stubbed his cigarette into the ashtray. He raised his eyes to meet hers. 'Then you had better marry me.'

Martha was stunned. He had to be making a joke. She bristled that he was trivialising her plight.

Dr Henderson got up from the desk and went to stand by the window.

'I can't replace what Captain Shipley meant to you. But perhaps I can understand what you are feeling. I lost my wife to the influenza during the war. My world fell apart. I lost all desire to go on. So I threw myself into my work. It has given me great consolation, but never removed the sadness. The loneliness.'

He stared out at the darkening garden. 'When I met you, I recognised a kindred spirit. Someone who has also known sadness. Someone who might assist me in my life's work.'

Turning to look at her, he said, 'I think we would make a good team. You would, of course, need to stop nursing once we were married, but you could continue to care for Jane. And the baby when it comes.'

Martha sat, rigid in her chair, unable to believe what she was hearing, her hands clasped in her lap.

'You've said nothing.'

'I don't know what to say. Why? Why would you want to marry me? I'm a nobody. I've no money. I'm carrying another man's child.'

He smiled at her and came around to sit on the edge of the desk again. He leaned forward and took her hands in his. 'I know you don't love me, Mrs Walters. How could you? We barely know each other. But maybe with time?'

'But you? You're a doctor. A man of importance. You could marry anyone.'

He laughed. It was a dry laugh, a bitter laugh. 'Who would want to marry me? A man past forty with one eye missing.'

She said nothing for a moment then said, 'But if you marry me, people will think it's your child. They'll think you... That won't be good for you.'

He smiled. 'There's something else you need to know. I can never be a proper husband to you. The war... I was injured... All the moving parts are there...' He gave a little chuckle, devoid of any humour. 'They just don't function any more. That's why I can't expect a woman to agree to marry me. You are my only hope, Mrs Walters.' He laughed. 'We are each other's only hope. I don't care if people think I am the father of your child. I want to be a father to him or her.'

'I don't know what to say.'

'Then say yes.'

'But why? Why do you even want a wife?'

He got up from the desk and walked towards the window. 'It sounds cynical, but people have greater trust in a man who is married.' He gave a deep sigh. 'No. It's more than that. I'm lonely. I want to come home at the end of the day and have someone waiting for me. Someone to talk to. Eat a meal with. Yes, and cook for me, care for me. Someone I can care for too. I think you are that person, Mrs Walters. Please, marry me.'

He bent his head over her hand and kissed it lightly. 'I realise that I will never be able to be everything to you that a husband should be, but I hope that with time, you might come to feel some affection and fondness for me as I already do for you.'

Her eyes were wet with tears. 'Thank you,' she said, her voice barely more than a whisper. 'Yes, I will marry you, Doctor.'

CHAPTER 18

The pain of being apart from Martha cut deep. Working in the sunken garden held no pleasure for Christopher when she wasn't there beside him. At night, he rolled around his bed, dreaming that she was there with him, only to wake with a start to find she was not. He closed his eyes and saw her sad eyes and her smile – a smile that transformed her face from impassivity and inscrutability into a joyful animation that made her beautiful. He saw her slender ankles, long legs, strong lean body, which responded to the slightest touch from him. Lying alone in bed, he longed to nestle against her, cup his hands around her breasts, breathe in the scent of her, lose himself with her.

Day after day, he rode over to the gamekeeper's cottage in the woods, hoping that she might have returned, but knowing that it was an impossible hope.

He sat on the doorstep, leaning against the door, remembering how he had come upon her there, shelling peas. He wandered around the outbuildings: the empty kennels, the deserted sitting house, scene of her rape by his own father. He forced himself to do this, trying to take her pain upon himself, hoping that somehow she would know he was here, keeping a lonely vigil for her.

Hooker cropped the grass, patient, as his master prowled around the house. Occasionally Kit went inside, lay down on his back on the bed, staring at the ceiling, where already a damp patch had formed. Replacing missing roof tiles was yet another task on the long list of neglected duties. He didn't want to do it. Why do something to make the place more habitable and appealing to a prospective tenant when the only tenant he wanted would never return? Better to let the place decay, a monument to the futility of their love.

After several months apart from Martha – months of mounting pressure from his increasingly impatient mother to marry Lavinia – Christopher decided he could stand it no longer. He had mooned around the estate and Martha's cottage for long enough. It was time he pulled himself together. He wasn't going to listen to his mother's threats to cut off Jane's payments and cut his own allowance. Money would not be used as weapon against him. He cared too little for it. Instead, he could seek legal help – the threat of a legal action and the associated scandal would be guaranteed to make Edwina Shipley back off. Why had this not occurred to him before?

But first he would go to St Crispin's and talk again with Martha, tell her his plan. Together they would find a way around the problem, so that they could marry and care for Jane.

It was a warm September day when he drove up the long driveway, lined with lime trees, that led to St Crispin's. The sky was a cloudless, brilliant blue and the trees had not yet started to lose their foliage. On a day like this nothing could be amiss. He was a fool to have waited so long, to have allowed Martha's caution to hold him back, to have let his mother's iron will subjugate his own. Not any more. From now on he would be his own man. Making his own decisions. Living his own life. Dreaming his own dreams.

He parked the Bentley and went inside the building.

Without stopping in the administrative section to announce his presence, he made his way towards Sycamore Ward. As he limped along the endless corridor, his uneven gait sounded on the wooden floor and echoed between the brown-tiled walls and the high ceiling.

He was halfway there when he saw Dr Henderson coming towards him, unmistakeable in his tweed sports jacket and military tie, black patch concealing the missing eye.

The doctor extended his hand to shake Christopher's. 'Glad to see you, Captain Shipley.' He put his other hand on Christopher's shoulder and steered him towards the doorway to his office. 'In fact, your arrival is most timely.'

Inside the office, Dr Henderson lit his customary cigarette and waved a hand to indicate that Christopher should sit down, before taking up his position behind the desk.

'You have come for a progress report on Miss Walters? I am delighted to inform you that she is doing very well indeed. She has learnt several nursery rhymes and loves to sing. In fact singing appears to unlock something inside her. It helps her remember words and make them flow. Her mother has spent a great deal of time teaching her, and Jane is responding well.'

'Her mother?'

Dr Henderson smiled. 'I know about Jane's parentage. Mar... Mrs Walters told me she is Jane's mother, and about the circumstances of her birth.'

Christopher suddenly felt uneasy.

'On behalf of Jane's mother, I would like to thank you and the Shipley family for so long supporting Jane's upkeep. But now Jane's mother and I have reached the conclusion that further visits from you would be counter-productive.'

'Counter-productive?' Christopher felt the blood draining from his face and a shot of fear ran through him.

'Confusing for Jane and upsetting for Mrs Henderson.'

The nerves in Christopher's leg seared through his body like an electric shock and his heart contracted inside his chest. He heard himself say, 'Mrs Henderson?'

Dr Henderson smiled broadly. 'I'm delighted to tell you that the former Mrs Martha Walters did me the honour of becoming my wife two weeks ago.'

The room lost focus. He struggled to breathe, gulped, trying to draw air into his lungs. Had he misheard? Was the doctor playing some kind of elaborate joke?

Christopher's eyes moved round the room, desperately hoping for some sign that this wasn't real. That he was dreaming. On the wall, a pair of framed certificates hung. Beside them a framed display case containing Dr Henderson's war medals. An ophthalmic chart, the letters on which swam in front of Christopher's eyes. Sunshine spilled into the office from the large window. Beyond he could see the extensive lawns, hear the sound of laughter, the clamour of rooks in the trees that bordered the lawn.

'You and Martha have married?' His words sounded displaced, disembodied, coming from somewhere else in the room.

'It was a small affair. Just ourselves and a witness. After-wards, we had a little tea party on the lawn. Mainly for Jane. Not that she understands. But these days she is mostly happy. Having her mother with her has been the best tonic for the poor creature.'

'Married.' Christopher repeated the word, as if uttering it might give the lie to it.

'My wife had been assisting me for some time, working as

an auxiliary on the ward. The close proximity which this necessitated caused me to depend on her, to grow an attachment. Fortunately, she felt the same.' He leaned back in the chair, exhaling the last of his cigarette before stubbing it out in the ashtray.

Christopher shuddered at the easy way Dr Henderson referred to Martha as his wife. He felt a sudden rush of loathing for the man.

'She keeps nagging me to give these things up.' Henderson laughed. 'That's women for you. They like to keep a fellow in his place.'

Nauseous, Christopher was desperate to get out of the smoky office, out of the building with its inescapable odour of disinfectant.

He got to his feet. 'Congratulations, Doctor. I... I... trust you and Mrs Henderson will be happy.' Then he turned and left the office.

He got in the Bentley and drove down the drive, his hands gripping the steering wheel tightly and his head pounding, barely seeing the road in front of him. As soon as the car was out of sight of the asylum, he pulled over to the side of the road, opened the door, got out and vomited onto the grass verge. Sweat stuck his hair to his forehead and his chest was heaving. A sour bilious taste filled his mouth and his throat burned with acid. He wanted to close his eyes and never wake up again.

Christopher barely registered the journey home to Newlands, driving like a machine, unconscious of the scenery, of the passing traffic and of any sense of time. He drove up the drive to the stable yard, got out of the Bentley, shouted to one of the grooms to saddle up Hooker, and walked back to the house, where he changed into his riding gear.

Back in the stable he breathed in the smell of clean straw,

the richness of fresh manure and the scent of leather. Hooker whinnied in welcome and turned to nuzzle his shoulder, eager to be going out after a day waiting inside in his stall.

Without hesitating, Christopher turned the horse in the direction of the woods. The only place he wanted to be now was the place where he had been with Martha.

Why had she married the doctor? Was the love Christopher thought he had shared with her completely one-sided? It was incomprehensible. When he had said goodbye to her she had told him she loved him. Why then marry another man and so rapidly? He asked himself why Henderson had asked her to be his wife after such a short acquaintance. Then he remembered he himself had fallen in love with her after only a few hours in her company.

He paced through the rooms of the house, running his hands over objects that she would have touched. Nothing made sense any more.

THAT EVENING he joined his mother in the library before dinner.

'You took the motor car today,' she said, her tone brusque. 'Where did you go?'

'You know perfectly well where I went. You seem to know everything that happens around here.' He knew he was being unfairly rude.

Edwina Shipley raised her eyebrows. 'Thank you for endowing me with supernatural powers, Christopher, but I can assure you I am not a fortune teller. My enquiry was simply out of curiosity and a concern for your welfare. You've been looking pale lately. Thin too. Maybe you should get back out into that garden of yours again. Working there might help you rebuild your strength. And give you a sense of purpose.' She sipped her drink.

Christopher gave a bitter laugh. 'Since when have you given a damn for my welfare? You have done everything possible to make my life miserable.'

Mrs Shipley groaned. 'Not that blessed Walters woman again. I thought you'd be over that infatuation by now.'

'Infatuation?' Christopher narrowed his eyes.

'Come on, darling. It can't possibly have been anything else.'

'I've told you a thousand times. I love Martha. And–' He was about to add that she loved him too, but now he was no longer sure.

'So that's where you were today? Visiting her?'

He said nothing.

'It has to stop, Christopher. I've made it clear. I will cut off the payments for her daughter if you don't stop seeing her.'

'You needn't worry on that account. I won't ever be seeing her again.' He ran his hands through his hair and exhaled loudly.

His mother's expression was curious.

Christopher glared at her. 'You've got what you want. I won't be seeing her again, as she's married someone else.' He flung himself into one of the fireside chairs, his head in his hands.

Mrs Shipley moved over to stand beside him, her hand stroking his hair. 'I hate to say I told you so, but I think that proves definitively that what I said about her was correct. A fortune-hunter. She played you for a fool. But don't worry, my love, you'll get over her. Especially now that you know what she's really like.'

The fight had gone out of him. He didn't even bother to argue with her. What was point?

It didn't take long for Christopher to realise that he might as well accede to his mother's wishes and marry Lady Lavinia Bourne. After all, his life no longer felt worth living. If doing this would make his mother happy, then so be it. He no longer cared what happened to himself.

The thought of Martha being married to Reggie Henderson was more than he could bear to think about. Not that he had anything against Henderson – he'd actually liked the man when he first met him. And how could he blame him for falling for Martha?

But Martha herself? How could she have done that to him? And so soon. It seemed out of character. She'd told him that if they couldn't be together she would rather be alone. She had promised she loved him. Hadn't she? Had that been a lie? Why marry Henderson? Surely, she couldn't love him? And there was no need to marry. Jane's upkeep was being paid. And he would go on paying it, despite this. Of that he was determined. Jane's birth and condition were a consequence of his father's actions – Christopher would not walk away from those responsibilities.

But now his thoughts and dreams were haunted by images of Martha in Reggie Henderson's arms. Reggie's hands on her body. Reggie looking into the dark pools of her eyes as they made love. Why? Why?

The meeting with Lord Bourne at his London club was not something Christopher wanted to repeat. His future father-in-law played for every possible advantage, dressing Christopher down, as if he were a naughty schoolboy caught scrumping apples. But ultimately the man's options were as limited as Christopher's were, with a shortage of eligible men and Lavinia's advancing age – she was already twenty-seven; he needed to grasp the opportunity to marry off his only living child, prop up his ailing fortunes and repair his dilapidated property.

'You have my permission to propose to the gal but, I warn you, she may well turn you down. You've not behaved like a gentleman. Buggering off, God knows where, when we were your mother's guests, leaving the poor gal on her own all weekend. Not showing up for Ascot, forcing your mother to cancel the visit to us at Harton Hall. Disgraceful.'

'I'm frightfully sorry, sir. Unless it had been a matter of some urgency, I would not have absented myself.' He was full of self-loathing as he spoke the words.

Lord Bourne muttered something to the effect that there could be nothing Christopher might need to do that was more pressing than attending upon his daughter. Christopher let the diatribe flow over him without further comment.

'So, I may speak with Lady Lavinia?'

'Yes,' he snapped. 'She and Lady Bourne are at my sister-in-law's in Eaton Square. You may turn up this afternoon and offer to take her to dinner or the theatre or something tonight. Up to you. I know they're planning to stay at home as I have a late sitting at the House. If she agrees to go, you can make your offer tonight. Don't waste any more time, Shipley. I won't have my daughter trifled with. Clear?'

Christopher assented.

He called on mother, aunt and daughter and endured a prolonged afternoon tea, in which Lady Bourne and her sister sustained the conversation, while Christopher chipped in when required – which was not often – and Lavinia maintained a nun-like silence unless addressed directly.

She did look uncommonly pretty, wearing a navy blue frock that stopped a good six inches short of her ankles, a loose tie belt above a dropped waist and pleated skirt. The biggest surprise though, was that she had had her blonde hair bobbed, the source of much disapproval from the older women. Christopher decided that gallantry was called for and told her that the new hairstyle was most becoming. He was rewarded with a radiant smile.

When he returned that evening to collect Lavinia, she appeared even more stunning. They were to go to the theatre – Christopher had managed to procure tickets for a light opera set in eighteenth century Bath. Lavinia wore a black silk gown, trimmed around the hem with ostrich feathers. As they took their seats in the stalls, Christopher saw heads turn to look at her.

The musical play was a complicated comedy adventure, involving the heir to the French throne masquerading as a humble barber.

Christopher was bored, irritated by the trivial nature of the piece. How quickly had England got over the horrors of war, keen now to indulge in a past where life was all masked balls, card games and fighting duels in which only minor wounds were inflicted. No death, maiming, destruction, annihilation and misery. Fancy costumes, clichéd lyrics, and mock sword fights were the diet craved by the London theatre-goers – and lapped up by an entranced Lavinia.

'What a wonderful evening,' she said as they left the theatre. 'Usually I find the theatre frightfully dull. I was jolly glad there was singing. And it was so romantic. Such gorgeous frocks. I would have loved to have lived in those times. So colourful. So splendid.'

'I'm delighted you enjoyed it.'

She beamed at him. 'Oh yes. Well, apart from the fights. It would have been better if all those parts had been cut out. But the dancing and singing and the love story...' She clasped her hands in delight. 'Didn't you like it?'

He summoned a smile. 'Most entertaining.' But all the

while he was filled with dread about the late supper ahead of them and how it would shape the rest of his life.

Once they were seated in the Savoy Grill and had ordered their food, they remained silent for an uncomfortable period. Lavinia's post-theatre ebullience had drained away and she seemed nervous. Christopher wanted to wait until they were served before making his proposal, anxious that they should not be interrupted by the reappearance of the waiter. The room was buzzing. It seemed they were the only diners who were not talking – shouting even, such was the cacophony. He glanced about him, hoping to take inspiration from his surroundings for some of the light-hearted banter that came so easily to other people. But all he could think of was that he wanted to be miles away from here, in the small, barely furnished bedroom in the little house in the woods, lying in the arms of Martha.

The waiter arrived with their Dover soles and, after refilling Christopher's wine glass, stepped away. They ate in silence, Christopher washing the fish down with the Pouilly-Fumé, finishing the bottle, while Lavinia's glass remained untouched.

Knowing he could delay no longer, he caught her eye and said, 'Lady Lavinia, I was wondering if... if you might... consent to be...'

'For heaven's sake, Captain Shipley. I thought we were going to be here all night. Daddy told me you intended to propose and the answer is yes, I accept.' She stretched her lips into a smile. 'Do you have a ring for me?'

He fumbled in his pocket. 'Yes of course.' His stomach hollow, he took out a small velvet box with the Garrard insignia, flipped it open and handed it over the table to her.

'Really, Captain Shipley! Surely you can do better than that! Especially after watching that French man proposing marriage to Lady Mary in the play. Down on your knees, please.' She looked at him archly.

Christopher's face burned and his gaze swept around the crowded restaurant. 'I was thinking… perhaps when we are alone. In the cab? It's so public here.'

Her face creased into a frown, and she narrowed her eyes. For an instant he thought of Martha and how, when she smiled, she became beautiful, while Lavinia frowned and her beauty faded.

He coughed, embarrassed, then said, 'Kneeling is difficult for me… my leg…'

She glared at him and wagged her finger. 'It doesn't stop you getting on a horse though, does it?'

Mortified, Christopher lowered himself awkwardly and unsteadily, choosing the side of the table furthest away from most of the diners. He held out the ring in its box.

'Put it on my finger then.'

He complied, and was about to rise, when a large party of nearby diners who had observed the scene, got to their feet and began to applaud. The clapping rippled from table to table, around the whole restaurant. Lavinia stood and acknowledged the homage with a graceful wave, while Christopher stumbled back up, and after a brisk nod at the appreciative diners, sank gratefully back into his chair. Desperate to settle the bill and make a rapid exit, he looked about for their waiter.

The wine waiter approached, smiling broadly and bearing a bucket of champagne. 'Compliments of the gentleman over there.' He nodded towards an adjacent table, where a man raised his hand in a mock salute. Christopher waved his thanks to the stranger. He had no appetite for champagne. It might as well have been the bitterest bile. Lavinia, on the other hand, had perked up. He remembered, too late, that she only drank champagne, watching glumly as the wine waiter filled a flute for her.

Half an hour later they were in a cab, heading back to Eaton Square. Relieved and tired now that the matter was dealt with, Kit couldn't wait to be alone.

CHAPTER 19

*I*t was several weeks after Christopher's meeting with Dr Henderson, that Reggie finally told Martha that Christopher Shipley had visited St Crispin's and was aware of their marriage.

Martha was startled. 'You told him of my condition? He knows?'

Reggie shook his head. 'I couldn't do that to him. The poor man looked wretched.' He smiled at her sadly. 'As wretched as you look now, my darling.'

His lips stretched into a grim smile. 'But it's as well he knows we are married. Now we can put all that behind us.' He hesitated, searching her eyes. 'Can't we, Martha?' His face was still anxious. 'We must think about the future. *Our* future.'

'Yes,' she said. 'You are right. We will never speak of this again.'

He moved towards her and took her hands in his. Bending forward he planted a kiss on the top of her head. 'You are such a comfort to me, my dearest.' He placed one hand on her belly, his fingers splayed out. 'Oh, Martha. It *will*

182

be my child. I promise you I will love and care for it as if it were my own. From now on I will only think of him or her as my own. And I hope that over time you will come to think that too.' He pulled her towards him, holding her against his chest, her face pressed against the roughness of his tweed jacket, his hand cupping the back of her head.

Martha bit her lip. She had promised herself she would do her utmost not to think about what had passed. To be grateful for what was present. To try to show affection to this man who had rescued her. This kind man.

There was no point in thinking about what might have been. No point in wondering whether, if she had told Kit about the baby, it would have made a difference. All that was past history. Reggie Henderson had steered her into a safe haven. He would care for her and Jane, and for her unborn child. Their child. Reggie was right – that's how she must think of it – this life pulsing inside her. Not Kit's child, but Reggie's. She must concentrate on the future.

'I was thinking...' Reggie's words were tentative. 'Wondering if perhaps we might occasionally bring Jane across here to the house. Only for an hour or so at first. A little longer once she's used to being here. Then, maybe, after some time, she might feel comfortable enough, familiar with the place... that she could live here all the time with us. What do you think? After all, we're still in the grounds. She can see her oak tree from the drawing room window.'

Martha felt a surge of joy inside her. 'You really think so? That she might be able to live outside the ward?'

'If we are patient and don't rush things. One step at a time, helping her get accustomed to new surroundings. But it may take months.'

She stretched her arms around him. 'Thank you, Reggie.'

A FEW WEEKS LATER, when Dr Henderson indicated Jane was ready to spend a few hours with them in their house in the grounds, the young woman suddenly developed a high fever and a terrible wracking cough. The home visit was postponed and Jane was put to bed in the ward. Soon after, she began to shake and shiver. A physician was summoned to her bedside and pronounced that she was suffering from pneumonia.

Martha watched helplessly as Jane struggled to breathe. Rasping sounds from her throat, lungs full, damaged, straining. Eyes wild, panic mounting, sweat soaking the sheets. Cries like an injured animal, caught in a trap, unable to break free.

Refusing to eat, Martha wouldn't leave her vigil at her daughter's bedside, accepting only water from the ward nurses when they or Reggie insisted. Reggie often sat with her too, holding Martha's hand in his, offering silent comfort. He would have stayed all through the night if Martha hadn't insisted that he needed his sleep and owed it to his patients.

The physician who attended, explained how the illness was likely to progress, that the crisis was a turning point, when Jane would be at her worst, and would either turn a corner and gradually recover or... But Martha wouldn't allow herself to think about the alternative.

In the gloom of the ward, she kept her vigil, alone save for the sleeping patients and one other nurse. Reggie had gone back to their house to snatch a few hours' sleep before his morning rounds. Martha stared up at the large wall clock above the desk at the nurses' station. She had been watching its progress all night, measuring Jane's against it. She monitored her daughter's temperature every hour, the lines on her face deepening as each time her hopes were dashed. The thermometer appeared to be stuck at 104: a dangerously high fever. Hair was plastered to Jane's forehead and Martha smoothed it away then wiped a cool cloth over her brow, soaking up the perspiration, praying that her daughter would recover.

There had been another patient on the ward, a month ago, who had contracted pneumonia. She had suffered for five or six days, until her body went into a shock reaction, sweating copiously and shaking violently. The woman's temperature had plummeted in the space of an hour and she had fallen into a deep and undisturbed sleep. The following morning she had sat up in bed asking for some tea. Within two days, she had recovered enough to get out of bed.

Martha clutched Jane's hands, whispering softly to her, telling her daughter she was there, promising she wouldn't leave her. She had no idea whether Jane could hear her, let alone understand her. The young woman lay, bathed in sweat, struggling to breathe, making little chuntering noises like a small animal. She had vomited bile and blood earlier, but now at least that appeared to have stopped.

The physician had ordered four-hourly doses of sulphate of quinine, alternating with tincture of chloride of iron. Glancing again at the clock on the wall, Martha saw that the hand had moved on only five minutes. It was twenty minutes before she needed to administer the next dose. She needed to sterilise the needle and syringe before giving the injection. That meant going into the nurses' room and leaving her daughter while she did so. What if, in the minutes she was away, Jane were to deteriorate, or wake and find her absent? She went through the same argument over and over again in her head. She didn't want anyone else to nurse her daughter but she didn't want to leave her bedside. Eventually, as the hands advanced around the clock-face, she knew she could postpone no longer and, after kissing her daughter's brow, she made her way to the room where the medicines were kept and took up a glass syringe and laid it on the counter while waiting for a pan of water to boil.

Terrified of missing a crucial development in her daughter's condition, she returned to the bedside. She knew she was not meant to leave water to boil unattended, but there was no one about to see this breach in protocol. The ward was quiet – only the sound of snoring, the odd sleeping groan and the faint noises from Jane as she struggled to find a breath. The noisiest woman on Sycamore had been screaming and tearing her bed sheets earlier, but had been dispatched to one of the two padded cells off the ward, where no one would hear her screaming and where a strait-jacket and the padded furnishings would be proof against her propensity for destruction.

After to-ing and fro-ing between bed and medicine room, at last the ten-minute boiling of the syringe was complete and Martha titrated the medicine into the glass tube. She went back to her daughter's bedside, rolled up the sleeve of Jane's nightdress, noting that it was soaking wet. She gave the injection, then turned her attention to wiping away the copious sweat on her daughter's face and neck. The clock was showing the time as ten minutes after three. The darkest hours of the night. Didn't they say that that was when people were most likely to die? She pushed away the thought. Believe. She had to believe. Trust in God.

In the distance along the ward she could see the duty nurse, snoozing in a chair. A quiet night for her.

Martha wanted to change her daughter's sweat-soaked nightclothes, wash her body and dress her in fresh dry linens but knew she couldn't do this without waking her and that might cause more distress. If only she could take all the agony her daughter was suffering upon herself. At least she would be able to understand what her body was going through, might find the strength and resources to fight the disease. But poor Jane felt only pain and was at a complete loss as to why it had afflicted her.

It was at half past three that Martha realised the crisis was happening. Sweat continued to pour from her daughter, more than should be possible, but there was no drop in Jane's temperature. Her face was red and blotchy, her tongue lolling in her throat and when Martha took her temperature again the thermometer showed it had increased to 106.

'Nurse Barker, come quickly.' When the snoozing nurse didn't reply, Martha screamed, 'Nurse Barker!'

The nurse jumped and hurried down to the bedside.

'It's the crisis and she seems to be getting worse. Her temperature has risen two degrees in the past half hour and she's sweating badly,' said Martha, her own heart pounding in her chest as she felt the clutch of rising panic. 'What should we do?'

Nurse Barker was taking Jane's pulse. 'It's racing. We need to get the duty doctor.'

'Then go. Go! Go! Please, I beg you. I can't leave her.'

The nurse seemed affronted, as if about to point out that while Martha may be Dr Henderson's wife, she was only an auxiliary, but must have thought better of it. She walked briskly out of the ward.

'Hurry.' Martha spoke more to herself than to the departing nurse. 'Oh, please, God, hurry.'

But she knew there was no point. By now Jane's breathing was so laboured it was like that of a drowning woman. She *was* a drowning woman. Drowning slowly and painfully from lungs filled with poison.

Martha slid off the chair and knelt by the bedside, her daughter's hand clasped inside her own, as she begged her to stay with her.

She wasn't aware of the exact moment of Jane's death – the last little flutter of breath drawn into those ravaged lungs. Instead she felt a sudden cooling in her hands, a stiffness and a silence that was so complete it was palpable. She gave a gulping sob and tried to rub the life back into her daughter's hands. Cold. Lifeless. It had happened so quickly. From one moment to the next. Life there, flickering, fragile, and then gone. Snuffed out. Blown away like autumn leaves.

Jane's birdlike, bony hands were now cold and white, like alabaster hands on a tomb. Frozen forever, they would no longer pluck at her bedding or tug at her sleeves. Giving a cry of pain, Martha bent over and kissed her dead daughter's head, then collapsed forward, her own head resting against the thin cold body under the blankets.

She lifted her head again, looking about her, at the line of beds with their sleeping occupants, at the brown ceramic half-tiled wall, the glow of the lamp on the nurses' station. The tick of the wall clock as it continued to mark the passage of time. All the little mundane things that were unchanged on the ward. How could these trivial things be the same when Martha's world was changed so utterly, with Jane in it no longer?

Looking down at her daughter, Martha saw Jane's face was now calm, her eyes closed, the chill of death spreading through her thin body. Beside the bed, the empty syringe lay in the enamel bowl where she'd left it. She should take it away and sterilise the glass tube and needle for the next patient. A little cry escaped her. Why was the world continuing as usual when her daughter was gone? Surely there should be some kind of pause, some acknowledgment of the passage of a life. Some momentous sign that nothing could ever be the same again.

Martha didn't even notice what the duty doctor did when he arrived. Didn't listen to his whispered instructions to the nurse as he told her to prepare Jane's body for removal to the mortuary. It felt as though she had been swept up by a huge tidal wave that was carrying her out to sea. She didn't care whether she would see land again or be dashed against the rocks.

Insensible to the hands that gently pulled her to her feet and held her against his chest, she barely registered Reggie's arrival at the scene. It was only when she felt a strange sensation inside her, a fluttering like tiny bubbles rising to the surface of a pool, that she remembered that she was bringing a new life into the world. As the spirit of Jane had left the world, that of her unborn baby was demanding her attention.

She tilted her head to look at Reggie Henderson. 'I felt our baby move,' she said.

The following evening, still red-eyed and exhausted from her lack of sleep, Martha told Reggie they would have to inform Kit of his half-sister's death.

'He hasn't visited her in months. I don't see why we should,' said Henderson.

'She was his sister. He didn't visit because I asked him not to.'

'All the same. Is it really necessary?'

'He has to be told. He has a right to come to the funeral. Besides the Shipleys must be informed as they pay Jane's fees.' As she spoke her daughter's name she gave an involuntary sob.

Dr Henderson placed an arm around his wife's shoulders. 'Very well, my dear, I will take care of it.'

'And the funeral?'

He hesitated.

'He must be invited.'

Henderson directed his eyes at his wife's swollen belly and nodded. 'Very well. But I doubt he will come.'

'He will come,' she said.

In the event, Dr Henderson requested the hospital superintendent to write an official letter to Mrs Edwina Shipley to inform her that, due to the demise of Miss Jane Walters from bronchial pneumonia, the standing order for payment of residency fees could be cancelled. A cheque for the amount overpaid on the quarterly advance payment was enclosed along with the final closing statement.

WHEN SHE STOOD at the hole in the ground into which her daughter's coffin had been consigned, Martha was beyond tears. She had known Jane for such a brief time, but her daughter had brought so much joy to her. She had hoped they would have years to make up for all those they had lost. Aching with grief that now she would have no chance to build on the progress Jane had made, Martha knew she could never replace the beauty of the quiet mornings she had spent holding her daughter's hand and singing to her. Jane's death was a loss she was sure she would never get over.

As she flung her handful of soil onto the lid of the coffin she raised her eyes to look around the churchyard, hoping against hope that Kit Shipley would appear to pay his respects to his half-sister. It was a miserable November day, with squally showers that cut into the faces of the small group of mourners. The graveyard was uniformly grey, except for the splash of colour from the flowers waiting to be placed on top of Jane's grave.

Why hadn't he come?

CHAPTER 20

*C*hristopher never got to read the letter from the asylum about his half-sister's death. Edwina Shipley locked it away in a drawer in the small escritoire she used for her own correspondence in the morning room.

She knew Christopher would eventually notice that the payments to St Crispin's had ceased but given the backlog of estate paperwork he was dealing with, it would probably be some time before he found out. She was confident that by then he would be safely married and the witless offspring of the gamekeeper's wife would be long buried.

CHRISTMAS 1919 WAS a miserable affair for Christopher. Not that any Christmas since the start of the war had been pleasurable. When he had been in Borneo it had passed like any other day – it had been hard to imagine a traditional festivity when in steaming heat and with so much work to be done. Yet that Borneo Christmas had been one of the happiest he had known. When at the Front, Christopher joined up too late for the famous but unofficial Christmas truces of 1914 when both sides had spontaneously laid down their arms to sing carols and join in an impromptu football game in no man's land. After that, a conscious effort had been made in subsequent years by the commanding powers to keep the intensity of the battle up. And as the war had progressed with its attendant annihilation, neither side had felt sufficiently well-disposed to the other to want a temporary ceasefire.

Christopher's only Christmas at the Front, in 1917, was memorable for the death of one of his men, caught by shrapnel from a stray shell on the night of Christmas Eve. Bleeding to death, the young Private was carried by his comrades to the nearest medical station, where he died soon after midnight. No, Christmas was not a cause for celebration, rather a time to remember that poor lad and all the others Kit had seen killed or wounded during the terrible years of the war.

This year, in the light of his engagement to Lady Lavinia Bourne, the Bournes were to join the Shipleys at Newlands. For Mrs Shipley, the festive season was an excuse for excess – with no expense spared on decking Newlands with elaborate decorations and a table groaning with food and treats.

Christopher stood in the entrance hall where there was a welcoming log fire burning in the grate and an enormous Christmas tree standing guard at the foot of the sweeping marble staircase. Such a sham! A waste, when people were hungry and jobless, when the recent war had wreaked havoc in so many lives. But for Edwina, it was a way to draw a line under the past, to be optimistic about the future. And that future included Christopher's marriage the following May to Lady Lavinia Bourne.

It was difficult for Christopher to absent himself from the

festivities, although Lavinia's unashamed refusal to emerge from her bed until late in the morning gave him some respite, and he was able to ride Hooker out in the mornings. On the night of Christmas Eve, Christopher and his mother distributed gifts to the servants, in line with tradition. His mother, determined to make it a memorable Christmas, volunteered to host the meet on Boxing Day for the local hunt, as had always happened when George Shipley was alive. She invited more guests to dine on the day after Boxing Day. Christopher had to give her credit, she was indefatigable in her attempts to put on a bright face and to re-establish Newlands as the centre of the social life of the area. He admired her energy and wished he could match it himself, but he felt hollow, empty, and desperately lonely.

As he watched Edwina moving effortlessly between her guests, ensuring glasses were charged and conversation was flowing, he had to admit his respect for her. He would have liked to be able to hate her, to punish her for what she had done to him, for being who she was – or rather for not being who he wanted her to be, but he was awed by her energy. From time to time, in an unguarded moment, the shadow of sadness in her eyes was apparent. When he saw this, Christopher reminded himself of what she had lost too. Her life had not been the one she had probably dreamed of. She had been married to an unfaithful, ambitious man, who had shown her no affection. She had lost her elder son in the first flush of his youth. She must be disappointed in her younger son, in his reluctance to do as she had done herself and knuckle down and play the game. Yes, she had a burden to carry and she didn't shirk from the task. But it was a burden of her own making. And in carrying it she was forcing him to carry it too.

The closer acquaintance that Christmas afforded them

did not do anything more to endear Lady Lavinia to him. She had arrived with her two precious chihuahuas in tow and talked to her pets constantly and in a loud and exaggerated baby voice that made Christopher shudder.

Now that they were engaged, she attempted to infantilise him too. 'Chrissy, do come and look at my babies,' she said one afternoon when he came upon her sitting with their mothers in the green drawing room. 'Come and stroke them. You haven't paid my lovelies the slightest attention and they will be very cross.' She pouted at him and turned her eyes down to reveal her long lashes to best effect.

He glanced at his mother to see if she had registered the exchange and would acknowledge the humiliation she had forced upon him. But she merely gave him a watery smile and turned back to her conversation with Lady Bourne.

Christopher approached Lavinia and peered down at the small big-eyed dogs. He liked dogs well enough, but thought these two resembled rodents more than dogs.

'Remind me of the dogs' names again.'

She obliged, wagging her finger at him. 'Now don't forget again or I will have to get very, very cross with you.'

He closed his eyes, wanting to turn around and walk away from her. 'In that case, remember *my* name is Christopher. If you refer to me as Chrissy I'm liable not to hear you.' He forced a beaming smile to his lips.

'Oh, Mr Spoilsport. You are such a bore. I was going to let you hold Popsy and Petal but now I won't. They don't want to be with such an old grump as you. So there.' That pout again.

'Ah, well, I'll have to find something else to do then.' He gave her another winning smile, nodded to their mothers and left the room.

Finding the atmosphere in the house oppressive, he went

outside. The weather was unseasonably mild – the thermometer on the wall in the stable yard showed it was fifty-four degrees. His mother had been disappointed by the absence of snow to show off Newlands to best effect. At least the constant rain and drizzle that had marked the beginning of the month had now passed on.

Christopher called in on Hooker, feeding him a handful of oats as he passed his stall. He strolled on to the sunken gardens, knowing he was unlikely to be disturbed there. Being Christmas, Fred would not be working and no one else ventured in there.

Once inside the quiet haven, he headed straight for the bench where he and Martha had enjoyed their first kiss. He sat there alone, lonely, unable to push Martha from his mind. The garden appeared sad, monochrome, tired. He and Fred had made massive inroads into the overgrowth and the pruning, but in the absence of new spring growth, the place was denuded, scalped. It looked like he felt.

Christopher thought of his sister, Jane. At least she would be spending Christmas for the first time in her life with her mother. At least she would be enveloped in Martha's love and affection. He squeezed his eyes tightly shut, trying not to think about them both and how much he wished he was with them now. All he wanted was to be in the company of the two people he loved the most, no matter how simple and humble the surroundings. Instead he was shut up in a house that was decked with holly and candles, with garlands arrayed like a magic kingdom, and filled with people he thought nothing of and who in turn cared nothing for him.

A robin appeared and settled itself on the handle of a spade standing upright in an adjacent bed. Fred must have left the spade out – unlike him to be so careless. The flash of red on the breast of the tiny creature was like a tongue of flame. As Christopher watched the little bird sitting there, surveying the drab grey world around it, he remembered some lines of a poem by Emily Dickinson he had been required to learn by rote at school. His housemaster was an American and had a passion for sharing the poetry of his homeland, in defiance of the more rigid British curriculum of the school.

HOPE IS the thing with feathers
  That perches in the soul,
  And sings the tune without the words,
  And never stops at all,

AS HE WATCHED THE BIRD, it began to sing, and Christopher felt it was singing for him alone: a command performance. The trilling and chirping was light, sonorous and was indeed a tune without words. For the first time since he had said goodbye to Martha, he felt his spirits lift. *Hope.* Did he dare to hope that his life might one day be better?

He remembered what Martha had said about hope when they were in that bedroom in the inn at Northington – that hope was a terrible burden. But she had meant the kind of hope that stopped you getting on with life, that froze you in time. He realised now that there was a different kind of hope, one that was about finding a way to go on living, to climb out of despair, perhaps not to attain happiness, but at least to reach some form of contentment, satisfaction, purpose.

He remembered how he had felt overseas. The freedom, the challenge, the strong sense of purpose. How the heat of the island of Borneo had seemed to infuse the blood in his veins with strength and energy. Returning there might restore his self-respect. Maybe he couldn't do it yet, perhaps not for four or five years, but once he and Lavinia had produced the heir to Newlands and to the Bourne title, or he had passed the age of thirty, he would be free to do as he wished. He determined to hold that memory of Borneo in his head as a source of hope, as his *'thing with feathers'*, perching in his soul.

*a*s Martha's confinement approached, she became more terrified every day. Her knowledge that her first pregnancy had resulted in Jane's brain damage caused her to fear what was about to befall her. On top of that, the longing for Kit that she had so long repressed came back to haunt her. She was about to give birth to their child; she wanted him to be with her.

But he had let her down. No. He had let his sister down. Martha still couldn't understand why he had failed to attend the funeral. Not even so much as a letter of condolence or a wreath of flowers. She could understand why he would be angry at her, after Reggie broke the news of her marriage to him. But to ignore the passing of his sister? Then she tried to rationalise his behaviour. He barely knew Jane. Only one morning fully in her company. Perhaps, now that Martha was out of his life, he had found it easy enough to set aside thoughts of his half-sister too. Maybe he had seen Jane only as a creature to be pitied and had not felt the strength of blood ties and the growing bonds of affection that she herself had experienced, so that every day, Jane's absence was like a dull ache inside her.

Her misery and anxiety were made worse by Reggie's excited anticipation. He brushed her concerns aside, telling her that as a second-time mother and now with a fully developed body, the problems she had experienced as a frightened fourteen-year-old would not be present this time. He reminded her so many times that he was a trained doctor, that there were other nurses and doctors at hand and that the midwife would attend her from the first signs of labour. Martha tried to repress her annoyance. It was all very well for him. He wasn't going to be the one bearing down in agony trying to push out a baby.

Despite her fears, Martha was eager for her child to be born. She wanted to fill the yawning hole that Jane's death had created in her life. This baby had been conceived in love. Since Kit wasn't here to share the joy of its birth with her, she had to take some consolation from the fact that Reggie Henderson was unequivocal in his longing for the child to be born. One thing was clear, her baby would not want for affection.

In the event, her delivery was rapid and uncomplicated. The midwife was efficient and reassuring, exercising a quiet authority and banishing Reggie from the house, to Martha's intense relief and despite his protests that he was a doctor. This time, no doctor was needed and Martha was cradling her new son in her arms only five hours after her contractions had started.

She relished the few brief moments she had alone with her baby before Reggie appeared at the bedside to look at the child. He stroked a finger along the infant's cheek then bent his head to kiss it. Martha tried not to recoil from the smell of tobacco.

'Well done, my dearest. I'm so happy it's a boy.' His face

was beaming. 'Now, we need to name him.'

Martha said nothing, still entranced by the tiny bundle lying in her arms, with his miniature snub nose, tightly closed eyes and thin covering of pale brown hair. She breathed in the warm, animal smell of the child and closed her eyes, bathed in happiness.

'I rather thought Kenneth, after my late father. We could call him Ken or Kenny. It's always struck me as a good solid name.'

'No,' she said, sharply, wanting to tell him it was her decision alone, but knowing that she must not.

'Very well.' He produced a piece of folded paper from his jacket pocket. 'What about George?'

Martha thought of George Shipley and snapped, 'Definitely not.'

'I'm starting to get the impression you have already decided, my dear.' He frowned. 'I hope you are not going to suggest calling him Christopher.'

She ignored the pointed remark. 'I want to give him a simple name. One that won't be shortened.'

Henderson bent his head over the piece of paper. 'John?'

'Maybe.' She tried to soften her tone.

'Or James?'

'Must we decide now?' She was drowsy, the tiredness after the exertions of birth kicking in.

'Well, no. But it's as well to settle these things quickly. A child needs a name. It doesn't seem right to leave him without one, and I was thinking of going to register the birth this afternoon.'

Weary and wanting to sleep, she said, 'David. Let's call him David.'

Dr Henderson frowned then, evidently deciding it was unwise to pursue the matter further, said, 'Very well. David it is.'

CHAPTER 22

*A*s his wedding to Lavinia approached, Christopher's sense of doom grew. Closer acquaintance with his bride-to-be had done nothing to endear her to him. He tried to blot the coming wedding out of his mind and steered clear of the planning, which had absorbed every waking moment for Edwina Shipley, Lady Lavinia and her mother.

In vain, Christopher tried to convince Edwina that a small-scale wedding with only family members would be more desirable – but his mother saw it as the means of cementing the Shipleys into the upper echelons of society and would not be swayed. And Lavinia had made her own views apparent – the bigger the better. The marriage was to be featured in *Tatler, Country Life* and the *Illustrated London News*, as well as the quality dailies.

The nuptials took place at St George's, Hanover Square. As Christopher waited at the altar, standing beside his best man, a fellow student from his Cambridge days, all he could think of was Martha. If only it were she, about to process up the aisle towards him. But were he to have married Martha it would have been a quiet affair. No pomp. No ceremony. Only love.

The organ roared into life, playing Handel. Christopher kept his eyes fixed on the altar, without turning to watch Lavinia approaching on the arm of her father. Eventually, Roddie, his best man, prodded him, at the same time throwing him a meaningful look. Christopher, resigned to his fate, turned towards his bride.

Lady Lavinia looked undeniably beautiful. Her gown was in ivory satin and lace with a train that seemed to run the length of the church, her veil a cascade of tulle and she carried a waterfall of white roses. She smiled a radiant smile and Christopher shaped his lips into a smile in return, his heart thumping like the organ.

The church was packed, both downstairs and in the upper gallery. All these people, here to witness what felt to Christopher like a public execution. He kept hoping for divine intervention: an earthquake, a bomb, a sudden unexplained flood – or an interruption from the back of the church calling a halt to the proceedings.

But there was no reprieve. They each made their vows and he slipped the ring on her finger, then it was all over. He was bound to Lady Lavinia Bourne for the rest of their lives.

The wedding breakfast was at Claridge's. Every minute was torture to Christopher. In the wedding portraits, he appeared either glum or bewildered. Lavinia made up for his dourness by flashing a smile whenever she was required to pose for the photographers, and when speaking to any of their guests. When not, her face was as miserable as his.

Christopher had put his foot down about a Paris honeymoon and a Calais crossing, declaring that Paris and northern France held too many bad wartime memories for him. Such was his ferocity on the point, that even his mother backed off. Instead they settled on Biarritz, sailing from

Portsmouth to Bilbao on a night crossing to avoid even having to pass through Paris.

Lavinia was seasick, confined to their cabin for most of the passage through the Bay of Biscay. Christopher spent the trip walking the decks, or reading in one of the salons, grateful that his new wife's illness had postponed any possibility of their consummating the marriage. By the time they landed and arrived at their hotel, Lavinia was pasty-faced and tired.

Their suite in *Le Palais* hotel was sumptuous and spacious, with twin bathrooms, a large bedroom and a comfortable drawing room. Chilled champagne, flowers and chocolates awaited them, and Lavinia immediately perked up. They retired after dinner, both exhausted from the journey. When Christopher returned from the bathroom and got into bed he found his wife was already sleeping or, he thought, more likely feigning sleep.

The following morning, he awoke and found the bed empty, and heard the sound of a bath running. Lady Lavinia was evidently as little eager for marital relations to commence as he was.

The day was cloudy and cold for May in the south of France. Christopher suggested a walk after breakfast and Lavinia, rather grudgingly, agreed. They trudged along the promenade, beside a windswept beach, the silence between them heavy. When they went into a café to take coffee, Christopher asked if there was anything she particularly wished to do.

'Go home and be with Popsy and Petal,' she said, her lips pouting and her brow furrowed. 'I still don't see why I couldn't have brought my darlings with me.'

'You know perfectly well the quarantine laws prevent that. We're only here for a week. Surely you can manage without them for that. And it *is* our honeymoon.'

'A week's a lifetime for me, without my girlies.'

He closed his eyes, he too wishing he were at home. Anywhere but sitting here in a crowded café with steamed-up windows, beside a woman with whom he was unable to communicate.

Lady Lavinia inspected the room, craning her head to see if there was anyone she knew – or wanted to know – among the clientele. Her frown deepened when she failed to find a familiar face. 'I knew we should have waited until June or July. Anyone who's anyone won't be here 'til next month. We're too early in the season.' She scowled at him.

They finished their coffee in silence. Once outside, Christopher said, 'Look, Lavinia, we have to find a way to rub along together. This may not be what you wanted, but we're married now and need to make the best of it.' He'd almost said 'what *we* wanted' but had caught himself in time.

She looked sideways at him. 'I didn't want to marry you. I only agreed because Daddy said I must.' She sounded petulant. 'It's jolly unfair that because Percy died, I had to marry you. Especially when you have a leg missing.' She started to cry.

Christopher stared at her in disbelief. 'Why didn't you tell me you didn't want to marry me beforehand? We could have called it off.'

'Daddy and Mummy said I absolutely couldn't.' Her sobbing grew louder.

Suddenly impatient, he said, 'If it's any consolation, I don't want to be married to you either.'

'What?' Her face was aghast.

'That's why we both need to make the best of a bad situation. Once we've had a child, I will free you of any further marital obligations. Our parents will be happy and we will have done our duty. We can lead separate lives.'

Tears flowed down her cheeks. 'You don't want me? You

only married me to have a child?' She blew her nose loudly. 'Don't you think I'm pretty?'

How was he going to spend the rest of the week in close confinement with a woman like her? She was a spoilt child. Infantile. And stupid. Very stupid. 'Of course, you're pretty,' he said.

'So why don't you want me? And you a cripple, after all.'

Christopher stopped dead. She waited for him to catch up with her, but he didn't, forcing her to step back towards him.

'I'm only stating facts. Don't you see it's horrid for me? Being married to a man with a missing leg? There's no point in trying to pretend otherwise. You are crippled. You have a limp and a false leg. I know it's not your fault but can't you see it from my point of view?' She sighed. 'I suppose as long as I don't ever have to see it… the stump, I mean. I talked to Mummy about it and she said that as you are a gentleman you would be considerate and maybe leave your false leg on in bed and keep it covered up whenever I am there. That way I can try to pretend it's not missing.'

He stared at her, unable to comprehend her insensitivity. How she could be so blind to the implications for him of the loss of a limb?

Realising words were pointless, he turned away and set off down the promenade away from her. He walked rapidly, moving as fast as he was able, conscious of his limping gait. He walked past their hotel and on to the end of the esplanade, taking a pathway up to the top of the cliffs above the beach. He turned his jacket collar up to afford some protection from the biting wind. Following a path along the top of the cliffs, he came to a rocky promontory, where the Biarritz lighthouse towered above the sea. He stood on the clifftop watching the waves crashing on the rocks below. The scene was wild and desolate and perfectly mirrored his mood.

He moved into the lee of the great lighthouse, sheltering from the worst of the wind. How had he got into this empty sham of a marriage? Condemned to a future with the prattling Lavinia. Worse, a life without Martha in it. He was only twenty-six and the best already lay behind him: his time at Oxford and in Borneo, his few precious stolen moments with Martha. Now he had to look forward to day after day of Lavinia's scowling face or simpering smile greeting him across the breakfast table: her mood based entirely on the presence or absence of her yapping lapdogs. And worse still, having to do what was required to give her a child. He shuddered at the thought of his humiliation in the face of her disgust at his physical disfigurement – and of her evident distaste for him and the prospect of him touching her.

Then he thought of his sister, Jane. It hurt him that because of Martha's marriage to Henderson he was prevented from seeing her too. Even though he had met her only for an hour or so, he felt sad that she was never to become a part of his life and his banishment from Martha meant also a banishment from her.

Nothing in his life had worked for him. His love for Martha. His career. His family. He was left with a loveless marriage, a harridan of a mother and the task of running Newlands, a task he had no stomach to do.

How hard would it be to move to the edge of the cliff and step out into the void? Death would come quickly, dashed to pieces on those rocks beaten by the great Atlantic breakers.

It was almost dark by the time he returned to *Le Palais*. A red-eyed Lavinia was waiting in the bedroom. She was stretched out on the bed, her frock creased and her hair dishevelled.

'You left me all alone,' she said, sounding peevish. 'You

went off and left me.' She scowled. 'It's not fair. It was mean of you.'

Christopher sat down in an armchair by the window staring out at the windblown gardens.

Lavinia began to cry. Little panting sobs.

He turned to look at her. What had he taken on, in agreeing to marry Lady Lavinia Bourne? Almost two years his senior, but like a small child throwing a temper tantrum because her favourite toy had been taken from her.

'I needed some time on my own,' he said, at last.

'You don't like me,' she whined, then broke again into sobs.

'Not when you cry like that. Not when you say the kind of things you said before.'

'You're mean. I want to go home. I want my dogs. I hate you.'

Christopher groaned. He was tempted to get up and leave the room, go down to one of the public rooms, find a news-paper, read a book, go to the bar. Anything to get away from her.

As if sensing that her self-pitying behaviour was making no impact on her husband, Lavinia got up off the bed and went into the bathroom. She was gone for more than ten minutes and when she emerged, she had dried her eyes, refreshed her face and tidied her hair.

'I don't want to quarrel,' she said. She moved across the room towards him, a shy smile on her face. 'Can't you be nice to me? Please?'

To his surprise, she reached for his hand. 'Mummy said to me that men are always nicer if one lets them have what they want. I think it's time we did what you want, then maybe you'll be nicer to me. I think we should get it over with. You know, so it won't be between us. You wanting it and me being afraid.'

She turned to him, her eyes large, her lips plump and moist. She was trembling and he saw that she was indeed afraid. The childishness that had irritated him now touched him. He saw that for her, like him, this honeymoon was something to be endured, got through, got over. His annoyance turned to pity. He wanted to tell her that no, he didn't want it. He didn't love her. Could never love her. But right now making love to her seemed inevitable.

'Shall I get undressed?' She spoke softly, almost a whisper.

He nodded. 'Would you like me to close the curtains?'

'Yes, please. Thank you.'

They took off their clothes in the darkened room and got into the bed. They lay side-by-side on their backs for a few minutes. Christopher realised that for Lavinia it was undoubtedly a frightening prospect.

'I won't hurt you,' he said. 'And if at any time you want me to stop, tell me. I promise to be gentle.'

He heard her small quick breaths. 'Thank you.'

As soon as he touched her she gave a gasp. Not of horror, but to Christopher's surprise it seemed to indicate pleasure.

'Is this all right?' he asked as he ran his hand over her body. 'Say if you want me to stop.'

'Don't stop.'

She took his hand and put it between her legs. To his surprise she was wet. Instinct took over and he manoeuvred himself over her. As he entered her, she cried out in pain, but then her arms wrapped around him, her legs rose to clamp him tighter to her and her hips moved under him, drawing him into her.

Christopher forced himself to blank out everything and concentrate only on what they were doing. He mustn't pretend that it was Martha underneath him now. He decided to let it all wash over him, relieved that he had not caused Lavinia distress and more tears. The act felt impersonal to him. How he imagined it might have been had he slept with that Belgian girl during the war. He relaxed into it, let the physical sensations seep into him, two young bodies acting reflexively, mindlessly, intent only on the pleasure of the moment.

Little gasps and groans from Lavinia signalled her own unexpected enjoyment at what they were doing. Christopher was grateful. If she had, as he had expected, hated what they were doing, it would have made the rest of the week hard to endure, but here she was, clutching at him, moving under him, arching her hips up to meet him, like a dairymaid having a romp in the hay with her lover.

When it was over, she curled her body up against his, and began to nuzzle at his neck, like a small animal. But Christopher didn't want this intimacy. Performing his marital obligations with her was one thing, and he was glad it had not proved to be a trial. But lying with her in his arms, as she clearly wanted, was another. He couldn't bring himself to offer that. He dropped a perfunctory kiss on her forehead, swung himself off the bed and went towards the bathroom. 'It's time we got ready for dinner,' he said, over his shoulder. 'It's getting late.'

Then, remembering that she did deserve some courtesy, he turned back and said, 'Thank you, Lavinia. I trust that was not too unpleasant for you?' Without waiting for her response, he went into his bathroom. He closed the door and leaned against it, eyes closed as he gathered himself together. A few moments later, from the adjoining bathroom, he could hear taps running and the sound of Lavinia singing to herself over the rush of the water.

He had a mix of emotions. Relief that, at last, they had got the act out of the way, that she had enjoyed it and that he had managed to perform. Sorrow and guilt, at what felt like a betrayal of Martha. Self-loathing that he had allowed himself to be put in this position by his mother. He was weak. Wasn't he? But what choice had he had? It had been this or Jane losing her place in St Crispin's. And Martha had chosen another. Reggie Henderson. Christopher hoped Henderson would make her happy. Then a wave of jealousy swept over him and all he wanted to do was punch Henderson on the nose.

He stared at his reflection in the mirror, realising he needed to shave. A longing for Martha ate into him, hollowing out his stomach. Why could it not have been her in the room with him? Why could it not be her on his arm when they descended to the dining room? Why was she not here to walk with him on those windswept clifftops, holding his hand as they stared out to sea, cocooned in their love for each other?

Christopher asked himself how he might have done things differently. Could there have been a better way? A way for him to defy his mother and marry the woman he loved? But as he asked the question, he knew there was not.

CHAPTER 23

The late afternoon's activity in the bedroom had evidently agreed with Lavinia. She dined with a hearty appetite and allowed the sommelier to keep her glass topped up with champagne without any sign of her usual moderation. She prattled away throughout the meal, talking of her pet dogs, of a new outfit she planned to wear tomorrow that she hoped Christopher would like, all the time looking around the dining room in her quest to find a face she recognised.

'I'm sure that's the Countess of Windermere,' she hissed at him. 'Don't look now but she's behind your right shoulder.'

Christopher felt no temptation to turn his head. 'I have absolutely no idea who the Countess of Windermere might be.'

'Really. You need to know these things.'

'Why?'

She was nonplussed for a moment. 'Because one must,' she said, fatuously.

Christopher sipped his wine and wished he were back in England. Back in the sunken garden, burning up his nervous energy, digging or tearing down ivy, stripping back the accumulated vegetation of six years of neglect. He stared across the table at the woman who was his wife. How had he been so lily-livered in agreeing to marry Lavinia? It had been unfair to her as well as himself. At least he had made her parents and his mother happy. Since happiness was something he no longer expected to experience for himself, then at least he'd achieved that. No doubt, plans were already advanced for the repairs to the Bournes' roof. Edwina Shipley, meanwhile, would be relishing the prospect of her eventual grandson inheriting a title. Christopher shuddered as he imagined her planning a party to mark his and Lavinia's return from honeymoon.

Lavinia had moved on to reciting her plans for how she intended them to spend the following day. These included a walk through the town to conduct some shopping at the *Bonheur* department store, followed by a stroll along the promenade to the old port before lunch. Christopher let her words flow over him, nodding occasionally and forcing an occasional smile to his lips.

Of course, he could have married someone else. Even a one-legged man was in demand in these post-war days, especially when he came with a sizeable fortune and a business with a healthy balance sheet. Notwithstanding heavy tax duties on the death of his father, Shipley Industries kept churning out profits faster than even his mother could spend them.

Perhaps Christopher could have found a more congenial woman, someone more intelligent, more *sympathique* as the French said. But if he couldn't be with Martha, then it might as well be Lavinia. Her shallowness, her prettiness, her general vacuity made her as far removed from Martha as any woman could be. Rationally, he knew he was behaving like a martyr, but such was the weight of his melancholy that he could do nothing about it.

The small orchestra in the corner of the palatial dining room struck up a waltz. One or two of the diners moved onto the dance floor. Christopher sensed Lavinia was keen to join them. Another ordeal to face. He hadn't even attempted to navigate his way around a dance floor with his wooden leg. There had been no dancing at the marriage celebrations, his mother declaring dancing at weddings to be vulgar. Lavinia was now twisting round in her chair watching the dancers eagerly. He muttered something about maybe having a turn after the pudding.

The waiter was serving their crèmes brûlées when someone slapped a hand on Christopher's back. He jumped and turned to see a tall man with an unkempt mass of wiry hair, towering over him.

'Well, well! Chris Shipley. I say, old boy. I thought it was you. Been craning my neck across the room all through dinner. Didn't expect to run into anyone I know here, in May.'

The man leaning over his chair had been at school with him. A bighead and a bully, a year older than Christopher.

'Algie,' he said. 'Good to see you.' But that was not an accurate expression of his feelings. He got to his feet and presented his wife. 'Lavinia, this is Algernon Belford-Webb. We were at school together. Algie, my wife, Lady Lavinia.'

'I say, Shippers, you lucky chap. I'd heard you'd got spliced, but had no idea that you'd plucked the fairest rose in the garden.' The man bent his head over Lavinia's hand, kissed it and was rewarded with a blush and a giggle.

'Mind if I join you?' Without waiting for a reply, Belford-Webb signalled a passing waiter to bring up a chair and, as soon as it was positioned, he sat down, turning in Lavinia's direction. 'So you're honeymooning then? And what do you think of Biarritz, Lady Lavinia?'

'It seems nice enough, but a little quiet. Rather early in the season.'

'Dead as a dodo. I'm only here as the mater hates the heat and expects me to bring her here for a week every year in May. Place is as dull as ditch water this time of year. Now, July's a different matter. Do you like to bathe?'

Lavinia told him she had never tried. 'Mummy and Daddy are frightfully old-fashioned about that kind of thing.'

'You must bring her again in July or August, Shippers.' He said this to Christopher without looking at him, keeping his eyes fixed on Lavinia.

Christopher said, 'Where is your mother? Perhaps she'd care to join us?' He had no real desire to engage an elderly dowager in conversation, but Belford-Webb's rudeness was annoying him.

'Turned in already. The old girl doesn't like staying up late and always scarpers as soon as the musicians start up. I say, why don't you two tootle along with me to the casino later? Have you been yet?'

Lavinia clasped her hands together. 'Ooh, do let's, Christopher.'

'I'm not sure–'

'Come, come, Shippers. How can you turn this divinely lovely creature down?'

Lavinia was giggling and making her eyes widen when they caught Belford-Webb's. 'Christopher's a mean old thing. He's been terribly grumpy since we got here. I sometimes think all he wants to do is disappoint me.' She pouted and looked down at the tablecloth, peering upwards through her long eyelashes at Algernon as he leaned closer.

'If we're to go to the casino I'll go back to the room and fetch my wrap,' she said.

Christopher got to his feet. 'I'll get it.'

'No, you stay here and talk with Mr Belford-Webb.' She gave Algie one of her winning smiles as the two men rose. 'I'm sure you've lots to catch up on since schooldays.'

A roll call of the dead and maimed, thought Christopher.

Algernon Belford-Webb had missed the war altogether. At least the active service part. His father was a Lieutenant General and had contrived for his son to get a desk job behind the lines. Algie had spent the war years in uniform, doing little more than rubber-stamping orders that came from further up the chain of command before transmitting them onward. He had emerged at the end of 1918 without a scratch and with his full complement of campaign medals.

Looking at Algernon now, Christopher felt only contempt for him. At school he had been a frequent snitch, in the pockets of the prefects, until he became one himself, doling out punishments with little cause. It rankled that he'd spent the war years safe behind the lines, pushing a pen, while men like Percy had paid the ultimate sacrifice.

'Hear you copped a Blighty before the war was over.' Belford-Webb turned to Christopher, sneering. 'Couldn't take the pressure any longer? Quick shot in the foot, eh?'

'Part of my leg was blown off.' Christopher ground his teeth, wanting to wipe the sneering expression off Algernon's face. 'How was your war? See much action?'

'Strategy.' Belford-Webb patted two fingers against his skull. 'Planning troop movements. Top secret stuff. They couldn't spare me for routine duties.'

Routine duties? Lying festering in filth and lice in the bottom of a muddy trench, while the Germans bombarded the lines with mortars. Stomachs rumbling from hunger. Eating worm-ridden or flyblown food. Dealing with diarrhoea and constipation with only a hastily-dug, stinking latrine to squat over – sometimes, just a corner of the trench.

Watching schoolboys being killed or maimed, their limbs blown off, their brains destroyed, their lives snuffed out or damaged utterly. The stench, the cold, the wet, the squalor. Night after night. Day after day. On and on. Men being fed into the meat-grinding machine that was the Western Front. Barbed wire, shell craters, the stink of rotting corpses from no man's land. Filth. Horror. Destruction. Men pointlessly pounding other men, whom they knew not and held no grudge against, with the destructive powers of industrial armaments. Routine duties?

Christopher imagined Algernon Belford-Webb billeted in some chateau or provincial inn, enjoying the contents of the wine cellars, while dining on the finest of food. He bit his tongue and clenched a fist under the table.

Lavinia returned, a cashmere wrap over one arm and a hat and gloves in the other. She had evidently taken advantage of her return to the room to apply lipstick and powder. 'Shall we go, chaps?' she said brightly.

'Oh, rather!' Algernon was already on his feet.

Christopher stood up. Could a trip to the casino be so terrible? At least if they were watching or playing the tables he wouldn't need to talk to either of them.

THE *BELLEVUE* CASINO was on a promontory at the southern end of the *Grande Plage*, above the sea. A large belle époque building, it was also home to musical concerts and a crowd of people were making their way up the stairs and under the portico.

'What's your vice?' Belford-Webb addressed Christopher. 'I'm a roulette man myself.'

'I don't care for gambling.' Christopher realised he sounded priggish but was past caring.

'Ooh, roulette! How wicked! May I have a go? Please,

darling.' Lavinia clasped her hands in front of her and turned her face up to Christopher's. She made a moue with her plump lips. 'Please!'

Christopher went to buy her some chips. When he returned, she was talking animatedly to Algernon. Christopher handed her the little tray of wooden chips. She beamed at him. At least she wasn't difficult to please. Like a small child, easily gratified.

'Have you ever played roulette, Lavinia?' he asked.

'No.' She drew her eyebrows together. 'But Algie has promised to show me how.'

So it was Algie already? Christopher followed the pair into the salon. Belford-Webb had a proprietary hand on Lavinia's arm as he steered her towards one of the tables. It was apparent that neither of them were interested in Christopher's presence. He watched as they exchanged their casino chips for coloured ones at the table.

Algernon whispered explanations to Lavinia about the different types of bets and the relative odds. She nodded as she listened, then slid one of her chips onto the intersection of four squares on the table, turning to smile uncertainly at her tutor.

'Have I got it right, Algie? A corner bet isn't it?' Her face was animated as she watched the wheel spinning and she groaned loudly when the ball predictably failed to land in any of her chosen slots.

'Lavinia, the only winner at roulette is the house,' said Christopher.

'I thought you said you didn't know anything about gambling.' Her tone was dismissive.

'I know that much. It's all you need to know.'

Losing her first bet seemed to do nothing to dampen Lavinia's enthusiasm and, as soon as the croupier cleared the table, she placed two more tokens down. The wheel spun again and this time the little ball landed in one of Lavinia's slots.

'There you are! That just shows you. I've jolly well won.'

The croupier placed the marker and cleared the table, then slid a pile of chips over to a delighted Lavinia.

'There's one other thing you need to know about gambling,' said Christopher.

'And what might that be, Mr Spoilsport?'

'Walk away as soon as you win.'

Lavinia glared at him then turned back to Belford-Webb. 'You're not ready to walk away yet, are you, Algie?'

'Certainly not.' He winked at Christopher.

Christopher decided to leave Lavinia and her new-found friend to get on with it. They didn't even look up when he wandered off.

He walked through the tall glass doors at the end of the room onto a stone-flagged terrace. The Atlantic breakers crashed onto the beach below. He moved towards the balustrade and leaned against it, watching the white peaks of waves bright in the darkness, riding in on a swell until they hit the shore and dissipated. A faint hint of mimosa reached him on the breeze, a sweet, warm, powdery scent that reminded him of his mother. *Acacia dealbata* he murmured to himself as he saw the heavy yellow blossoms trailing over the wall at the end of the terrace. He sat down on a stone bench. There was no one else out here, the lure of the gaming tables proving irresistible to all but him. He settled back against the balustrade and thought about the future.

Was this to be his life from now on? Saddled to a dim-witted, shallow wife, who had as little interest in him as he had in her. Lacking any sense of purpose in life, he was now cut off from the career as a botanist and explorer that he had wanted to pursue. Moving papers around a desk every morning, to keep Newlands running smoothly, was his fate now, when all he wanted was to be as far away from the place as possible. And worst of all – a life without Martha in it, knowing that she was out of his reach for ever.

LAVINIA CONTINUED to accompany Belford-Webb to the casino every night, not returning until after Christopher had gone to sleep. He went along with them to the Bellevue for the first two nights, but found the atmosphere oppressive and the gambling boring. While money meant little to him, he didn't enjoy watching Lavinia throwing it away, night after night. Instead, he had taken to retiring to one of the public rooms in the *Hotel du Palais*, with a book, while listening to the string quartet that played there most evenings.

They had two more days left of their honeymoon. Christopher couldn't wait for it to be over, even though Biarritz was a pleasant enough place. He had enjoyed his walks along the beaches and the clifftops. He walked alone, as Lavinia had taken to lying in bed until luncheon, after coming in late every night from the casino with Belford-Webb. Christopher rarely saw her in the afternoons either. Mrs Belford-Webb, the large, matronly and loudly-spoken mother of Algernon, had taken Lavinia under her wing – a place Lavinia was only too happy to occupy, once she met her new friend's pug dog.

'Look, darling,' she said excitedly to Christopher, when he walked into the grand salon after one of his walks. 'Mrs Belford-Webb has the darlingest little pug. His name is Punch. Isn't that the cutest name?'

Christopher ignored his wife's lack of politeness in introducing the dog rather than its owner, and introduced himself to the lady.

Mrs Belford-Webb frowned at him. 'Your delightful wife

has told me you travelled here by ship and she was dreadfully seasick.'

'It was rather a rough crossing.'

'It's always a rough crossing through the Bay of Biscay. Surely you know that?' Without waiting for an answer, she added, 'I've told Lady Lavinia she must travel back to England with Algernon and me. We are leaving the day before you, but we should be back in London around the same time. I've invited Lady Lavinia to spend a night with us in Paris and then to stay with us in Berkeley Square until you arrive in London. You're welcome to join us for another night or two when you return. Then you can travel home to Newlands together.'

It was happening to him again – another woman wanting to run his life for him. He bristled and started to speak, but Lavinia interrupted.

'Isn't it marvellous? I couldn't face that horrible ship pitching about again. The train is a much better way to travel. And we're going to spend a night in Paris. Isn't that wonderful, darling? You don't mind, do you?'

Algernon threw him an expression that indicated he'd had nothing to do with the new arrangements. He shrugged and rolled his eyes at Christopher as if to say they were both powerless in the face of the women's casting votes.

Christopher had mixed emotions. A journey home without Lavinia's prattle was appealing, but it was bizarre for a husband and wife to return from their honeymoon separately. What would his mother say? But he didn't give a damn what she'd say. And anyway, she didn't have to know.

In their suite, dressing for dinner that evening, he raised the subject again with Lavinia.

She said, 'It makes perfect sense. You don't want to travel through northern France and I don't want a long boat trip. It will be bad enough for me crossing the Channel.' She formed her lips into her familiar pout. 'And it's all above board as Mrs Belford-Webb will be with us.'

She smiled at Christopher, then said, 'Don't get dressed yet.' She pushed him onto the bed and climbed on top of him. This had become a daily ritual.

If Lavinia found Algie's company more congenial than his, it didn't stop her appetite for marital relations. Contrary to Christopher's expectations, once Lavinia had got over her scruples about making love with a one-legged man, she had demonstrated a healthy enthusiasm for it. With a bit of luck she might fall pregnant before too long and Christopher told himself he would have fulfilled the Bourne family's expectations and the bargain he had made with his mother. He was already mentally planning his escape to Borneo on a long expedition.

CHAPTER 24

*M*artha had to admit that her husband was a devoted and attentive father. Over the six months since David's birth, he had given no indication that David was anything other than his blood son, always keen to hold the baby, and constantly enquiring of Martha as to his welfare.

David was a healthy baby, pleasing his father with rapid progress in all the frequent checks he made of weight, feeding patterns and general development. Dr Henderson gave Martha a notebook and asked her to keep a record of each breast feeding, the time it occurred and its duration and he checked her entries every evening. The attention he paid to the child was close to obsessional, and Martha had to suppress her irritation when Reggie questioned or corrected virtually everything she did. She kept reminding herself that he had rescued her and her child from a likely penurious future and she owed him so much. It seemed ungrateful that her only complaint was her husband's solicitude. The kindness he had shown to Jane had also touched Martha. And he was full of affection and generosity bringing her posies of flowers, enquiring as to her well-being and eloquent in his gratitude for everything she did for him. Reggie Henderson was a model husband in so many ways.

Since marrying, they had maintained separate bedrooms and he had never ventured across the landing to visit her at night. His assertion, when he had asked her to marry him, that he had been rendered impotent by war injuries, had been a relief to Martha and a major factor in her agreeing to marry him – the thought of making love with anyone other than Kit was abhorrent.

One night, in August 1920, when David was seven months old, Reggie came to her bed. The baby was sleeping quietly in his cot on the other side of the room. Martha jumped in fright as her husband climbed onto the bed beside her and curled his body against her back. He placed one arm around her waist and drew her tighter against him. To her alarm she felt his erection pressing against her and his breath was hot against her neck.

She twisted away from him. 'What are you doing?'

He ignored her question and whispered, 'I love you, Martha. You're my wife and I want you.'

She jerked upright and sat up in the bed, astonished. 'You told me... you said you couldn't... said that you were...'

'Impotent?'

She couldn't see his face in the dark and was glad he couldn't see hers, as it was burning with embarrassment and mortification. This couldn't be happening.

'I *was* impotent. At least I thought I was. But it seems not to be the case any longer. I owe that to you, Martha. You have given me a son. You have been my companion and friend. Now I would like you to be my wife.'

'But you said...' She struggled to find the right words. She was unprepared for this, embarrassed and shocked. Until this moment, he had shown no inkling of any sexual desire. Affection, yes – he kissed her every day, but always a chaste kiss on the cheek in the morning and the same before retiring at night.

He pulled her down beside him on the bed and his hands began to move over her body, cupping her breasts and stroking her stomach through her linen nightgown.

'Stop!'

'I've asked so little of you until now.'

'I know. But you told me it was all you expected. You led me to believe that ours would be a marriage based on friendship and support.'

'I didn't know then that my feelings for you would change.'

'It's not your feelings,' she gasped, still seeking the right words. 'You told me ours could not be a physical marriage.'

Henderson continued to run his hands over her body, trying to work her nightdress up her legs. She pushed his hand away.

'I thought it wouldn't be,' he said. 'I had had no feelings at all in that way. I believed my body incapable... the war... my injuries... but you... you changed all that and I am so grateful, my darling. You've made me feel desire again. You've awakened me.' His hands tugged at her nightgown.

She pushed him away again, clamping her legs together and drawing her nightdress down over her legs.

'You made vows. You stood beside me in church and promised to obey me, to worship me with your body, to be my *wife*. I have waited patiently until you were delivered of David. I've waited for your body to recover.' Henderson's was now peevish. 'I have been an honourable man and a dutiful husband. Now I want to make love to you. That is all I ask. I don't expect you to *love* me. All I want is for you to do your duty as a wife. That is what every husband expects and has a right to. It is so little to ask of you.'

Martha shuddered. 'It may seem little – but it's more than I can give. And it's more than you told me I would need to give. You led me to believe you were incapable of fulfilling that aspect of marriage. Did you only say that so I'd agree to marry you? Because you knew I wouldn't consent otherwise?'

Reggie was silent. All she could hear was his breathing in the dark. For a moment she thought he was acknowledging the truth in what she was saying.

The blow across her face happened so suddenly she didn't see it coming, had no time to duck to avoid it. His palm hit her cheek with force. Face burning, she raised her hands to protect herself against another blow. Eyes streaming. Heart pounding. Nerves screaming in pain and shock.

The next blow didn't come. Martha only realised David was crying after she felt the mattress shift under her as Henderson got off the bed and went across to the cot. He bent down and lifted the wailing child into his arms. Suddenly she was filled with a greater alarm – this time for the welfare of her baby. Crawling to the end of the bed, she reached out for the child. Her husband took a step backwards, holding the boy tightly in his arms. By now, David was howling.

'Please, please!' she begged. 'Please, give him to me. He needs a feed.'

She couldn't see Henderson's face in the darkness of the room, but she saw the shape of his body, heard his breathing and sensed his hesitation. Then he moved towards her, placed her child in her arms and went across to the door.

Martha put the baby to her breast, afraid that the pounding of her heart would further unsettle the child and put him off feeding, but he immediately began to suckle hungrily.

Reggie opened the door and stood in the frame, illuminated by the landing light. 'We will speak of this tomorrow,' he said, and closed the door quietly behind him.

WHILE MARTHA WAS PREPARING BREAKFAST, she kept running over the events of the previous night. Reggie's behaviour had been so out of character that she asked herself if she had dreamt the incident. But the smarting of her cheek and the burgeoning blueness under her left eye was proof that she hadn't.

It was so uncharacteristic of the usually gentle and jovial Dr Henderson that Martha wondered if it were a hangover from his experiences in the war. Had he mistaken her for the enemy and lashed out? But the words he'd spoken were clearly directed at her alone. He had meant what he said.

He arrived in the room and sat down at the table as she finished cooking his bacon and eggs. Instead of his customary good morning kiss on the cheek, he unfolded his newspaper and began to read.

Martha placed the food in front of him and he said nothing. She returned to the kitchen to make his pot of tea, standing nervously in front of the stove waiting for the whistle of the boiling kettle.

Was he going to maintain this stony silence? Should she say something? Ask him to talk about what happened? Had he forgotten what he had done to her? Maybe it had been some kind of waking dream that he had acted out and now forgotten.

When she returned with his tea, Reggie had set aside his newspaper and was tucking into his breakfast. He asked her to sit down.

She pulled out her chair, opposite his, and sat with her hands twitching in her lap under the tablecloth.

'Not eating?'

'I'm not hungry now. I'll eat later.'

He cut a piece off his bacon, dipping it into the egg and put it in his mouth. Chewing slowly, he studied her face across the table. She lowered her eyes.

'I prefer you to eat when I do. And you need to eat regularly for the sake of the baby.'

Martha said nothing, her heart pounding inside her chest. She was afraid of this man, this cold stranger who had struck her and tried to force himself upon her.

'I will maintain my bedroom as a dressing room but, as of tonight, I intend to share your bed. I'll send one of the porters over to move David's cot into my room. It's time he started to sleep in his own bedroom.'

'But he needs feeding throughout the night.'

'Then you will go to him. There is a nursing chair that you can move in there. You can feed him then return to bed.'

She started to speak but there was something in his eyes that stopped her. His stare was penetrating, as if he held her in contempt. It was as though a different man were seated on the other side of the table.

Henderson took another mouthful of his fried breakfast, his eyes fixed on her face. He chewed, swallowed, then took a drink of tea and wiped his mouth with his napkin. 'Perhaps I owe you an explanation as to what happened last night, what has changed.'

Martha waited.

He pushed his plate aside. 'Last week, I read an article in *The Lancet*. Since the war I have been taking medication. It was intended to help with certain symptoms, to help me feel calmer. The medication helped restore me to a state of equilibrium. I believed that my injuries had resulted in my inability to achieve and sustain an erection.'

Martha shuddered, embarrassed at the nature of what he was saying. Henderson's medical background meant he showed none of the restraint in his choice of words that a layman would have done.

He continued, his tone brisk and matter-of-fact, no trace of embarrassment on his face. 'The *Lancet* article posited that this particular medication contraindicates impotence. I had in any event been considering ceasing to take it, as I no longer have the symptoms for which I needed it, so I decided to stop altogether. As a result, after some weeks, I find I am able to function fully once again. That is why I intend to consummate our marriage at last and to live a normal married life.' He leaned back in his chair, arms folded.

Martha noticed a fleck of egg yolk adhering to his moustache. She felt a shiver of loathing for him.

'But if you stop the medication, your symptoms will surely return?' She was thinking of the violence with which he had struck her face.

'No. It's six years since I was injured and last saw action. Plenty of time to heal. Now it's time to live a normal life. And part of that is living a normal married life. Sexual intercourse is an essential means of the mind and body being healthy. I have been reading a lot of journals and papers on the subject. Any slight increase in nervous tension as a result of stopping the pills will soon be offset by the benefits of enjoying full marital relations.'

'And the fact that you told me you would not expect to have a normal marriage when you asked me to marry you?'

'Is immaterial.' He glanced at his watch and pushed back his chair. 'If I had known that my impotence was not permanent I would not have said that. I can assure you, my dear, it was not said to mislead. It was a statement of the facts as they were at the time.'

Dr Henderson got to his feet and, without his customary peck on the cheek, left the room. Martha heard the front door close behind him and slumped down, her head on her arms on the table.

THAT NIGHT they ate dinner in silence. After Martha settled David down in his cot, in what was to be his new bedroom, she looked down at her sleeping son, at his soft downy cheeks and rosebud mouth. As always, she searched for resemblances to Kit in his slowly evolving features, but had to acknowledge that at the moment resembled neither of them, only a baby, a very beautiful baby. Her stomach clenched with fear at the thought that, just as his behaviour towards her had changed, so too might Reggie's attitude to David, once he did start to resemble Kit. She shuddered. It left her no choice. She must behave with compliance to her husband or risk retaliation.

They undressed silently in the bedroom. Martha was grateful for the heavy brocade curtains that blocked out all trace of moonlight and left the bedroom pitch dark. She fumbled her way into her nightgown and could sense Reggie's movements on the other side of the bed. She slipped under the covers and waited for him to join her, her eyes squeezed tightly shut and her heart thumping under her ribs.

The springs creaked and she felt the mattress shift underneath her as he got into bed. She lay motionless, neither helping nor hindering as he pulled up her nightdress and eased himself on top of her. He was hard and she squeezed her eyes tightly shut as she waited for him to push inside her. He was straddling her body, then he raised himself up on his elbows and jerked her legs apart, kneeling between them.

Martha braced herself for the moment of entry, but nothing happened. She was conscious of his now limp penis pushing flabbily against her. One of his hands moved down to coax it back to attention, while she lay motionless, waiting. His efforts became frantic but were pointless. As she was feeling a sense of relief and reprieve, he jerked his upper body back and struck her across the face.

The pain was even sharper than the previous night, coming on top of the already bruised and tender tissues. Her eye stung where he had clipped the edge and she could feel tears coursing down her cheek. Henderson's body slumped beside hers, his back to her. He jerked the covers, pulling them to his side of the bed, so that she was barely covered, and fell asleep immediately.

Martha lay beside him, shivering, skin smarting where he had hit her, anger rising in waves through her body. After a few minutes, she got out of bed, pattered barefoot across the floor and opened the door. David was still sleeping, so she slipped between the covers of what had been her husband's bed.

Sleep was impossible. Her mind was racing, her face burning. She knew it would be badly bruised and would mean she'd have to stay in the house until the inflammation passed, or invent a reason for a fall if any of the nurses saw her.

Later that night, while feeding David, a plan came to her. She would find the medicine that Henderson had abandoned. Since he now refused to take it, she'd have to find a way to administer it to him without his knowledge. She had to suppress this sudden explosion of violence in him. If Reggie had stopped taking the pills suddenly, his rapid behaviour change was unsurprising.

The following morning, Martha's face was puffed up and painful. She stared at her reflection in the mirror and was horrified to see that she had ugly purple bruising across her left cheek bone and eye.

As she served her husband his breakfast, she avoided looking at Henderson but could sense his gaze and knew he was looking at her. They ate the meal in silence. If he was feeling ashamed, he said nothing.

After a silent and morose Dr Henderson left the house, Martha searched his chest of drawers and the small cabinet in the bathroom. Eventually she found a discarded bottle of pills in the waste-basket in the little room off the half landing that he used as an occasional study. She stuffed the bottle into the pocket of her apron and went about her tasks for the day.

While preparing the vegetables for a lamb stew she put her plan into action. The instructions on the medicine bottle were for two tablets, morning and evening. After setting the vegetable peelings aside to put on the compost heap later, Martha took a pestle and mortar down from the shelf and ground up four of the tablets into a fine powder. Licking a finger she put a tiny amount in her mouth to see if it had a discernible or bitter taste but, to her intense relief, there was none. It would be easy enough to mix this into his serving of the stew. It could also be hidden in soups, mashed potatoes and gravy. Breakfast was a problem and Reggie often failed to come home at lunchtime if he was busy on the ward, so she would add the full four tablet dose to his evening meal.

Relieved that she had a way to restore the status quo, Martha went about readying the rest of the supper. Then it occurred to her that the bottle was only half-full. How would she obtain more of the pills? She had recognised the name on the label – it was a medication often prescribed to calm down and pacify violent and aggressive patients on the wards. There would be supplies in the medicine cupboard on the ward, but that was kept locked and she had no key. Even were she to get hold of a key, how would she be able to access the cupboard without raising the suspicions of the nursing staff? How to steal supplies without anyone noticing they were missing? By her calculations, she had only five days left before the pills ran out.

Then it struck her. Five days might be long enough for the pills to work in calming her husband. If that were achieved, she could appeal to his more rational nature – cessation of the pills had failed to cure his impotence and had caused him to be violent. The old Reggie would have been mortified. She had to pray that five days was long enough to bring the old Reggie back.

REGGIE WAS SMOKING in the small parlour when Martha came downstairs, after settling the baby for the night. She had fed her husband the last of the pills that evening, mixed into a lamb hotpot. If she were to talk to him, it had to be now.

He hadn't raised his hand to her again, although he had made one more attempt to have sexual relations with her, but his erection had failed before he could penetrate her. To Martha's relief he had turned over and gone to sleep.

She sat down opposite him. He was staring at the fire. Martha felt herself shaking with fear as she summoned up the courage to speak to him. How had it come to this? That she was afraid of her husband.

Clearing her throat, she started to speak, but he raised his hand to halt her and said, 'I know you've been feeding me the pills.'

Martha's heart almost stopped. 'What do you mean?'

'Don't take me for a fool, Martha. The bottle disappeared from my litter bin.'

She was about to tell him she emptied the basket daily,

but stopped herself. After all, she had planned to confess to him and try to persuade him to start taking the medication again. He was actually making it easier for her.

'I know I hurt you. I'm sorry I hit you.' He reached across the gap between them to touch her cheek.

Martha flinched and drew back.

'My hope that stopping the medication would restore my manhood was ill-founded. Instead it has removed the restraints on the violent tendencies that caused me to take it in the first place.' He buried his head in his hands.

Martha faced him across the silence that followed, unsure what to say or do next.

After a while, he lifted his head. 'I wanted to be a proper husband to you. I hoped – no, I believed – that you would in time want that too. Maybe another child. *Our* child.' He quickly corrected himself. 'Not that I see dear David as anything other than that, I promise you.'

'Where does the violence come from? All that anger? You frightened me.'

He seemed ashamed, his face contrite. 'I suppose it's the war. They treated me here in 1914. Then I returned to Nottingham until my wife died, when I came back to St Crispin's, this time to join the medical staff.' He twisted his hands together. 'The condition for my being allowed to resume practising was taking those pills.' He made a long sigh. 'And I would have kept taking them, were it not for you, my dearest. I so want to be whole for you. To love you. To be your husband in every sense.'

'But I don't want that, Reggie. Nothing will change that.'

'You're only saying that because I'm a disappointment to you.'

'No. My disappointment is that you tried to force yourself on me. And that you struck me.'

He gave another deep sigh. 'Forgive me, Martha.'

'All I ask is for things to be as they were before.' She shaped her mouth into a reluctant smile. 'I'd like the old Reggie back.'

He bent forward, then moved to his knees in front of her, placing his head in her lap.

Martha tried not to shudder, forcing herself to lay her hand on his head and stroke his hair.

CHAPTER 25

The passage back to Southampton was calm. Even the Bay of Biscay was placid. Christopher was relieved that Lavinia wasn't with him, but at the same time he couldn't help feeling a sense of shame and guilt that she had chosen to return from their honeymoon without him. He hoped his mother wouldn't find out, as it would give her yet another cause for complaint, another of his perceived shortcomings to rail about. He didn't give a damn for her opinion any more, but didn't want to fuel her carping.

Lavinia had done nothing to win his affection or respect during their time together. On his last morning, he had gone to the casino to settle the account he had reluctantly agreed to set up for her, only to discover she had run up a debt of over eight hundred pounds. She hadn't even seen fit to mention it. Whatever else he did, he had to make sure she spent no more time in Algernon Belford-Webb's company once they were back in England. While Christopher had no love of money, he had no wish to set fire to it either – and, until his thirtieth birthday, he had to account for it to his mother.

As for Lavinia's sexual desire, that had been a surprise to him. She had given no indication of feeling anything but revulsion for him before they were married, but during their time in Biarritz she had seized on any opportunity to have intercourse. To Christopher it was a soulless experience. He was a man with normal desires and instincts, but with Lavinia it felt impersonal, lacking affection – two people separated by their very physical proximity.

Back in England, the weather was cool and showery with dull grey skies that made him feel glummer. After the mild winter, it seemed as if they were in for a miserable summer. Maybe that was no bad thing – the summer before the war had been an endless sun-filled balmy time and yet had presaged the long depressing years of the war. In that summer of 1914 Christopher had come down from Cambridge and had been getting ready to leave for his expedition to Borneo. The talk at dinner every night had been of the possibility of war and Percy's intention to take a commission in the army. Christopher had had to withstand the pressure from his father to cancel his voyage and join up himself. He had been resolute, refusing to be bullied out of a lifetime's opportunity – because of a war that may never happen and, if it did, everyone believed would be over in a matter of weeks. Two years later, both his brother and his father were dead and he was heading to France to join his regiment.

The Belford-Webbs had a town house in Berkeley Square. Algie's father, the lieutenant general, had left the army after the war and now had a seat in the House of Lords. Hating to travel, he left his only son to accompany his wife on her annual holiday to south-west France. Christopher had met General Belford-Webb twice before, when he had given out the prizes at the school he and Algie had attended, and once when he had made a brief visit to the frontline to inspect the troops. Neither of those encounters had endeared him to Christopher, who was not eager to renew the acquaintance.

Lavinia protested volubly when Christopher arrived at Berkeley Square and announced they were leaving immediately for Newlands.

'But Algie has promised to take us to a jazz club tonight.'

'You told me you hate jazz.'

'A girl can change her mind.' She gave him one of her artificial smiles.

They were sitting in the drawing room of the Belford-Webb's house. There was no sign of Algie, and Mrs Belford-Webb had removed herself discreetly for Christopher's reunion with his wife, muttering something about organising for tea to be served.

'We are going back to Newlands today. It's all arranged. There's a train at four o'clock and I've telegraphed for the car to meet us at the station. Mother is expecting us for dinner tonight.'

'But that's not fair. You're so mean, Mr Spoilsport. You seem to enjoy making me miserable.' Her lower lip protruded in her customary pout.

Christopher looked at her with dislike. The easy way would be to give in but he knew that, if he capitulated now, he would never be able to exert any influence over Lavinia again.

'If we leave in an hour we can call on your parents and pick up your dogs.'

Lavinia's face transformed immediately into a smile. 'My babies! Yes. That will be wonderful. Do you know, Chrissy, I'd almost forgotten about them. Isn't that terrible of me. Naughty old mummy!'

The *entente cordiale* was a brief one. By the time they were settled into their compartment on the train, a sulk had returned to Lavinia's face and she passed the journey in a sullen silence. Christopher was grateful for the peace.

CHAPTER 26

*B*ack at Newlands, Christopher continued his work in the sunken garden – retreating there every afternoon had become an even greater imperative since his marriage. Lavinia rarely left the house, only emerging to walk her dogs on the paved terraces or in the rose garden, maintaining that her hay fever prevented her venturing further afield. Christopher saw it as a manifestation of her passive resistance to him and his refusal to take a property in London.

She occupied a separate bedroom and never ventured across the corridor to his. On a couple of occasions, mindful of his mother's promise that she would loosen the reins on her control of his inheritance as soon as Lavinia produced an heir, he tried her door, but it was always locked. Secretly relieved, he did not raise the issue with her. He suspected she might already be pregnant but hadn't yet asked her. It seemed a likely explanation for her changed attitude regarding marital relations.

She was spending a lot of time in London, informing him that she and her mother were shopping for the winter season. Christopher welcomed these absences and the peace that returned to Newlands without her prattle and the yapping of her small dogs. Sometimes it was almost possible to pretend to himself that he wasn't married at all.

One afternoon, as he was clearing vegetation from around an ornamental Chinese summer house, he heard a high-pitched scream coming from the nearby stable yard. It was unmistakably Lavinia.

Christopher and Fred, who was working alongside him, exchanged looks. They both downed their tools and ran up the stone stairway out of the garden.

One of the grooms was standing in the stable yard, hands on hips staring down towards the lake. When Christopher asked him about the commotion the lad replied, 'Her Ladyship just ran past. She seems to have lost one of her dogs. Ran away, I think. Willie's gone after her.'

Inwardly groaning at what was no doubt exaggerated concern for her pampered lapdogs, and Lavinia's overdeveloped sense of drama, Christopher set off in the direction the groom indicated, instructing Fred to go back to work.

He walked rapidly across the park, following Willie, the stable boy, who was by now a couple of hundred yards ahead. As Christopher reached the top of the slope that led down to the lakeside, he saw Lavinia at the edge of the lake, running up and down frantically. She was screaming for Popsy, cradling the other dog, Petal, in her arms.

As Christopher drew nearer, Lavinia shouted at the stable boy who was trying to prevent her from going after Popsy. She pushed the lad away, laid Petal on the ground, screamed to the boy to watch Petal, then kicked off her shoes and waded, fully clothed, into the lake. Christopher called out to her in alarm. The lake was deep in places, shelving abruptly, where the quarry edges had been, and he doubted that his wife was a strong swimmer, or even that she could swim at all.

'Stop, Lavinia! Get out! It's dangerous.'

She turned her head, saw him and pointed a finger at the island in the centre of the expanse of lake. He looked over to where she was pointing and saw the missing dog caught up in a floating conglomeration of twigs and leaves which was drifting towards the island. Without answering or waiting for Christopher, Lavinia waded in further, the skirt of her silk dress billowing up around her, the water already waist-high. As Christopher reached the shore, she must have stepped off a ledge, as she dropped down and disappeared under the water.

Without pausing to think, Christopher ran to the water's edge, encumbered by his artificial leg. He burst into the lake then dived forward, striking out to where Lavinia had been. Her head bobbed back up above the water a few feet in front of him and her hands flailed frenziedly as she fought to keep herself above the surface. Christopher ploughed through the water towards her, but she sank below as he was almost upon her.

He dived down underwater, struggling to orientate himself in the murky depths. Moving blindly, he caught hold of one of her arms, but she jerked it away from him as she burst upwards in panic towards the surface again. He broke through the water as she spluttered and kicked out, her terror causing her to sink beneath once more. Christopher stretched his hand out to grab her as she went under, but she was already gone. He dived below the surface again. Lavinia's frantic struggles had churned up the mud on the lake bed and he could see nothing. Groping about in the dark, he plunged down deep towards the lake bottom. Thick, foggy water made it impossible to see anything. Lungs bursting, he kicked his way back up to the surface, gulping in air, chest burning, then dived down again. And again. Arms extended, hands outreached, fingers probing, feeling sightlessly for a limb to hold onto. Darkness. Silence. His hand snagged on something. An arm. He tugged at it, trying to haul Lavinia back up to the surface but her body wouldn't follow. Wouldn't budge. In a swoosh, he burst up to the surface, gulped air, dived again. Fumbling in the dark, head throbbing, this time he found her waist, grabbed onto it with both hands and tugged. Desperate. Heaving. Dragging. Trying to get purchase on the muddy lake bed. Darkness all around. Swallowing water, he choked, tried to find the surface, the light, the air. Then everything went black.

WHEN CHRISTOPHER AWOKE, he was in his bed. He tried to focus. Two shapes at the far side of the room. A low buzz of conversation. He breathed, trying to orientate himself. The local doctor and his mother were speaking quietly, as his vision blurred and he slipped into unconsciousness.

Next time he became aware of his surroundings, Christopher was alone in the bedroom with no idea how long he had been asleep. His head throbbed and he needed several seconds to recognise the familiar surroundings. He reached for the water glass on the table beside the bed and drank thirstily, downing it in one long gulp. With effort, he pulled himself upright, reaching towards the end of his bed where his artificial limb usually lay on top of a wooden trunk while he slept. It wasn't there. Looking around, he saw it on the far side of the room, leaning against a chair. Levering himself up onto his good leg, holding onto the bedpost, he hopped across the room to reach the prosthesis. The movement made him feel dizzy, lightheaded, weak.

Once his leg was strapped on, he caught his breath. He was exhausted, as though he had undertaken the labours of

Hercules. Gradually the events at the lake came back to him. The cold murky water. Clutching and straining in the dark gloom of the depths. The suck of the mud on his foot as he'd tried to gain purchase. The thrashing panic of Lavinia as he'd tried to pull her free of whatever was holding her on the lake bed. Lavinia. Where was Lavinia? Had he got her out of the water?

Christopher stumbled across the room, wrenching open the door. Even the slightest movement took a huge effort. His head was throbbing and there was a hollowness in his stomach and a burning in the back of his throat.

The door to Lavinia's bedroom was wide open and the room was unoccupied. It was uncharacteristically tidy, missing the usual clutter of perfumes, potions and lipsticks on her dressing table. The scarves and necklaces she tended to drape over the chair or scatter on the chaise longue, were absent.

His fears mounted as he made his way downstairs. The long-case clock in the hall told him it was after nine o'clock. He found his mother in the summer dining room eating breakfast. She looked up as he entered, her eyes full of concern. Opening her arms wide, she got up from the table and moved forward to embrace her son. This unusual display of maternal affection filled him with dread. Something was wrong.

'Where's Lavinia?' he asked, already knowing what the answer would be.

Edwina Shipley stretched her lips into a grim line. 'I'm sorry, Christopher. She's gone. She drowned.'

He pulled out a chair beside his mother's and sank into it. 'Drowned?'

'You nearly drowned yourself. You were so brave. You did everything you could to try to save her. I'm so proud of you.'

Lost for words, he stared down at the table, conscious

only of the solemn ticking of the clock on the marble mantelpiece. It was a chilly morning and a fire had been lit in the grate. He heard the spit and crackle of a log.

Edwina shook out her napkin and replaced it on her lap. 'Try to eat something, darling. You've had nothing for three days.'

'Three days?' he echoed. 'I don't understand.'

'I told you. You nearly drowned. The stable boy and the groom dragged you from the lake. You'd passed out.'

Bewildered, he shook his head. 'I couldn't get Lavinia out. I had hold of her but she wouldn't budge. It was as though she were stuck to the bottom.'

'She was.' Mrs Shipley poured a cup of tea and passed it to him. 'Here, drink this. Then try and eat something.' She topped up her own tea and took a sip. 'Her foot was trapped.'

'Trapped?'

'An old man-trap. You know, that they used to use for poachers. Someone, one of the keepers probably, must have thrown it into the lake. Been there for years I expect. Lavinia stepped on it.'

Christopher felt sick. He bent over the table, his head in his hands. The heat from the fire was oppressive. Dizziness struck him and the room spun around him. While he had no affection for Lavinia, the thought of her suffering such a terrible death chilled him to the core. What she must have been feeling as she tried to break free, as he tugged at her. To be trapped liked that, knowing she was going to die.

'Drink some tea.' His mother got up, stirred some sugar into his tea, then placed one hand on his head and lifted the teacup to his mouth with the other. 'You're shocked, darling. It's understandable. But you mustn't blame yourself. You did everything you could to try to save her. It took four of them to get her out. Apparently the chain on the man-trap was wedged under a rock.'

'She just walked into the water. I called out to her. Told her it was dangerous.'

'I know. I used to worry whenever you and Percy swam there.'

'Lavinia couldn't swim.' The memory was now vivid. 'She was trying to reach the island to get her wretched dog.'

'The dog was fine, of course. Floated back to the edge and they fished the horrible thing out. Stupid girl. She should have realised.'

'Where is she?'

'Her parents arranged for her body to be taken to Harton Hall. They want her to be buried in the family vault there. I presumed you would have no objection?'

Christopher nodded, still numb.

'Fortunately, they took her dogs back with them. I'm glad to see the back of those creatures. As are Rockie and Cocoa.' She indicated her spaniels, who were lying in their usual places at the fireside. 'The funeral is next week. The coroner is a friend of Lord Bourne and the circumstances surrounding her death were confirmed by several witnesses, so they've hurried things through. The verdict was death by misadventure as she walked into the lake of her own volition. Lord Bourne argued hard for accidental death but the stable lad said he'd offered to go in but Lavinia insisted on fetching her precious dog herself. I think His Lordship is worried the newspapers might make more of a misadventure verdict than they should. Any excuse to attach blame, point fingers or raise rumours.' She made a tutting sound. 'Still, they hurried matters through and dealt with it all without an autopsy, so we have to be thankful for that.'

Mrs Shipley turned her head towards the windows. Outside, a morning mist was still lingering in the distance where the land dipped down towards the lake. Christopher noticed her shivering. Then she said, 'Did you know that Lavinia was pregnant?'

Christopher felt the blood drain from his face. 'Pregnant?'

She nodded. 'According to the doctor, she consulted him a few days before she died. She was four months into her term. The baby would have been due in March. I'm so terribly sorry, Christopher.'

His mouth was dry and his forehead was clammy. 'Four months?'

'Yes. So easy to conceal with these loose low-waisted dresses.' She frowned. 'What's the matter?'

'Since our honeymoon... since we've been back in England... well, we haven't... she wouldn't... I didn't...'

Edwina Shipley closed her eyes. 'You're trying to say you weren't the father?'

Christopher shook his head.

'Couldn't you manage even that?' Her voice was cold.

'Are you asking me whether I was prepared to force myself on my wife? If so, the answer is no, I wasn't.'

'So you never slept with her at all? Never consummated the darned marriage?' In her irritation with him, her American accent surfaced briefly.

'Yes. We consummated the marriage.' Christopher swallowed then decided bluntness was the best course where his mother was concerned. 'Numerous times, if you must know. Lavinia had rather a taste for it. In fact you could say she couldn't get enough of it on our honeymoon.'

He saw Edwina's mouth curl in distaste and he took some satisfaction from that. 'But after we got back to England, she didn't want me near her.'

'And it didn't occur to you that must mean she was having an affair?'

'As it happened, I didn't care. But since you ask, I actually thought it was because she was pregnant. That it had happened while we were in Biarritz and as a result she didn't want to… Look, this is embarrassing, Mother.'

'You never asked her if she was?'

'I hadn't got around to it. In case you hadn't noticed, Lavinia and I didn't exactly spend a lot of time in each other's company.'

Mrs Shipley was frowning again. 'And yet you risked your life to try to save her from drowning? Why?'

He stared at her in astonishment. 'Of course I did. What did you expect me to do? Stand by and watch her drown?'

Mrs Shipley shrugged. She turned her head towards the window again. 'Do you think she was going to bolt? Do you know who she was seeing? And when?'

'Bolt?' He hated the way his mother made such efforts to slip into the speech patterns of her society friends.

'Run off with this man, whoever he is.'

'Algernon Belford-Webb. Must be him. I was at school with him. We ran into him in Biarritz. With his mother. He introduced Lavinia to the casino. She took to it rather too well.'

Edwina snorted and said, 'It sounds like it wasn't only the gambling she took to.' She gave a long sigh. 'Well, what's done is done. She's out of our lives forever, once the funeral is over. I never liked the girl. Shallow and vain.'

Christopher stared at her, shocked, but she avoided his eyes, folding her napkin and drawing back her chair from the table. She touched his arm. 'Thank heavens you're still with us, darling. I couldn't have borne losing you as well as Percy.' Her tone switched from tender to brisk. 'No riding for a few days. Get plenty of rest. The doctor's orders.' And with another pat of his arm she left the room, her two dogs in her wake.

$\mathcal{T}$he death of Lavinia affected Christopher deeply. It was not that it had altered his feelings about her in any way. He hadn't loved her – or even liked her. And he didn't feel proud about the fact that she had sought comfort in another man's bed – and done so under his nose. How long had it been going on? She had played him for a fool. Belford-Webb had too.

But the real impact of her death was the shame Christopher felt at his failure to save her from drowning. No matter how many times he was told that one man alone could never have raised her from the trap that tethered her to the lake bed, he knew that had it been Martha under the water he would have saved her or died trying.

It was ironic that his mother treated him as though he was a hero – for the first time in his life. His period in uniform had counted for nothing with her, compared with Percy and his distinguished service on the battlefield, but the fact that Christopher had risked his own life to try to save Lavinia's made him a brave man in her eyes. Perhaps it was the proximity of his action, the fact that Lavinia's lifeless body had been laid out in the house and Edwina forced to confront it, unlike the faceless dead of the war. Apart, of course, from Percy – his death had deified him for her.

As soon as Christopher's strength was restored and the funeral over, he returned to work in the sunken garden. The building works had been completed, the ingress of brambles and weeds had been curtailed and Fred had begun work on restoring the condition of the lawns and digging over the flower beds.

He stood in front of the single storey building that might have become Martha's home. Deep sadness and a sense of loss came over him. What was the point of any of this? Why was he bothering with the restoration of the gardens if she wasn't ever going to be here with him to enjoy it? He had made a complete hash of his life.

A few minutes later, slumped on the bench where he had first kissed Martha, he realised he was indulging himself, allowing himself to wallow in self-pity. Yes, he had some right to feel aggrieved with what life had handed to him, but he remembered how he had felt when he'd sat here that Christmas before he married Lavinia. His eyes searched around for the robin that had reminded him to hope, telling himself that if the robin appeared, hope would be justified. But there was no sign of the little bird.

He leaned back against the bench and closed his eyes, breathing slowly. He would count to ten.

When he finished the count, there was still no sign of the robin redbreast. He closed his eyes and started counting again. Then again. And again. Still no robin.

It dawned on him that this refusal to give in and accept the robin's absence was in itself a sign of hope. He got up and walked around the garden, looking at the transformation he had effected with Fred's help. This was something to be proud of, achieved in spite of the lack of skilled gardeners, his own disability and in defiance of his mother's wishes. And hadn't the work in itself been a source of strength to him?

He headed over to the steps that led out of the garden. As he drew near to the brick arch that spanned the steps, something caught his peripheral vision. He turned his head. His robin was sitting on one of the lower branches of a maple tree. *'Hope is the thing with feathers.'* Smiling, he quickened his pace and headed up the steps and out of the garden.

Back in the house, he found his mother sitting in the conservatory, drinking tea while flicking through a copy of *Tatler*. She looked up when he entered the room. 'Hello, darling. How are you feeling today?'

'I've made a decision, Mother.'

'Oh dear!' She gave a little laugh. 'That sounds ominous.'

'I'm going back to the Far East.' He exhaled deeply when the words were out. Relief spread through him.

Edwina frowned. 'But why? There's so much to do here.'

'I've had enough of doing what other people want. I've done nothing else all my life, apart from when I went to Borneo. That's the only thing I've ever done that was wholly of my own volition.' He mentally added *and falling in love with Martha,* but decided not to antagonise his mother by saying that.

'But when you went there before, you were...stronger.'

'You mean I had two legs?'

'I'm only saying it was a long time ago. And your father and Percy were here. It was different. You didn't have the responsibilities you have now.' She put down her teacup and swivelled in the chair, facing him directly.

'My mind's made up,' said Christopher. 'I'm going to hire someone to run the estate. I won't leave you in the lurch. Don't try to persuade me otherwise. I fulfilled my side of the bargain and did what you wanted when I married Lavinia. A woman whom you yourself now describe as shallow and vain. My life, ever since I came back from Borneo, has been an unmitigated disaster and that's because I've allowed it to be controlled by others.'

Ignoring Edwina's furrowed brows, he carried on, determined to say everything he had been bottling up. 'During the war, I had to follow orders that went against my better judgement and that I knew would cost lives. Since the war, I've allowed you to rule my life.' He felt the relief mounting as the words spilled out of him. 'Enough is enough, Mother. From now on, I'm going to do what *I* want to do. I'm going to make choices that are right for *me*, not someone else's idea of what they want me to be.'

'Am I to assume you plan to take that woman with you?'

Christopher could see his mother's knuckles were white as she squeezed her hands tightly.

'If you mean Martha Walters, no, I don't. I can't take her, much as I would love to, as she has married someone else.' Christopher struggled to keep the emotion from his voice.

There was a silence for several seconds. Rockie padded across the floor to lie beside Cocoa, next to Edwina's chair.

Eventually, his mother said, 'I thought perhaps…' Whatever else she was about to say she must have thought better of. She leaned down to stroke the dogs. 'That's just as well then. I'm glad you're not contemplating doing something foolish.'

Resentment surged inside him at the way his mother so obviously despised Martha and the fact that he had had the temerity to fall in love with her. 'My decision to go away has nothing to do with Martha and everything to do with getting away from you.' Then, ashamed at his own words, he added, 'It's about doing something for me. Something I care passionately about.' He paused, breathing deeply.

'Have you finished?'

'Yes.'

'Well, I don't like it. Not one little bit. Can you imagine what it will be like for me living here without you? In fact I may well return to the States. I'll be wretched here all on my own.' She made a self-pitying sound.

Christopher groaned. 'Don't play the martyr card, Mother. Go back to America if that's what you want to do. Although personally, I think you'd be better off moving to London.'

'London?' She spoke in high-pitched indignation. 'I couldn't possibly live in London. All that smog and filth. All those people. Staying for a few days is one thing, but living there all the time is another.' She stretched a hand out and stroked one of the spaniels. The other dog got up and went to snuffle about under one of the potted palms.

'Suit yourself,' Christopher said. 'I wouldn't presume to advise you. It's *your* life, after all.'

Edwina drew her brows into a frown, then allowed it to drift into a smile. 'You're trying to make a point, aren't you, you naughty boy?'

'Hardly a boy.'

She gave an exaggerated sigh. 'You're right. You aren't a boy any more. Perhaps I have been a bit selfish.' She wagged a finger at him. 'But I've never intended to be. Everything I've ever done has been because I believed it was the right thing for you.'

'It's my life. Let me live it.'

She nodded, gave a long sigh, then glanced at her wrist-watch. 'Almost time for cocktails. Let's move to the library – I've asked Bannister to mix us gin rickeys.' She touched his arm. 'You will indulge me tonight, darling, won't you? I suppose we must drink to your foolhardy venture, although I'd prefer to be drinking to staying here.'

He leaned over, kissed her on the cheek and pulled her to her feet.

Over dinner Edwina resumed her efforts to persuade her son to change his mind. Unused to being denied her own way, she was like a terrier in pursuing every possible means. She sulked, she complained, she pleaded, she cajoled but her efforts made no impact on Christopher. By the time the meal was almost finished she appeared to have reached a grudging acceptance of her son's impending desertion and moved onto her favourite subject – society gossip.

'If you're going to be in Sarawak, you'll have to call on the Brookes. Vyner Brooke is married to that awful Sylvia Brett. Must be nearly ten years now. You know, darling, Lord Esher's daughter. I never liked the girl. Common as muck and so lacking any dignity. And I hear since she's been out in Borneo she's got even worse.' She tutted and gave her head a little shake.

Christopher let her words drift over him, relieved that he had got through the worst part – telling her – and now he had the delightful prospect ahead of him – his return to the island he loved.

CHAPTER 28

*M*artha had put David down for his afternoon sleep and was planning to make herself a pot of tea, before catching up with her chores. It was harder, since the baby had arrived, to keep on top of things.

Humiliation at his failure to perform in the marital bed, and David's need for night-feeds, had led to Reggie making no protest when Martha started sleeping in the single bed in David's bedroom. Slowly their marriage was reverting to the amicable partnership on which it had been founded. The difference was that now Martha knew she could never completely trust Reggie again and was always on her guard.

There was a knock at the front door. She wiped her hands, took off her apron and went to answer the door, unused to unexpected callers. When her former nursing colleagues dropped by they always gave her forewarning.

Standing on the doorstep was a woman, slightly older than Martha. She was smartly dressed, but gaunt, with angular features, her body painfully thin, her eyes anxious. The woman made no attempt to smile at Martha.

'Are you Mrs Henderson?' There was a hint of an Irish accent.

'Yes.' Martha was puzzled. 'And you?'

Ignoring the question, 'Mrs *Reginald* Henderson?'

Martha frowned. 'Yes. What's this about?'

The woman looked around then said, 'May I come inside? It's of a personal nature. We need to talk.'

Unease gripped Martha but she nodded and stepped aside to allow the woman passage. She led her into the parlour and offered to make tea, which the woman refused.

'Excuse me, but you haven't told me your name, who you are,' said Martha, sitting down opposite the stranger.

'The name's Henderson. Mrs Reginald Henderson.'

A clutch of fear gripped Martha. The woman was too young to be Reggie's mother. 'I don't understand.'

'My husband was not in a position to marry you, Mrs Henderson. He is still married to me.'

Martha stared at her, unable to believe what she was hearing.

The other Mrs Henderson pursed her lips. 'I'm sorry. It has clearly come as a shock to you. I need to ask you a question. Did you get married or do you style yourself as his wife?'

Martha clenched her hands together. 'Of course we got married. The ceremony was in a local church.' She felt her cheeks burning. 'St Matthews. It's on the Highgrove Road.' Why was she behaving defensively? She had done nothing wrong. 'There must be some mistake.'

'No mistake.' The woman opened her handbag and took out an envelope and handed it to Martha.

Her hands shaking, Martha opened it and took out a photograph. It showed a couple in wedding clothes – younger incarnations of Reginald Henderson and the woman sitting opposite.

'Eighteenth of April, 1908. St Anselm's church in Nottingham. See for yourself.'

Martha unfolded the other piece of paper and saw it was a marriage certificate for Reginald Henderson, profession, student doctor, and Miss Eileen O'Hara, spinster.

'But this isn't possible. How can it be?'

'When my husband returned from his brief time at the Front he was a changed man in so many ways. He had lost his eye but he had also lost himself. The kind and loving man I married had changed into a violent and angry person, who beat me without cause and with regularity. Life with him became a living hell.' She raised her eyes to meet Martha's. 'I tried to persuade him to seek help. He of all people, being a medical man with a specialisation in psychiatric health, should have known that was the right course. But he refused. What is it they say? "Physician heal thyself"?' She studied Martha's face, assessing her. 'So he didn't tell you he was married?'

'He said his wife had died of the influenza. During the war.'

Mrs Henderson gave a hollow laugh. 'He did, did he? Killed me off then? Metaphorically speaking.'

Martha said nothing.

'I begged him to get help but he took no notice. I stuck it out until 1917, when one night he punched me so hard he broke my jaw.' She lifted her hand and touched her chin. 'So I left him. I went home to Ireland. My mother took me in. I've been caring for her in her old age, but she passed away almost a year ago. All the time I was gone I heard not a single word from Reginald. He must have known I would have gone back to Ireland.' She shook her head lightly. 'He was probably ashamed of what he had done. After Mother died, I returned to Nottingham to find him, hoping he might by now have sought help for his condition. My mother's death made me take stock of my life. I began to remember the good things about Reginald.'

She dropped her eyes for a moment, then fixed them on Martha again. 'I decided to do what I could to save my marriage, convince him to seek treatment if he hadn't already done so.' She looked down at her hands, fingering her gold wedding band. 'It took me until now to track him down. I met one of his army colleagues who told me he transferred to the asylum here before the end of the war.'

They were interrupted by the howling of the baby. Martha jumped to her feet. 'The child's not Reggie's,' she said quickly. 'Please wait. I'll be back in a few minutes.'

She went upstairs and picked David up from his cot, holding him against her, dropping kisses on his soft hair, stroking his back to comfort him. The child calmed. 'Did you have a bad dream, David, my darling boy?' she murmured. She tried to lay him down but he began to cry again. Conscious of the waiting woman in the parlour, she wrapped his shawl around him and carried him downstairs.

She paced in front of the fireplace, hoping movement would keep the child quiet. Turning to the other woman, she said, 'I was working here in the asylum when I discovered I was expecting my son. There was no question of me marrying the father for reasons I would prefer not to discuss. I thought I would end up in the workhouse, but Regg... Dr Henderson offered to marry me and give the child a name.' She paused. 'He and I have never... Ours is a marriage in name only. He married me out of kindness. I had no idea you were alive.'

The woman studied her sceptically. 'You're trying to tell me that he has never had sexual relations with you? You can't expect me to believe that.'

'He takes medication.' Martha didn't want to tell this

stranger all the details. It was up to Reggie to tell her the details, not her. 'It affects him.'

'Are you trying to say he's impotent? He certainly wasn't when we were married.'

'He wasn't taking the pills then. And he was aggressive then, you said?'

The woman nodded. But her expression indicated she was suspicious.

Martha adjusted David's shawl and avoided looking at Mrs Henderson.

'You swear that child is not my husband's?'

'On my baby's life. David's father is the only man I have ever loved. He loved me too. Sadly, we could not be together.'

'He was married too.' The question was spoken rhetorically.

'I don't want to talk about that.' As the baby had fallen asleep again in her arms, she sat down. 'What happens now? What do you intend to do?'

Mrs Henderson sighed. 'I will go the police and they will probably take him into custody. My husband is a bigamist and whether he has had relations with you or not, he must be punished for it. I'm sorry that you and your child will have to suffer the consequences of his deceit. I intend to tell the police that I believe you were duped by him. They will probably want to talk to you themselves. I can't help that. And there will be a scandal. And of course you are no longer married. Your marriage is void.'

Martha didn't know how to take all this in. It was too much.

'I came here this afternoon because I wanted to find out whether you knew the truth. Apparently the second wife rarely does, but I had to be sure for myself. And I thought it would be better that you heard it first from me rather than from the police.'

Martha nodded. They sat for few moments in silence.

Eventually Martha said, 'What about you? What will you do?'

The woman touched her wedding ring again. 'I don't know. Divorce possibly. But... I loved my husband and I believe it's medical help he needs. I hope that he will get that help while he's in prison. My going to the police is the only way to clear all this up. All the lies. The deceit.'

'Prison? Will it come to that?' Martha felt a sudden rush of horror, as well as pity for the man who had deceived her. After all, he had given her shelter, made her son legitimate, and apart from the brief spell when his rages caused him to physically attack her, he had shown her kindness and affection.

'Bigamy is a crime.'

'But prison? That would be such a waste. He does good work here at St Crispin's.'

'They will doubtless take that into consideration. I've talked to a lawyer. He told me bigamy carries up to seven years, but given Reginald's circumstances, and assuming neither you nor I are screaming for blood, he could receive a sentence of as little as six months. Given his professional reputation and the fact that his mental state traces to his war service, the solicitor believes he would get a minimal custodial sentence.'

When Mrs Henderson had left, Martha paced up and down, trying to make sense of what had taken place. She was still trying to take in the full import of what had happened that afternoon. Initial pity for Henderson was soon replaced by anger. He had married her under false pretences. He had lied to her when he had promised their marriage would never be consummated. And he had attacked her – and his legitimate wife – with callous violence. And now, his irresponsible actions would have terrible consequences for her and for David.

As her baby stirred in her arms, purred and went back to sleep, she felt a stab of fear. What would become of her? And what would become of her child?

CHAPTER 29

*T*he superintendent narrowed his eyes at Martha with ill-disguised disgust. 'You and your child can stay at St Crispin's until the end of the month, then I want you out of the house and gone from here.'

Martha lowered her eyes. Only three weeks to find somewhere to go.

'I'm only letting you stay here as long as that because Dr Henderson begged me to do so when they took him away.' He glared over the desk at her with loathing. 'It always went against my better judgement agreeing that you could work as an auxiliary here, when you had a relative as a patient. Most improper. And I had a feeling a woman like you would take advantage of Reggie. I'll be honest, when he said he was going to marry you I tried to dissuade him but he wouldn't listen.'

'A woman like me?' She lifted her eyes to look at him.

The superintendent's gaze was cold. 'A woman of another class. A cleaner. And a woman of low morals.'

She said nothing. What was the point of arguing with him? His mind was clearly made up.

'You gave away your daughter and didn't visit her in twenty years.' He picked up a piece of paper from his desk, glanced at it without reading then put it down again. 'As soon as you met Dr Henderson you conceived the plan of marrying him. Poor Reggie.' The last two words were muttered half under his breath.

He got up and walked over to stand by the window. 'Dr Henderson has told me the child isn't his. That he offered to marry you to make your son legitimate.' He twiddled the wooden pull from the window-blind between his fingers. 'You have ruined the life and reputation of a good man, Mrs Walters. Dr Henderson was doing great work here, ground-breaking work. Even if he avoids a lengthy prison sentence, he will never work in medicine again.'

He stared out of the window, his back to Martha. 'End of the month. No longer. After that don't come anywhere near St Crispin's again.'

There was no point in protesting. Martha knew he wasn't alone in his sentiments. Not a single one of the nurses – women she had thought of as her friends – had come near her since the news erupted. She wasn't surprised. They had all adored Dr Henderson.

She got up and left the superintendent's office without further words, and walked across the lawn to the small house that had been her home. One of the hospital cleaners, glad to make an extra shilling, was sitting with David. When the woman left, Martha scooped up her son from the hearth rug where he was playing with some wooden bricks. She held him against her body, breathing in his soft, powdery smell. 'Oh, my darling boy, what's to become of us?'

That night, Martha sat up late, thinking, in the glow of the firelight. After examining all the possible options, she reached a conclusion. Her son's welfare was paramount. She would have to swallow her pride and seek help from the

Shipleys. From Kit. He would have to be told about his son. If his father had paid for the support of Jane all those years, then Kit must now do something to help David.

She hadn't wanted him to know about David. Jane had still been alive and dependent on the Shipleys when she'd discovered her pregnancy. Doing anything that might have jeopardised her daughter's future had been out of the question. She didn't want to think about how Mrs Shipley would have reacted. She couldn't have risked her cutting off the payments. But now that Jane was gone, David was everything to her. In fact he was the only thing she cared about now. Seeking Kit's help was her only hope. And Mrs Shipley wouldn't have to find out.

Martha knew Kit had married – she'd seen the photographs in a magazine she found the previous spring, in the ward sister's office. She remembered how she felt when she saw those photographs – Lady Lavinia looking radiant and Kit looking as though he were about to mount the scaffold. Her heart had swelled with love for him, twinned with sadness that they were now lost to each other for ever. She couldn't have hoped for anything else, but it still cut her to the quick, knowing that they would never be together. If she had known when Henderson asked her to marry him that Jane would be dead a few weeks later, she would never have agreed. It was hard not to think what if…

Discovering his son's existence would be a shock to Kit. Martha didn't want to make matters worse for him. By now, surely he would be reconciled to life with Lady Lavinia. Martha's appearance with his child would throw everything into confusion. But what choice did she have?

TWO WEEKS LATER, Martha walked up the long driveway to Newlands, having left David in the village in the care of the retired schoolmistress. There was a frost on the grass and little indication of the coming of spring. Martha breathed in lungfuls of air, conscious of the hammering of her heart in her chest. How would Kit react to her turning up out of the blue? Would he be pleased to see her? Angry? Distressed? She was filled with trepidation. One thing she was certain about – however he felt about her, he would not shirk his responsibility towards his son.

When she reached the top of the sweeping drive, Martha hesitated. Should she go round to the back of the house and knock at the servants' door? She had never used the grand porticoed front entrance. But this was not servants' business.

Nerves on edge, she ascended the stone steps and tugged on the bell-pull.

It was a few minutes before Bannister appeared. When he saw Martha, his face registered surprise. The elderly butler had known her all her life and, she suspected, like all the servants at Newlands, probably knew about her brief relationship with Kit. Gossip travelled at lightning speed on a country estate.

'Mrs Walters?' He frowned and turned to look over his shoulder, then moved towards her. 'You'll have to go round to the back.'

'I'm here to see Captain Shipley.' She stood her ground.

'Captain Shipley is overseas.'

'Overseas?' She hadn't anticipated that possibility. 'For how long?'

'Indefinitely.'

Martha bit her lip, disappointment surging through her, but told herself she had to think of her son. 'In that case I would like to see Mrs Shipley.' Then, afraid that he might think she meant Lady Lavinia, she added, 'His mother.'

Bannister frowned again. 'Wait here,' he said curtly, then disappeared inside the house, closing the door behind him.

She stood under the stone portico, shivering. There was a sharp wind and the daffodils growing along the edges of the gravel driveway were bent over sideways. The prospect of telling Mrs Shipley about her situation was not an appealing one. If Martha had been nervous before, she was petrified now.

The door opened wide and Bannister ushered her inside.

Martha remembered her last audience with Edwina Shipley – standing, humiliated, in front of a big oak desk while the woman handed her a cheque. Would this be a repeat of that experience? But today she was shown into a small parlour, unexpectedly cosy, with a crackling fire burning in the grate, a couple of sleeping spaniels and there in an armchair, Mrs Shipley herself. She waved a hand to indicate that Martha should sit down opposite her.

Martha's nerves evaporated. Why should she be afraid? All she was about to do was ask for the right thing to be done for the support of her son. David was, after all, Mrs Shipley's grandson.

Her adversary spoke first. 'I heard you had married again? Why have you come? Why did you ask to see my son?'

'Mr Bannister says he's overseas.'

'Mr Bannister is correct. Captain Shipley is in the Far East.'

'I see.' She hesitated a moment. 'And Lady Lavinia?'

Mrs Shipley narrowed her eyes. 'My daughter-in-law is dead. I presumed that was the reason for your visit.' Her expression was cold, hostile.

Martha's heart began to race. 'I didn't know. When? How?'

'October. She drowned. Here in the lake. Some fool, probably your late husband or father, had thrown an old man-trap in there and her foot was caught in it.' She inserted a cigarette into a long black holder and lit it, exhaling the smoke slowly. 'Why are you here?'

Deciding the truth was the best choice, Martha told her about her marriage and recent discovery that it was invalid. 'I married Dr Henderson, believing him to be a widower and because I was carrying your son's child.' She felt herself shaking as she got the words out, afraid to look Edwina Shipley in the eye.

'You were pregnant with Christopher's child?' Mrs Shipley's words were hesitant, her characteristic confidence now absent. 'Did my son know?'

'No, he did not. My son's name is David. He is fourteen months old.' She could see Mrs Shipley mentally doing a calculation.

'Where is the child?'

'He's in the village. Miss Edmonds is looking after him while I'm here.'

'You're sure my son knows nothing about the baby?'

Martha nodded.

'Why didn't you tell him?'

Martha hesitated. 'Because of you. Because you would have cut off his allowance and stopped the payments for Jane.'

'Ah, yes. They wrote to tell me she'd died, poor creature.'

Martha clenched her fists, angry at the woman's tone. 'They told *you*? Not Captain Shipley? Didn't he know?'

Mrs Shipley turned her head away. 'I thought it better he didn't.'

So that was why he hadn't come to the funeral. Martha closed her eyes, relieved to know that Kit hadn't simply ignored his sister's death, but angry that Mrs Shipley had continued to exercise control over him.

'And you are now homeless?' Edwina Shipley asked curtly.

Martha nodded.

'Then you will bring the boy to me. I will give him a home here. Wait.' She left the room and returned with an alligator skin handbag and pulled out a cheque book and fountain pen.

Martha watched, horrified as Edwina Shipley filled out a cheque, and handed it to her. 'That should take care of things for you. Bring the child to me this afternoon. I'll see that he is cared for. He is after all a Shipley and needs to be brought up as one. I don't want to see or hear from you again, Mrs... Mrs whatever your name happens to be now.'

Martha stood up, holding the cheque in her hand. She tore it into pieces and let them flutter to the floor. Both dogs raised their heads as the shower of paper scattered, then finding it of no interest, dropped them and closed their eyes again.

'That's your answer to everything, isn't it? That little book of cheques. A flourish of your pen and you think you can buy me. Is your opinion of motherhood so low that you imagine a mother would be prepared to hand over her baby in exchange for money? Would you have done that with your own son? You are a monster, Mrs Shipley.'

'Sit down!' Mrs Shipley barked. 'Tell me why you came to me, if not for money.'

Martha remained standing. 'I did come here for money. Money to help me support my son. I am alone in the world. I have no means to earn a living with a small child to bring up, with no references, no roof over our heads. All I want is a modest allowance to help me bring up my child. Your son's child. Your late husband at least saw fit to do that for my daughter.'

Stuffing her hand in the pocket of her coat, Martha squeezed her fist tightly, trying to summon up her courage.

'Do you think I *want* to ask this? Do you think it gives me any pleasure to come to you with a begging bowl?'

Edwina Shipley leaned forward, elbows on her knees. She was wearing cream and navy – a long, fine-knit jumper over a pleated silk skirt, with a string of pearls almost as long as the jumper. Even angry, and past fifty, she was an elegant and beautiful woman.

'You have to admit, Martha Tubbs, you do have a habit of having illegitimate children with the men of this family.'

Martha resisted the urge to slap the woman. 'How dare you! How dare you equate what your husband did to me when I was a fourteen-year-old child and didn't even know how babies were made, with what I had with Kit. How dare you, you... you cruel woman!' She stood in the doorway. 'Your son loved me and I loved him. David was a child born out of love. But you wouldn't even know what that is.'

Without waiting for a reply, Martha stormed out of the parlour and towards the front door, her heels clacking on the marble floor of the hallway.

'Stop! Come back.' Mrs Shipley's voice echoed through the hall as she followed Martha. 'I shouldn't have said that. Come back... please.'

Martha hesitated. Bannister had appeared in the hallway and was standing in front of the door.

'Bring us a pot of coffee, Bannister. Right away, please.'

Mrs Shipley stretched out a hand and touched Martha's sleeve. 'Please come back. I spoke in haste. I was shocked at what you told me. I will help you.'

It took them over an hour to thrash out the details. Initially, Mrs Shipley tried to insist David must stay in the house.

'He can have the nursery. It's on the top floor and you can have one of the maids' rooms so you'll be near him. I'll hire a nanny. Later on a tutor. And of course when he's old enough, he can board at Christopher and Percy's old school.'

Martha had to summon up all her courage to stand up to the onslaught from Kit's mother. She refused to entertain the idea of her child living anywhere but with her, and ruled the nanny out of the question.

'As to schooling, David's only fourteen months old. We don't need to discuss it at this stage.' She said it knowing she would never agree to her son being sent to boarding school, but thought it prudent not to fight all her battles at once.

Edwina Shipley was used to getting her own way but, faced with Martha's intransigence, eventually agreed to a compromise. They settled on David living with his mother but spending time every day with his grandmother. To Martha's surprise, Mrs Shipley suggested she and her son might move back into the gamekeeper's cottage.

'The place has been empty since you left. My son never got round to hiring a new gamekeeper and there's little point in getting one now since he isn't here. I can't very well host shooting parties myself.'

Martha's face lit up, her past antipathy for the keeper's lodge had evaporated after the time she had spent with Kit there. Now it would be a place full of joyful memories, the place where her son was conceived and she had experienced real and lasting love for the only time.

'Mind you,' Mrs Shipley went on. 'It's probably thick with dust and cobwebs and the whole place will need a good airing. Likely damp too as it's been unoccupied for so long. You'll have to be prepared to roll your sleeves up.'

'I have no fear of hard work. And thank you, Mrs Shipley. That's a very generous offer. David and I will be no trouble.'

'Very well. Now I would like to meet my grandson. Why don't you fetch him here now. You can leave him with me while you get the cottage ready.'

Martha hesitated, nervous at the idea of leaving this cold-hearted woman in charge of her son.

'I have brought up two sons of my own, Mrs Walters, and it appears you'd agree I did a reasonable job as far as Christopher is concerned. The baby will be safe with me. I presume he has been weaned?'

Martha nodded.

When she returned with David an hour or so later, Martha was shocked at the reaction her son provoked in his grandmother. When Edwina Shipley leaned over the straw bassinet and saw her dozing grandson, her eyes welled with tears. 'May I hold him?' she asked.

She cradled David in her arms and made a little breathy sound. Turning to Martha, she said, 'He's beautiful. The living image of his father.' She held the baby against her, stroking the back of his head and Martha was amazed to see that she was weeping. 'Thank you,' she said. 'Thank you, Martha. You have made me very happy.'

The baby stirred and looked up at his grandmother, stretching out one chubby hand. Mrs Shipley hesitated for a moment, then moved her own hand, allowing the child to grab her finger. She smiled to herself as the baby clutched it ferociously, hanging on tight. Martha watched as the older woman lowered her head and brushed her lips over David's soft cheek.

As the days turned into weeks and months, Mrs Shipley's unashamed adoration of her grandchild did not abate. The little boy became fond of her too and happily accompanied her and the dogs around the house and gardens. She had endless patience with the child, reading him stories and playing him music on the wind-up gramophone.

The two women gradually moved from their uneasy truce

to mutual respect, united by their love for David. Martha would walk over to the big house every day after lunch and leave her child there in the care of his grandmother, while she herself had taken to joining Fred in the sunken garden in the afternoons. At four o'clock she would duck into the gardeners' cottage and change out of her work clothes, ready to return to collect David.

Being in the garden helped her feel close to Kit again. How he would have loved it. The structure of the place was now more apparent, with the gravelled pathways clearly defined, a small chain of ponds linked by a stream that meandered between them, all cleared of pondweed and algae. A variety of different focal points had emerged: some across the wide, open lawns, others through shrubbery or clusters of specimen trees. There was a tranquillity and peace about the place that Martha found restorative.

Kit's absence was a constant ache. Everywhere at Newlands made her think of him. Every day she passed by the stable or the paddock and fed a carrot to Hooker, knowing he must be missing his master too. She imagined Kit climbing through dense forests and walking alongside mountain streams, hunting for exotic plants. She pictured him sitting outside a tent or a hut as the day faded into evening, drawing and painting the plants he had seen, or eating a simple meal with his guides. Her sorrow at being apart from him was tempered by her knowledge that he was doing what he loved in the place where he had once been so happy. Martha wondered if he ever thought of her. It saddened her to think that, if he did, it would be a cause for pain – as he would believe her to be with Henderson. If only he knew she were here, that he had a beautiful son and that she longed for him to come home every waking moment. Sometimes she doubted he would ever return.

Mrs Shipley told her she had received only short letters

posted from ports during the voyage out and a couple since he had arrived in Sarawak. The older woman tried to brush off her anxiety, making light of Kit's failure to make the effort to keep in touch.

'It was the same when he was at boarding school, and at the Front. And last time he was in Borneo I think we had only three letters the whole time he was there.' She smiled. 'Nowhere to post letters in the jungle apparently.'

After her work in the garden, when she went up to the house, Mrs Shipley now expected her to join her for tea, so that she could update her on what she and David had done each day. By now, the child was running around the house as if he owned it and Martha realised that perhaps one day he might.

Mrs Shipley delighted in David calling her Granny. The cold hard shell of the woman melted completely in her grandson's company and the respect she had begun to show Martha, over time, softened into a genuine friendship.

It was obvious that Edwina Shipley had been a lonely woman. Martha recognised and understood loneliness in others, as it had governed her own life until she'd met Kit. They had both been victims of an unhappy marriage, both knew what it meant to grieve for someone, and now, in David, to feel abounding and unconditional love. The other thing that united them was the hole that Kit had left in their lives. But this was at first a taboo subject, Mrs Shipley brushing off his absence as though it didn't matter to her.

One afternoon, in late summer, eighteen months after her return to Newlands, Martha walked back to the house from the sunken garden and saw Mrs Shipley sitting on the terrace, while David rode up and down in front of her on his new pride and joy: a wooden tricycle that she had bought for him.

They sat together in quiet companionship, sipping tea

and watching David play. The heat of the summer was softening into a gentler warmth that signalled the coming autumn.

Several times, Martha thought Mrs Shipley was about to say something, but she remained silent. Martha finished her tea and was about to call to David and head back to the cottage, when the other woman said, 'I can see now what my son must have seen in you, Martha.'

Martha was taken aback, tongue-tied.

'Did you really love him as much as I know he loved you?'

Martha turned to face her. 'More than I ever thought possible.' She added, 'And I love him still. Not an hour passes when I don't think of him, when I don't miss him.'

The older woman nodded. 'I miss him too. I think the hardest part is not hearing from him. Only those two brief letters since he arrived in Borneo. A few lines to say he had arrived safely and then another to tell me he was setting off into the interior.' She sighed. 'Almost two years now. I know he would write if he could, but most of the time he is in the middle of nowhere with no means of sending any post.' She paused, squinting into the sun. 'I don't know what I'd have done if you and David hadn't come. It has meant so much to me being able to spend all this precious time with my grandson. Thank you, Martha.'

'David loves you, Mrs Shipley. That's clear.'

Edwina smiled. 'I think he does. He is a miracle I thank God for every day.' She turned to Martha and laid a hand on her arm. 'Please call me Edwina. I think we have got past the need for formality.' She put down her teacup and smiled. 'And I have grown fond of you, Martha. I think of you as my friend.' She paused. 'I hope you can forgive me for the wrongs I did to you. I was only doing what I believed to be best for Christopher.'

Martha felt a rush of emotion. 'Thank you,' was all she managed to say.

Edwina continued. 'I think you and I are alike in many ways. My marriage was not a happy one but I was blessed in both my sons. My greatest regret is that I didn't show them the love and affection they deserved.' She turned to gaze over the rolling parkland. 'My husband was a bully and a compulsive adulterer. Not that I need to tell you that. He believed any woman was his for the taking. If they turned him down he'd take them by force if they were weaker than him, or find some way of ruining them if they weren't. I watched it all from a distance. Day by day my resentment grew. I became bitter and angry. And you, dear Martha, you were the butt of that anger. Losing Percy was such a terrible shock to me. So much pain. I couldn't bear the thought of losing Christopher too.' She closed her eyes, but Martha could see she was close to tears. 'And now I *have* lost him.'

'What do you mean?' Ice froze Martha's veins. Had she heard some news of him?

'I drove him away. He told me he wanted to get away from me.' She gulped. 'I am afraid he will never come back.'

Martha reached out and squeezed her hand. 'He will come back. I am sure of it.' But as she said the words they felt hollow. She bit her lip and choked back her own tears.

CHAPTER 30

$\mathcal{T}$he kingdom of Sarawak was an anomaly within the British Empire – and within the Far East in general. Ruled by the Brooke family, known as the White Rajahs, and now a British protectorate, its current monarch, Charles Vyner Brooke, had succeeded to the throne on the death of his uncle in 1917.

A land of fertile coastal plains, lush forests and an inhospitable, virtually impassable interior, Sarawak had been home to pirates, Christian missionaries and – hardest of the three for the rajahs to stamp out – headhunters. The hunting of heads was imbued in the culture of Borneo and the indigenous people, the Dyaks, had perfected the art of decapitation, displaying the heads as trophies. Their headhunting was not born of cruelty or savagery – it was a social norm, practised through the centuries to deal with enemies and mete out justice. For the most part, the Dyaks were a friendly and hospitable people and, by now, headhunting was rarely practised in Sarawak.

For a naturalist, the island was both a paradise and a challenge. Rich in flora and fauna, with many unique species, its interior of mountains and dense jungle was almost impenetrable. The main settlements clung to the coastal areas, while the basalt mountains were steep, slippery and treacherous to climb, with thick pathless jungle, lacking any form of sustenance to the traveller. Those who did persist in exploring the interior needed to carry with them enough provisions to last the entire trip. Progress could be as slow as half a mile a day on the steeper reaches.

The boat Christopher was travelling on passed houses close to the water's edge, constructed of palm leaves. Women and children gathered on the banks to watch the steamer's passage, their chatter drifting across the water to where he leaned against the rail of the deck. Alligators basked in the mud shallows and, as they passed by areas of forest, he could hear the scream of monkeys as they leapt between the branches of the trees. The smell of nutmeg and spices mingled with the scent of hibiscus and gardenia. In the distance, above the trees, the mountains of Matong and Santubong rose, heavily wooded, with the odd rocky outcrop.

Christopher had been relieved to discover that the Brookes were out of the country, thus removing the need for him to call on them. Everything his mother had told him about Sylvia, the Ranee, convinced him he'd had a lucky escape.

He spent a few days resting and visiting a British clergyman and his wife, the Lawrences, who had befriended him on his previous expedition. On that occasion there had been four Englishmen on the trip. Now he would be alone. The Lawrences had started a family since Christopher was there – three daughters, born in rapid succession.

'I'd love to join you, but my days of hill climbing and tramping through forests are done,' said the Reverend Lawrence. 'Your best bet is to hire a Malay guide to take you into the jungle to one of the Dyak villages where you can hire local guides. You won't be able to keep the same ones for the whole trip – they don't like to be away from their village for long – but they'll get you to the next settlement and you can engage some more there.'

'How do I communicate with them?'

'The Malay guide will translate. I know just the fellow. Name's Hilmi. Decent chap. Go light on the luggage though – you can leave some baggage here. The Dyaks aren't so great at carrying a lot of weight.' He gave a wry laugh. 'Well, the women are, but they won't be guiding you. They're hard at work in the fields. Dyak men are rather lazy in comparison to their womenfolk.'

After a day's gentle climb through the forest, Christopher and his guide reached a small Dyak settlement, surrounded by rice and vegetable fields. They were shown to a circular hut built on raised posts, which the villagers used as a council chamber and to conduct trade, and where the young single men and any visiting strangers slept. There was a fireplace in the centre of the building, the smoke issuing through an opening in the roof.

Soon after their arrival, the villagers gathered to inspect the visiting white man. The men wore traditional loin cloths, known as *chawats*, tied two or three times around the waist and between the legs with the long ends left to dangle at the front and rear. Their necks were adorned with necklaces made from shells and they wore brass bangles, earrings and belts.

Negotiations with the head man, the *orang kaya*, were protracted and Christopher got the sense that the chief was holding out for a better price. Christopher turned his head from his translator to the *orang kaya*, trying to follow the progress of the discussion. Once arrangements were eventually agreed they settled back to eat – a meal of rice and vegetables, with gifts of eggs which he wasn't sure whether he was expected to eat or keep. Rice wine was passed around, then the company watched as the villagers danced, accompanied by Chinese gongs.

The following day, Hilmi and Christopher set off upstream with a small group of young men, pushing higher into the hills and deeper into the forest. Every now and then they had to divert from the stream they were following in order to get past dense thickets of bamboo. After several hours walking, Christopher's leg was chafing, but his body was full of energy and he was exhilarated by his surroundings.

The plan was to move as deeply as possible into the lower reaches of the jungle. Climbing up to the summit of the mountains was out of the question, given Christopher's disability.

Each time they reached a village, they were obliged to recruit another set of guides, entailing lengthy discussions with the village head men and occasional delays. Christopher was both frustrated by the process and grateful – it gave him ample opportunity to rest between bouts of walking. Leaving Hilmi to handle the arrangements, he explored the area around the villages, where every available strip of land was used to grow rice. Reverend Lawrence was right – the hardest labour was done by women, who spent all day working in the fields, carrying heavy loads of vegetables or firewood back to their villages at the end of the day, often for miles and over difficult terrain. Their domestic duties then began with pounding rice to powder, before cooking the evening meal. Meanwhile, the men sat around talking and chewing betel nuts.

Each night, when he lay on a bed of palm matting, he would look up and see the small, dark outlines of shrunken heads hanging from the rafters. After a while he began to find these departed spirits oddly comforting.

Where possible, they travelled by canoe, the Dyaks propelling the boats forward with long poles. While he had little personal luggage, Christopher's boxes and bags for transporting seeds and specimens took up a lot of space. As the journey progressed they gradually filled up. Christopher realised that would determine the time of their return, as he would need to get the boxes back to Kuching and acquire new ones.

Parts of the forest were bright with colour, flowers growing up the trees and hanging down in vibrant red and orange festoons, like curtains. During the day, the jungle was eerily quiet, coming alive at dusk with the sound of birds, the cooing of pigeons and the beating of wings, and, if they were close to the river, the croaking of frogs.

After three weeks in the jungle, Christopher had collected a substantial quantity of seeds, as well as photographing and sketching numerous different species of the pitcher plants which were the main object of the expedition. As he was considering it was time to undertake the long trek back down to Kuching, he heard the Dyaks talking rapidly to Hilmi. The Malay told him they had news of a rumoured flowering of the giant rafflesia plant, a little higher up and across a river, close to a section of rapids.

As Hilmi translated their words for him, Christopher brimmed with excitement. He thought of that afternoon when, after they had made love, he had described the rafflesia to Martha, telling her how he regretted failing to photograph the plant, due to the fading light and the steep slopes, where setting up a tripod was well-nigh impossible. How could he miss another opportunity now?

His original plan had been to return to Kuching for a

couple of weeks, catch up on letters to his mother, his tutor and the Horticultural Society, and fulfil a promise to dine with the Lawrences before heading back towards the heart of the island for another trip. However, the opportunity to see the rafflesia was too significant to pass up. And it would delay him by only one or two days, three at the most. Were he to postpone hunting for it, it would be dead by the time he returned.

Hilmi was reluctant, presumably keen to return to Kuching and his family. Christopher persuaded the Malay to travel back without him and convey his apologies to the Lawrences for his delay. He asked him to take the boxes of specimens with him and arrange their shipment back to England.

The guide protested, pointing out Christopher's lack of the local language.

'As long as they return me to the same villages I can pick up new guides as I go. The *orang kaya* know me now so I should be able to get by without the language.'

Hilmi shook his head, unhappy, but torn between a desire to go home and a wish to stand by the Englishman. He tried again to dissuade Christopher from the enterprise but Christopher was determined. So Hilmi left, accompanied by one of the Dyaks in the canoe with the seed collection.

It took Christopher and the three remaining Dyaks six hours hard trekking to reach the river they needed to cross. The fast-flowing river was several feet below them in a deep gorge. Christopher could see no means of crossing it. He peered down at the clear stream. Rocks protruded through the water in several places, forming rapids. The bed of the river was covered in pebbles, white quartz, and semi-precious stones that Christopher thought were agates and jaspers, their bright colours shining in the sunlight that filtered through the trees. They followed the banks of the stream for about a mile until they reached a makeshift bridge, suspended between overhanging trees on each bank and also supported by wooden struts set diagonally into the riverbanks on each side. By a process of sign language, Christopher understood that they were to camp here for the night and cross the bridge the following morning.

When he woke up next morning, the Dyaks appeared to be arguing, something Christopher had not witnessed until now. For the first time, he wished he had not persuaded Hilmi to return without him. After five minutes' heated debate the men fell silent, and one of them gestured to Christopher to follow him. The other two hung back, sitting down on the riverbank, chewing betel nuts which they cracked open with the daggers they wore tucked in the waistbands of their *chawats*.

The bridge swayed and creaked as Christopher and the single guide made their way across. Christopher tried to keep his eyes fixed on the back of the man in front of him, avoiding looking down into the river ten or twelve feet below. The sound of rushing water as it hit the rocks and tumbled downwards, was disturbing as the bridge wobbled under their weight.

He turned his head back, expecting the other two men to follow them across the bridge but they remained, squatting on the bank, chewing and watching.

It took Christopher and his single guide a couple of hours to reach the rafflesia plant. The leafless parasite was showing two buds and one single bloom which had burst through the bark of the vine which hosted the body of the plant. Christopher measured the span of the open flower at an inch under three feet wide. Carrion flies were buzzing around the bloom, dipping inside the central bowl, attracted by the foul smell of the plant. He was overjoyed. The plant was rare and was concealed inside the vine stems until the buds burst through for their brief lives.

The Dyak guide was talking to him rapidly. Shaking his head and gesturing with his hands to convey his bewilderment, Christopher set up his tripod and began to photograph the plant. The light was less than perfect, so after getting what he could, he sat down on a nearby tree trunk and took out his sketchbook and began to draw the rafflesia.

When he had finished, he moved back to the enormous flower and took some more measurements. The Dyak man began to speak again, pointing to the two unopened buds. Before Christopher had a chance to sketch these, the man had taken out his betel knife from his waistband and cut the buds off. He wrapped them in a fold of his *chawat*, which he tucked back into his waist. Christopher, annoyed, remembered the Dyaks believed the buds of the rafflesia had aphrodisiac properties and were also used to facilitate childbirth. He could hardly begrudge the man his harvest, and he couldn't take it back to England, where it would never survive without its host and in a hostile climate.

Their mission complete, the two men headed back to the stream and the bridge. The other Dyaks were still waiting on the opposite bank.

The Dyak stepped onto the structure which shook under his weight. As Christopher followed him, he could hear the voices of the others. One called something to Christopher's guide, but the man ignored it.

A sudden cracking noise. Christopher looked towards the bank, six feet away. Before he could turn around again, he felt a heaving movement, then the flimsy platform beneath him jerked and fell away and he found himself lurching forward and pitching towards the river below. A scream penetrated his consciousness, sharp, strident, raw with emotion. He'd heard that sound before – far away on the muddy fields of the Somme, the cry of a man certain in the knowledge he was confronting his own death.

Christopher's hand flew out, desperate to gain purchase on the twisted palm-leaf guide rope, but as he grabbed hold of it, it tore through his hand, ripping his skin, burning like a brand. The rope bridge bounced back upwards, part of it rebounding on him like the lash of bullwhip. He hurtled through space. Time stopped as the shallow rapids below rose up to meet him. His last thought was of Martha, before he hit the rock-strewn river.

CHAPTER 31

$\mathcal{C}$hristopher never found out how he had been rescued from the river, how the Dyaks had fished his body from the rapids and hauled him up the steep banks, then carried him, unconscious, back to their village.

When he eventually awoke, back in the Dyak village, Christopher was disorientated. He was lying on a pallet in a corner of the otherwise deserted circular hut. He could smell the smoke from the fire. Turning his head he saw sunlight shafting through the aperture in the roof, setting dust motes dancing. It was evidently the middle of the day, but which day?

His artificial limb was missing, whether lost, damaged or removed by the Dyaks for his comfort. Head throbbing he raised a hand to his brow and felt a cloth bandage there. A sweet smell of some kind of poultice struck him as he touched the barkcloth. How had he got here?

The bridge. His heart constricted in remembered fear. Swinging above the water by one arm until the force of the rebounding structure had caused him to lose his grip and sent him plummeting to the river. After that, nothing.

His whole body ached. Running his hand down his arms and leg and over his stump, he checked to see if he had broken any bones. Miraculously he appeared to be intact, just bruised and battered. There was a gash along his left arm and his right hand was bandaged in a dressing that seemed to be made of woven leaves, underneath which he felt a burning across his palm where the skin had been torn off.

Looking around the room from his horizontal position he could see no one and no sign of his missing wooden limb. He tried to ease himself up into a sitting position but the room swam around him, pains shafted up his back and he fell back again, unconscious.

When Christopher came to, Hilmi and the Reverend Lawrence were sitting cross-legged on mats on the floor beside his bed.

'Ah! Christopher,' said Lawrence. 'Welcome back to the land of the living. You gave us quite a scare. We weren't sure you were going to make it.' His tone was jovial but his eyes were filled with concern.

'How long have I been here?'

'Almost two weeks. Two of the Dyaks came down to Kuching to bring us here. Apparently you fell from a bridge?'

'I didn't fall. The bridge collapsed underneath me. There was another chap in front of me. Is he all right?'

'He die. Head crack open on rocks. You lucky, sir.' Hilmi grinned at Christopher. 'Yes, you very lucky.'

Christopher thought of the young man who would never have a chance to test the aphrodisiac powers of the buds he had plucked. He said a silent prayer of thanks for his own life.

'Thank you for coming here. Both of you. Sorry to have been the cause of so much trouble.'

'No trouble. I was happy to have an excuse to use with Mrs Lawrence to come up here. Bit of an adventure for me.

Oh, and she sends you her best wishes. Wants you to stay with us when we get back to Kuching. Until you're fighting fit again, old boy.'

Christopher nodded his thanks. 'Have you seen my leg? It's missing.'

Hilmi said. 'Gone in river. Leg save you life. Catch in rocks. Dyaks cut leg off to get you free. In Kuching make new one.'

Christopher's heart sank. How was he to manage without his custom-made limb? But when he thought about it later he realised it was a strange irony that his missing leg had been the means of his escaping death.

THEY BROUGHT him back to Kuching in a rough and ready open palanquin, made by the Dyaks from long bamboo poles with palm matting stretched between. It was a journey that took several days, stopping in different villages overnight. Time passed in a daze for Christopher, mingled with moments of vivid consciousness as they passed through the forest and he spotted a plant he wanted to stop and examine. But there were no halts or diversions for plant collecting on this trip. Straight down to the coastal plain. The stretcher lurched about as the Dyaks negotiated obstacles, but Christopher must have been weary or drugged in some way – who knew what concoctions his hosts had administered to ease his pain and aid his recovery?

The day before they were due to reach Kuching, Christopher's temperature rose and he felt alternately feverish and chilled. Even though he was lying motionless, he felt the weight of exhaustion upon him and all his muscles ached – a different kind of pain to the background pain from his injuries. He began vomiting as they were moving through the woods on the last leg of the journey. Voices carried on the air towards him, but Christopher could not hear what they were saying. The canopy of forest above his head seemed to be moving down towards him, as though to crush him under the weight of leaves and branches.

When he was next aware of anything, he was lying in a comfortable bed, shrouded by mosquito netting. A cool breeze drifted through an open door from a veranda, carrying the scent of hibiscus and jasmine. There was a Bible on the nightstand beside the bed and the room was sparsely furnished but clean and bright.

As he was taking this in, a woman came through the doorway and drew back the net to look at him. 'You're awake, Captain Shipley. I hope you're feeling a little better at last?'

'Mrs Lawrence,' he said, smiling up at her kind face.

The woman took his temperature and ran her fingers over his brow, pushing his unkempt hair away. 'You had us extremely worried for a time.'

'I had a fall. From a bridge.'

'More than that. You've had malaria. A very bad bout. We didn't think you were going to make it. Your body was run-down after your accident, so the disease took a firm hold.' She pulled her lips into a tight smile. 'My husband wanted to inform your family – but we couldn't find anything to tell us their address. There was only your trunk but it was locked and he didn't want to break into it unless...'

'Unless I'd actually died?'

She nodded, embarrassed. 'But fortunately it didn't come to that.'

'How long have I been ill?'

'Several weeks. And you must rest for weeks more. We have to rebuild your strength. But the good news is that a letter arrived for you today.' She flipped over the envelope. 'It's from your mother! Now you'll be able to write to her and tell her you are on the road to recovery, so I am rather glad we didn't find her address and give her cause for worry. But no letter-writing until you are feeling strong enough.'

'Thank you.' He sank back into the pillows. A sudden thought occurred to him. 'My plant specimens? My camera and sketch books?'

'Your specimen boxes have all been dispatched to the botanic gardens at Kew in accordance with your instructions. As to your camera equipment and sketch books I've no idea. I fear they may have been lost when the bridge collapsed.'

Christopher closed his eyes and groaned inwardly. After all that, he would have no record of the rafflesia. He opened them again, a worse fear hitting him. 'Please could you pass me my jacket.' He nodded towards the chair where the jacket hung over the back.

Mrs Lawrence passed it to him and he felt inside the top pocket. Relief washed over his face as he pulled out a piece of folded card, crumpled and water-stained. He opened it and inside was a small pressed flower, a fading yellow buttercup.

'A buttercup!' said Mrs Lawrence, nostalgically. 'I haven't seen one of those in a long time. Is it a special type?'

'No. A common or garden one. But precious to me as it was a gift from a very special person.'

The woman smiled at him, then moved to the door. 'I'll leave you in peace now.'

The loss of the sketchbooks and photographic plates were a blow – but losing Jane's buttercup would have been more than he could have borne.

LATER, when a bowl of broth had helped restore a little strength, Christopher remembered the letter from his mother. It lay on his trunk beside the bed, Edwina's hand-writing unmistakeable.

My dear Christopher,

Why haven't you written to me? I am living in daily terror that a wire will come to tell me I have lost you. There has been nothing since you wrote to tell me you were heading off into the jungle. Surely you must be back in Kuching by now?

If you'd any idea how much I worry about you, you wouldn't be such a poor correspondent. The other day, Margaret Bennet was telling me there are cannibals in Borneo. I was worried sick that you'd been stuck in a cooking pot and boiled alive. I only calmed down when Mr Bennet assured me that there were no cannibals. But then yesterday I bumped into Mrs Collerton in the village and she told me there are headhunters. You can imagine what kind of state I was in at the thought of your head being hung on a string round some native's neck, until Major Collerton appeared and assured me that they don't do it any more in Sarawak and are really quite friendly. Apparently his brother, who is something to do with oil prospecting, passed though Sarawak a few years ago on his way to somewhere else.

But I digress. Please, please, darling, come home. You have had plenty of time now to get your botanical adventures out of your system. Now it's time to return to your responsibilities. Your sunken garden is looking marvellous. Yes, I have actually been to have a look! What a fantastic job you have done, but the young man who is working there needs more help and it would be such a shame to let it fall back into a wilderness again.

I miss you so much, darling boy. You know I'm not good at saying this kind of thing, but I think of you all the time. I feel so guilty that I drove you away. That I was the cause of the very thing I didn't want to happen. I know I was wrong to push you into marrying Lavinia, to keep trying to make you the person I thought you ought to be, rather than the one you are – which, now that you aren't here, I realise is the very best person – a son to make any mother proud. Oh dear, I am now doing what I've just admitted I shouldn't do – trying to get you to do what I want rather than what you want, but I can't help it.

I do hate to think of you all alone. I know marriage to Lavinia was a terrible and tragic mistake but, once some time has passed, perhaps you should think of marrying again? It would be wonderful for you to be settled, with a wife and children. I so want to see you happy.

Now don't be cross with me but there is someone whom I think you could be happy with one day. But I promise you, Christopher, I have no intention of compelling you or coercing you into marrying anyone. I have a feeling that if you come home, things will be better for you in so many ways.

Please come home! Quickly!

Your loving mother.

CHRISTOPHER SHOVED the letter back into the envelope, irritated. Edwina couldn't resist interfering. She had probably already got a selection of marriageable women lined up as potential replacements for Lavinia. Well, he wasn't playing her game. It was his life and he had no intention of going home to Newlands.

Two days later, Christopher's bubble was burst when the doctor told him that as soon as he was fit to travel he would be best advised to return to England and avoid returning to the tropics again.

'Malaria's a tricky disease,' the man said. 'You can go for as long as a year, feeling fit as a fiddle before it strikes you down.'

'I don't understand.'

'Plasmodium. It's a parasite. Can take months after you're infected before you get the symptoms. The problem is that the damn things can lurk in your liver for years and then re-emerge. You were very sick, my friend. My advice to you is to get well, get home and get yourself along to the Tropical Diseases Hospital in London and have them take a look at you. Then stick to temperate climates. You may appear physically strong, Captain Shipley, but you've been through a lot. Your war injuries, the head injuries you sustained when you fell in that river, and now this. Don't make things too hard for yourself.'

'But I'm a botanist. This is what I do.'

'That's fine but do it somewhere else. There are plenty of plants to study in Europe. I can't believe they've found them all, have they?' The doctor put his stethoscope back inside his bag. 'Or you could work in a laboratory or a hothouse. Let some other fools go climbing through tropical jungles for you.'

WHEN CHRISTOPHER DISEMBARKED from the steamship at Southampton, he was unsteady on his feet. After two months at sea, the ground seemed to roll underneath him as he made his way up the quayside. Today there were no gangs of leaflet-waving women, no men in uniform crowding the dockside. Just the departing passengers and crew and a few dockers to unload the cargo.

The makeshift prosthetic leg he'd had made for him by a Chinese carpenter in Kuching was causing him pain – he would have to get fitted for a new one as soon as possible. It was scuffed and splintered in places and the straps were wearing thin and kept slipping out of place.

Arriving in London, he debated whether to stop off for a couple of days there, sort out a new prosthesis, get the once-over from the Tropical Diseases Hospital and call in at Kew Gardens to find out whether the plant specimens he had sent four months ago, before his accident, had arrived safely. But now he was back in London he was suddenly impatient to be home.

Newlands had never exerted such a pull on him before. He was keen to see how much further Fred had progressed with the sunken garden. He couldn't wait to ride out with Hooker again. But most of all, he realised he actually wanted to see his mother.

The long absence and his near-death experience had made Christopher feel a fondness towards Edwina Shipley that he'd rarely felt when in her company. He imagined her standing in front of the fireplace, a cocktail in her hand and her dogs in attendance, and smiled to himself. When he had written to her before leaving Kuching, he had been vague about his future plans. Anxious not to worry her he hadn't mentioned the malaria. There was still that doubt in him that as soon as he were home she would start her scheming again. And yet... she was lonely and did what she did with the best of intentions. Surely his unexpected return would be welcome?

His mind made up to surprise his mother and travel straight to Newlands, he took the train and then a taxicab from the local station. He had made arrangements in London for his trunks to be sent on separately, along with a wooden crate containing more specimen plants – these destined for the greenhouse in the sunken garden.

Telling the driver to drop him at the main gates, he walked up the long sweep of the drive. The trees were turning gold and brown and there was a smell of burning leaves in the air. It was so different from the heat of the tropics, the dank smell of the jungle, the oppressive humidity of the island that had been his home for almost a year. He breathed deeply, enjoying the fresh air and the crunch of crisp leaves under his feet.

It was a few minutes after three. Edwina would doubtless

be reading in the small parlour, as she usually did in the afternoons. Christopher pushed open the front door and, after dropping his overnight bag onto the floor by the door, hurried across the large expanse of hallway.

Swing-doors at the rear of the hall, behind the sweep of the staircase, led to the service areas. With a crash, the doors burst open and a small boy shot through on a tricycle, wearing a pirate costume.

Christopher stopped in his tracks, astonished. Edwina Shipley must be away from home. Were she present, no servant would dare to bring a child into the house, much less allow him to run rampant.

The boy skidded to a halt, looked up at Kit and said, 'Are you looking for Granny?'

Kit echoed him, 'Granny?'

The boy smiled. 'Granny's with her doggies.' He pivoted his tricycle around towards the corridor that led to the parlour. 'Come on!'

Stepping in front of the little boy, and despite the awkwardness of his homemade leg, Christopher squatted down in front of him, blocking his passage. He studied the child's features.

The boy's dark eyes had a solemn expression and the possibility formed in Christopher's mind that this was Martha's child. But how could that be? And who was Granny? Overcome with emotion and confusion, he held out a hand to shake the little boy's. 'Hello, what's your name?'

Suddenly shy, the boy shook hands and whispered, 'David.'

'David? That's a good strong name.' As he squatted beside the boy, heart thumping, a mixture of confusion, fear and joy in his head, he was unable to think straight. Who was the boy? Why was he here? Could he really be Martha's son? But it wasn't possible. How could it be? And yet? Tears pricked at his eyes and he wiped a hand over them.

David studied him, expression curious. 'Are you my daddy? You look like the picture Granny has on top of the piano. But my daddy's gone away.'

Christopher gasped, his heart bursting with a rush of joy and love as he leaned forward and lifted his son off the tricycle and into his arms. Kissing the soft silky hair on his head, he breathed in the smell of the little boy. 'Yes, David. I'm your daddy. I've come home.'

The child moved his head back so he could see Kit's face. 'Will you go away again?'

'No. Never. I'm here for good now, David. I won't be going away.' Holding the small body against him, a sudden rush of fear spread through him. David's presence could only mean one thing. Martha must have died. Why else would the child be here? Martha would never have given up her son. What was going on? And Edwina would never have let Martha return. Besides, Martha was married to Henderson.

He was struggling how to ask the boy, when a familiar voice interrupted them. 'Darling! You've come home! And you and David have met each other. But why didn't you tell me you were coming? I'd have asked cook to do something special.' His mother was standing in the arch leading to the east wing. He could see she was on the point of tears.

Christopher put down his son and still holding onto the little boy's hand, moved to greet his mother, putting his free arm around her and drawing her towards him. For once she didn't resist.

'Come and get warm in the parlour. There's a fire blazing. I'll ask Bannister to bring us some tea. Oh, darling, I've worried so much about you. All this time with no word. I'd begun to fear the worst. I thought something terrible had happened to you. Or that you'd decided to stay in Sarawak.'

'I was ill. Malaria.'

She squeezed his hand, then flung her arms around him in a most uncharacteristic display of emotion. 'My poor darling. I can't tell you how happy I am that you're home. And, David! Isn't it marvellous that Daddy is home again?'

Christopher had never seen his mother in such a state of unbridled joy. He let her lead him along the corridor and into the warm, cheerful room. The two dogs stirred from their habitual places in front of the grate and came to greet him, tails wagging as he bent down to stroke them.

A little voice chimed. 'Can I keep on riding, Granny?'

Edwina turned a beaming smile upon her grandson. 'Of course, my angel. Daddy and I have lots to talk about.'

Kit watched the boy pedalling out of the room, then turned to look at his mother. His hands were shaking as he said, 'She's dead, isn't she. Martha's dead. Tell me what happened.'

Edwina Shipley looked astonished. 'Dead? Of course she's not dead. To the best of my knowledge she's where she always is in the afternoons, messing about in your sunken garden. She'll be back for tea later. The dear girl does insist on staying in the keeper's cottage, even though I'd much rather they moved in here.'

Kit's heart soared inside him. Relief, joy, overwhelming gratitude. She was alive. She had given him a son. A beautiful healthy son. And, miracle of miracles, Edwina was happy about it – even wanting Martha to move into the big house.

The door opened and Bannister put his head around it. Seeing Kit, his face lit up. 'I saw the bag in the hall and I did wonder. Good to see you home again, Captain Shipley.'

'It's good to see you too, Mr Bannister.' Christopher got up and shook the elderly retainer's hand.

'I'll bring tea and then I'll put your bag upstairs, sir.'

When he had gone, Christopher said, 'But I don't understand, why is Martha here? I thought she'd married the doctor at the asylum.'

His mother gave her head a shake. 'A bad business. He married her bigamously. Poor Martha had no idea. But I'll leave her to tell you all that.'

Christopher gasped in disbelief. 'She's not married?'

'Not any more. She agreed to marry him unaware of the wife and only because she was expecting David.' Edwina reached out her hand to touch his arm. 'I am sorry, Christopher. From the bottom of my heart. I've been a selfish woman and I know now I hurt you very much. I had no right to do what I did.' She looked at him intently. 'As I've come to know Martha, I've become increasingly fond of her.' She swallowed. 'In fact, I've come to think of her as a daughter.' She squeezed her lips tightly together. 'I hope that perhaps one day she might become that. My daughter-in-law. Your wife. You do still love her?' Her face was anxious.

Christopher closed his eyes. Shaking his head slowly, he said, 'More than ever. If that's possible. And David. Oh, Mother, I have a son, a beautiful son.' He got to his feet. 'I must see her. I must go and find her right away.'

'Sit down. Please wait. I haven't finished yet.'

Bannister came in and served them tea. Christopher sat, fists clenched in impatience, longing to be making his way to the sunken garden and Martha.

When they were alone again, Edwina said, 'I did something else that was unforgivable. But I hope you will find it in your heart to forgive me.' She looked down, her face anxious. Kit saw her hands were twisting together in her lap. 'Your sister died. Jane. It happened before you went away. Before Lavinia drowned. I didn't tell you. They wrote to me from St Crispin's to say she had passed away and I could cancel the payments for her keep. I'm so sorry I didn't tell you. I was afraid. I didn't want you to go to Martha. You'd only recently married Lavinia. I thought it better you didn't know.' She gave a little sob. 'And I didn't want you to be hurt. To drag all that up. I kept hoping against hope that you would eventually be happy with Lavinia. I was wrong. I should have told you. You had a right to mourn your sister.' Edwina closed her eyes and then looked up at him. 'I'm so sorry, Christopher. Martha thought you knew and had decided not to attend the funeral.'

'No! Not dead. Not Jane.' Christopher let out a long groan. 'I should have gone back again. I should have visited her.' He felt in his pocket for the piece of card with the pressed buttercup that he always kept there.

'I am so terribly sorry, my darling. For that poor girl and for not telling you. I don't know why I thought I had the right to play God.' She took out her handkerchief and wiped her eyes. 'Can you ever forgive me? I was only trying to do what was best for you. And I have explained to Martha. I think she has forgiven me, so I hope you will.'

She picked up the teapot and was about to pour more tea for him, when she put the pot down. 'I'm doing it again,' she said. 'Being selfish. Go to Martha. Go now. It's what you want to do. And if you see David on your way out, tell him his granny is ready to read him his story.'

Christopher needed no further invitation. Throwing a grateful look to his mother, he raced out of the house, across the lawns and the stable yard to the sunken garden, heedless of the discomfort from his battered leg.

At first he didn't see her. The large garden was criss-crossed by winding paths with trees and shrubs obscuring the view of different areas, creating a series of gardens within a garden. Then, as he turned past a small Chinese-style summerhouse and headed towards the rear of the garden, he saw her.

Martha had her back to him, bending over to prune and

shape a line of lavender bushes in a border in front of one of the red-brick boundary walls. It was only when he was a few feet away that she turned around and saw him.

For a moment it was as though time had stopped. They both stood motionless, staring at each other. Then Martha dropped the secateurs and ran into Kit's arms. Their kiss was long, passionate and hungry, then tender and searching, followed by countless light kisses, as they kept breaking off to seek out each other's eyes.

'I thought you might never come home. I was so afraid. Oh, Kit, I couldn't have borne it if you'd died out there. So far away and without seeing...' She pulled her head back and looked at him. 'You've seen him? You've met David?'

'I knew almost as soon as I set on eyes on him that he was yours. Then he recognised me from a photograph. He called me Daddy.' Kit's eyes filled with tears. 'When I knew he was our son I can't begin to say how that felt. ' He crushed her against him. 'My first thought was that you must have died. I couldn't believe Mother had taken him in.'

'Your mother has been marvellous. She and David adore each other – and she has been so good to me.' Hesitating a moment she added, 'She has become for me the mother I never had.' She looked up at him. 'It's hard to believe but it's true.'

'She said the same of you. She loves you.' He smiled at her, his heart swelling as he saw the love in her eyes. 'Mother told me you're not married. That you never were, as far as the law is concerned. Oh, Martha, will you marry me? Please say you'll marry me.'

'Of course I'll marry you, my love, my life, my Kit.'

Kit gasped, holding her against his pounding chest. 'We'll have to tell Mother the news. And we have so much to ask each other. So many gaps to fill in. All that lost time apart. And Jane – oh, my dearest, I am so terribly sorry about Jane.

I had no idea.' He looked into her eyes. 'How you must have suffered, losing her. And I knew nothing of it. You know I would have come. I'd have been there. To share your grief. To say goodbye.'

'I knew you would have come if you'd known.'

He pulled her against him again, scarcely able to believe that at last they were to be together. He smiled at her and pushed a stray lock of hair away from her forehead. 'There's something we must do first. Before we tell Mother, before we do anything else.'

'What's that?'

'I'm going to saddle up Hooker, lift you up in front of me and we're going to ride as fast as we can to that little cottage in the woods so I can take those ridiculous breeches off you and make love to you until you beg me for mercy.'

Martha laughed. 'That will never happen.'

'What? You won't let me make love to you?'

'I'll never beg you for mercy. I'll never ask you to stop.' She lifted her face and kissed him again.

As they walked hand-in-hand out of the garden, the robin fluttered down from the branch of a maple tree and perched on the edge of a sundial.

The End

If you enjoyed The Gamekeeper's Wife, it would be fantastic if you could spare a few minutes to leave a review at the retailer where you bought the book.

Reviews make a massive difference to authors - they help books get discovered by other readers, they make it easier for authors to get promotional support – some promotions require a minimum number of reviews in order for a book to be accepted. Your words can make a difference.

Thank you!

JOIN CLARE'S MAILING LIST

CLARE'S SHORT STORY COLLECTION

To get Clare's newsletter, click below or go to clareflynn.co.uk to the sign-up form. We'll send you a link to a free download of A Fine Pair of Shoes as a thank you gift. You can unsubscribe any time. (Privacy Policy on Clare's website clareflynn.co.uk

https://www.subscribepage.com/r4w1u5

ALSO BY CLARE FLYNN - THE CANADIANS

The Chalky Sea

The first in the trilogy, *The Chalky Sea* tells the stories of Gwen Collingwood, an English woman and Jim Armstrong, a young Canadian soldier during World War Two.

" A stylish, unusual and well-written Second World War story" (Discovering Diamonds, Historical Fiction Blog)

The Alien Corn

The follow up to The Chalky Sea, *The Alien Corn* is set in rural Canada in the aftermath of World War 2. Jim Armstrong has returned to his farm in Ontario where he is joined by his English war bride, Joan. Jim suffers from the after effects of the horrors he has witnessed in the Italian campaign while Joan struggles to adapt to her new life and family.

COMING SOON

The Frozen River will be published in 2018 and will complete the trilogy.

ACKNOWLEDGMENTS

With thanks to Clare O'Brien, Mary Longhurst, Susannah Sewell, Lynn Osborne and JT Carey for your helpful pre-publication read-throughs. Thanks to my editor Debi Alper, my cover designer Jane Dixon-Smith and to Helen Baggott my proof-reader. And to Roz Morris who inspired me to try out a short break in a property of The Landmark Trust – it was there that the initial idea for this book came to me.

Last but not least to Jay, Jill, Margaret and Maureen for your always insightful Friday feedback.

ABOUT THE AUTHOR

Clare Flynn is the author of seven historical novels and a collection of short stories.

A former Marketing Director and strategy consultant, she was born in Liverpool and has lived in London, Newcastle, Paris, Milan, Brussels and Sydney and is now enjoying being in Eastbourne on the Sussex coast where she can see the sea and the Downs from her windows.

When not writing, she loves to travel (often for research purposes) and enjoys painting in oils and watercolours as well as making patchwork quilts and learning to play the piano again.

facebook.com/authorclareflynn

twitter.com/clarefly

instagram.com/clarefly